AFTER WE DROWNED

❊ ADVANCE PRAISE ❊

"In *After We Drowned*, Jesse's spirit and devotion to his family shine in a coming-of-age journey that is equal parts raw and tender. With haunting lyricism and unflinching candour, Jill Yonit Goldberg depicts the profound human cost of reckless environmental exploitation. This is an impressive debut that introduces Goldberg as an exceptional new voice in CanLit."

— Ellen Keith, bestselling author of *The Dutch Wife* and *The Dutch Orphan*

"*After We Drowned* is a haunting, raw, propulsive read. Jill Yonit Goldberg crafts authentic characters, an immersive world, and a gripping story that builds to an ending that left me breathless. This stellar novel announces Goldberg as a writer to watch."

— Daniel Scott Tysdal, author of *Wave Forms and Doom Scrolls*

AFTER WE DROWNED

A NOVEL BY

JILL YONIT GOLDBERG

anvil PRESS

Anvil Press | Vancouver

ANVIL PRESS PUBLISHERS // VANCOUVER, BC

LIBRARY AND ARCHIVES CANADA CATALOGUING IN PUBLICATION

Title: After we drowned / a novel by Jill Yonit Goldberg.
Names: Goldberg, Jill Yonit, author.
Identifiers: Canadiana 20240359348 | ISBN 9781772142273 (softcover)
Subjects: LCGFT: Novels.
Classification: LCC PS8613.O4337 A69 2024 | DDC C813/.6—dc23

Cover by rayola.com
Cover illustration by Meags Fitzgerald
Interior layout: Derek von Essen
Represented in Canada by Publishers Group Canada
Distributed by Raincoast Books

The publisher gratefully acknowledges the financial assistance of the Canada Council for the Arts and the Province of British Columbia through the B.C. Arts Council.

Anvil Press Publishers Inc.
P.O. Box 3008, Station Terminal
Vancouver, B.C. V6B 3X5
www.anvilpress.com

Printed and bound in Canada.

For Willie
and
In memory of Charlie

PART ONE

ONE

JESSE – CRUEL SUMMER

EVER SINCE THE OIL rig exploded, Daddy's been obsessed with killing things. Small animals mostly, so we can eat, but his bloodlust has gotten so bad that lately, when I catch his eye, all I can think of are the glowing, leaden pupils of the alligators that float up Bayou Lafourche near the four-room shack with the rotting wood and peeling paint that we've been living in. Daddy nearly died in that explosion, so he moved us here to get rid of his memories. Now he acts like life is a punishment, a bitter drink he swallows every single day.

Around here, water and death come together like twins. Daddy and I have waded into the bayou, and he's bent over noodling for catfish, sticking his hand under a log, into a nest where he swears he can feel a big one. He stumbles back and yanks from the water a beast whose mouth closes around his elbow. The fish is longer than Daddy's ropey, muscled arm and it thrashes as it bites into his flesh. On its side, dark wet holes big enough to stick your thumb into gape open, belch sludge.

"Fucking oil," Daddy says, fingering one of the holes. The catfish lets go, and my father rubs his bloody arm on his bare stomach then holds the bite to his mouth as if to suck out venom. His jaw is narrow, grizzled with stubble.

"Kill it." He throws me the fish and then his knife.

"We ain't even going to eat it." I'm not the son my father wants. At fifteen, I haven't even had sex yet.

The fish's tail twitches like an electric charge runs through it.

My father pulls his rough-skinned hand through his wavy hair, rubbing heat from the ridge of his forehead. His eyes are closed as if looking at me will hurt. I grunt and fling the huge fish into the murky water of the lonely estuary where no one else ever comes.

"Pussy." That's what my father calls me now. I clench my fists so hard I think my nails will draw blood from my palms and I whisper that I wish he was dead. He puts the cigarette from above his ear between his thin lips. "That don't make you special," he says. I look straight ahead at the sluggish water and breathe in the stink of swamp that is always there.

Daddy and I went fishing four days before the explosion, when we still lived in Grand Isle, and he would come home for three weeks then fly off to his job on the rig for three weeks. He was a roughneck — the lowest job on the platform — but it was the first time we'd ever had enough money to survive on anything more than peanut butter and Cup Noodles. In the weeks he'd be gone, everything at home would get real peaceful — my father had always been a drunk, even before everything happened, before his bad moods swelled like the tides of the Gulf during a hurricane. But the rig job changed him. Every time he came home, he'd be real tired, but happy, at least at first. That time we fished at the far end of the Island where the beach is wide, and we watched the sun the colour of peach flesh melt way out over the water where the rigs are like alien ships in the distance. We waited at the end of the long pier and watched a flock of noisy gulls disappear into the dusk until a fat red snapper showed up at the end of our line. My father laughed when he saw it: a real fighter, writhing and slapping its tail until Daddy yanked it from the hook and sliced its head right off. My father never left a fishing trip without catching something big.

On the way home, Daddy turned up the radio in his dusty pickup and we sang the words to that song "Mama He's Crazy," pretending we were the mother and daughter crooning at each other like that and laughing. When we burst into the kitchen with our sandy shoes and bucket of fish, Mama and my sister, Willow Rose sat there eating burgers from Jo-Bob's Gas and Grill. The smell of fried meat filled the room.

"Emmett!" Mama said, as if we startled her. And then, "We were hungry." She hid her guilty smile in her burger, letting her long, dark hair fall into her face.

Willow Rose, who is not even two years younger than me, has the same long, messy hair as Mama, but light like Daddy's, and the blue eyes we all have in our family. She looked up from her half-eaten burger, mayonnaise and bloody juices running off her hands, dripping into her lap. "Want some?" she offered, holding the bitten-up meat and bun out to us. Willow Rose was the clown, the fearless jester, and now she looked straight at Daddy even when even Mama didn't. If that happened today, my father would holler, maybe even slam his fist on the table and let Mama and Willow Rose have it real good, but that day, even though his face crumbled like a sandcastle, all he did was mumble, "Who do you think paid for those?" Then he snatched up Willow Rose's fries and gobbled them down, Willow Rose protesting the whole time until Daddy tossed the last three fries into her mouth like she was a sea lion on TV, and made her laugh.

Three days later my father came home looking like he'd already turned corpse. They'd given him a clean company T-shirt — white with that slick green logo on it — at the hotel where they'd flown all the men who survived, but he came back to us like a man who didn't know how to be alive anymore. His face was shadowed and wild. He became a stranger who needed and hated us at once. During the days he'd close himself in the bedroom or scream at us for making noise, for every little thing we did. One time at night, I woke to the sound of his sobs.

By the day after the explosion, the stench of smoke and chemicals drifted over the water and squeezed our lungs so hard it felt like they got turned inside out, while our eyes grew red with stinging tears. Then the tar started showing up on the shore. Two weeks after it happened, Willow Rose and I went looking for Daddy at dusk and found him at the beach where we always went, where the dolphins used to swim so close, and we watched as our father dug the sticky balls of oil from the sand, his fingers turning greasy and black. He piled the tar into a gummy welt and then went to put the whole mess into a plastic garbage bag. He paused at the sight of a dead fish washed to shore, picked at it and then touched his hand to his eye, smudging his face with dark ooze.

"Fuck," he whispered, his voice a hammer whacking a nail. He rubbed his eye with his arm and cussed again.

I yanked my shirt off and ran to offer it to him.

"Get away from here," he said, his now-pink eye blinking fast, tears coming. "This beach ain't no place for you no more."

TWO

EMMETT – TWIST OF FATE

SMOKE. THAT'S WHAT I remember. Black smoke like a beast trying to kill me a dozen different ways. Even now I can smell it, taste it in my sleep. It pushes into my throat, and I sweat so that the sheets become wet like I pissed them. I wake, but the beast has already got me.

I should have died that night. No one was supposed to be drinking on the rig, but I was the guy no one ever noticed. I figured nobody would care, so I brought the stuff on board hidden in metal canteens — real smart, I thought. That night, I holed myself up in my room and I drank. We'd been working hard and the weariness was deep in me. At first I went slow, flicking through pages of the book I was reading: a history of oil exploration in the Gulf. I wanted the whisky to last until my next trip home. I sipped from a plastic cup like I was some kind of gentleman, but I had no one to lie to, and pretty soon I swigged straight from the canteen. I guzzled until I felt real happy and until I nearly fell over when I got up to piss. And still, I went back for the last drops. I'd told myself I could hold back, but I couldn't. Real drunks can't. I lay down and panicked at how I'd get through the next weeks without anything to help. Real smart, I told myself. Real smart.

No one would believe me now, but things were good for me on the rig. I kept my problems to myself and did my job. In the early days, I didn't know if I'd make it past being the lowest of the low — a worm. I thought I'd die grappling tongs, jerking slip, pushing this, pulling that. And there was all that noise all the time, but it turned out that working that made my brain grow quiet and my body get real tired. I moved up to roustabout — still the lowest man on payroll, but not a worm. Days on were the good days. I learned fast and the next guy up — the tool pusher — he joked that I should be employee of the month because of how much work I did, even scrubbing and painting the rig when I had to, just to keep busy. On shift, I acted like everyone else, talking fast and laughing. The men I worked with even gave me a nickname — Skinny Jones, or just Skinny. On the rig, I felt something different, like for once in my life, I could see past today. But then the nights would come, and I'd be alone in my tiny room, and the noise of all the machinery couldn't drown out the truths I knew. I'd always drink. I'd always be the lowest rank. A man can't escape himself.

That night when the siren blared, I grumbled to myself about too many fucking drills, and I waited for it to stop. I pressed my hands to my ears, but the pulsing noise kept on. I figured it couldn't be real. Plus, I was too drunk to run. The rig had never had a problem before, so I lay in my bed, and worried about my empty canteen.

The explosion threw me across the room so hard that after I hit the wall, I lay there unsure if I was alive or dead, my insides vibrating, my vision doubled or tripled. My head had slammed against the wall and so did my shoulder, but the pain felt far off, like it was someone else's. I could feel wetness seep down my cheek. I tasted it with my tongue: blood. When I opened my eyes, the room spun and swooped, so I closed them and let the blackness come over me. How long did I lie there? A minute? A lifetime?

From the hallway, I could hear the sounds of panic and of running. Someone banged on all the doors, hollering at us to get to the lifeboats. They screamed *Fire, Fire, Fire!* But I waited, dazed. I stumbled to the sink and, like a fool, I squirted toothpaste in my mouth. *No one had to know,* I told myself. And then I smelled the smoke. Run, I told myself, but like with everything else, I was too late.

Inside my room, the lights flickered off and on and then off again to total blackness. I started to move, my left arm dangling from my side like a dead animal. I felt my way to the door of my room and into the corridor, into the hellscape of black smoke. Slowly, I guided myself down the long hallway towards the light. Other men ran past me, their wailing voices a blur of sound. When the next explosion came, the force rammed me into the far wall and the world went silent except for a high-pitched ringing. I couldn't call out because I had no breath. I lay there and I listened to the sound of other men's feet race past. I grew real warm as I let myself drift off. I thought how easy it would be to die. I thought I was already a goner. And then, I felt something collapse beside me, something warm and heavy. Through the haze, I realized I wasn't alone. I gasped myself awake.

Frank. A guy I'd worked with, the nicest guy I'd ever met, the kind of guy who laughs at all your dumb jokes, lay near me in a heap. I could hear his shallow breath. He groaned. The smell of crude oil, of gas, thickened around us. I could taste it. I had to help Frank, I thought. I had to get my ass up and save him. His head lolled on his chest and his eyes were closed. I shook him real hard until he shuddered awake, wiped his face and felt the moist droplets on his cheeks. He whispered, "Methane," and then he looked straight at me, and I swear I could see his blue eyes piercing all that smoke around us, and he said, "I don't want to die."

I hoisted Frank up from where he lay and we leaned into each other — him much bigger, much taller than me — and we inched our way down the hallway. The siren blasted over and over. He'd been with others but got left behind after the first blast, he said. His ankle was bust, so I wrapped his arm around my shoulder and took his body onto mine. A man is a heavy weight to carry. Beyond the hallway, the blistering heat licked our skin, and the fire on the derrick roared. The beast was on the move.

We'd practised this during drills every week. We knew our way to the lifeboats. They weren't far from the sleeping quarters, but now it was night, and the smoke took up all the space. If there's such a thing as Satan, he was in that inferno. I dragged Frank to the deck where I thought the lifeboats would be, I ran up to the edge and looked over. Nothing. The boats were gone. The light from the fire made Frank's eyes glow like trapped prey.

All I wanted was to spare Frank. He didn't deserve to get left behind like that. I did, but not Frank. Whoever left him like that — injured and alone — if I ever found out, I swore I would kill him. From across the platform the blaze swept towards us. There was nowhere left to go. Beneath us, the rig groaned like a dying man. I turned to Frank and pleaded with him to crawl, to do anything it took to inch his way up to the metal railings.

"I can't swim." The sound of the fire and the siren swallowed Frank's sobs. Beneath us the Gulf was more than six storeys down.

I half wrestled, half tugged him to the edge. I held his hand. I forced him.

I don't remember letting go. I remember thinking the wind would tear my limbs from my body so that death would meet me before I crashed into the water.

Alone I plunged into the Gulf, as if drilling into concrete with my body. The water rushed past me and when I stopped going down, I had to guess which way was up. I thought my lungs would burst. I broke the surface. The taste of salt and oil fouled my mouth. I was swimming in gas. Flames raced across the water.

When the men on board the lifeboat pulled me out, I hurled myself to the floor, puked up water, fuel, and salt, and I pissed myself thinking the flames would get me. I shrieked against the night sky until right in front of our eyes, the whole rig erupted in one more explosion. I screamed for Frank. He didn't surface.

I should have died that night. The greater punishment is to live.

Hours later in a hotel room in Houma, I signed my name on the dotted line of a piece of paper and then I ran through rooms looking for Frank until all the rooms were empty. I went home and tried to forget.

For weeks it was all over the TV. Every goddamn time I turned it on, there was the smoke, the fire, the oil that kept gushing into the Gulf for weeks, but from the TV, you couldn't smell the gas or feel the flames scorching your flesh. Yet all those talking heads thought they knew something. Even the president himself, old Ronny Reagan, was everywhere, looking all concerned, but I knew he was an actor, a son of a bitch pretending to give a crap about men like me who do real work, while men like him get rich just for looking like they care. One night I turned on the TV and there he was, finally shown up in Grand Isle, but only after he visited that big fair in New Orleans and showed off riding some gondola, posing on that goddamn oil platform they put on display, and jabbering about America's oil boom. Next thing you know he's put a sad face on, and he's standing on the shore of the Gulf in front of all those white wooden crosses and he's reading the names of the men who are gone, but I refused to listen. I turned off the TV and shoved it into a closet, and then I put my fist into the wall.

It was a pushy broad from the newspaper in New Orleans who called and wanted to know how it felt to jump and how it felt to survive when others didn't. How in hell she knew any of that, or if she knew about my booze and Frank and how he died on my watch, I didn't want to know, so I slammed down the phone. After that, I cut the cord with a pair of kid's scissors. I closed my bank account and took all my money in cash. I found us a new place to live.

If I never see the Gulf and its stinking beaches again, I'll be lucky. Let death find me but find me on dry land.

THREE

JESSE – SAY IT ISN'T SO

THE BLACK-FEATHERED ROOSTER crows like the devil on a bender before dawn. I thrust my head under my pillow trying to sleep, but the rooster and the heat and the pit in my stomach keep me awake as I wait for the sound of Daddy's footsteps that will tell me it's time to go.

The only good things me and Willow Rose have in the room we now share is a faded world map that hangs, creased, on the wall right beside my bed and the radio with the tape recorder that I take from the kitchen each night so I can listen to it while I fall asleep. The map is torn all down the Atlantic and the Pacific Oceans and fixed with tape. I stole it from my homeroom class last year before school ended. I wanted it so bad. When I look at the map I think about how if you live somewhere important like New York, Houston, or even New Orleans, it must feel real different than if you're like me and you're just one person clinging to a tiny spot on the map, in a place so small no one else knows it's there. The place where we live now doesn't even have a name. I trace my finger up the line that runs from Louisiana west to Texas and then down to Mexico, wishing I could be anywhere but here, in this house, in this place. All summer long on the radio, I've listened to WRNO, the radio station coming from the World's Fair in New Orleans. There they have a Space Shuttle on display and a 3-D movie about lakes and rivers that they say makes you feel like you're really on the water. Everything and everyone is at the fair but us. If I could drive, I would take Daddy's truck up the highway and see all of it — the gondola over the Mississippi, the Aquacade shows with the pretty girls in swimsuits, the Wonderwall with its temples and towers, I would see the whole city — for myself.

"Hurry up, Jess. Sun up soon." My father sticks his head in our room as he pulls on a shirt. Since he stopped working on the rig, Daddy has grown thinner than he ever was; all there is to him now is bone and stringy muscles and skin that covers him like a bag. He could be a scarecrow in a field, or a skeleton at Halloween, but still strong, his big hands tough enough to put out a match between his fingers, or crush a beer can flat in his palm.

On the floor, Willow Rose sleeps on her mattress, long legs flung out like wild vines of morning glory. She looks close to grown up, except that she sleeps with a ratty brown stuffed dog that she yanked from the trash before we moved from the old house.

I pull on this week's shirt, loose with heat, and my jeans and a pair of ancient, cracked waders, and slink into the kitchen where my father pours black coffee made with yesterday's grounds into an old blue lunch thermos. He screws on the stained lid and together we slip out of the pressing warmth of the house. Outside, under the sky still streaked with traces of indigo, the rooster struts in circles at our feet. Daddy kicks gravel at him, but the rooster doesn't care; he just pecks and crows some more.

"Sometimes I think I ought to put a bullet through that shit-for-brains bird just to get some quiet around here," he says. I reach down to stroke the rooster's feathers. I like the bird. He has nerve. My father watches and grunts at me to move my ass. He cups his left ear in the way he has ever since the explosion, like there's a mosquito in there that won't stop buzzing.

I know you shouldn't hunt small game in August, and my father knows it too, but it's one of two things he wants to do these days: kill animals and drink cans of Bud. Though we have no hunting permit, we set out water traps and snares last night and now we're going to check them. Daddy has his .22 rifle — a Winchester single shot — strapped across his shoulder as we walk through the cypress trees, covered with Spanish moss like a ghost veil, and down to where the long grass slips into marsh. I pray we've caught nothing. Sometimes there are squirrels or rabbits in the traps, but a few times we've caught raccoons. The raccoons are the worst. They stay alive, struggling, terror in their eyes. Last time that happened Daddy made me club one unconscious and then stand on its chest until it heaved its final breath. There's nothing but sorrow in looking a dying raccoon in the eye. At least other animals — squirrels, rabbits — they die easy, like they don't even know they're alive.

Two of the snares have brown marsh rabbits with bloody fur pulled back on raw pink muscle. One has an open mouth and a jaw covered in blood; he tried to chew his way out of death. I ease them from the snares like they're babies and close their bulging eyes before putting them into the burlap bag we've brought.

I wade into the water, lean in and shuffle along the bottom of the marsh, careful as though searching for treasure with the soles of my feet, my strides still shorter than my father's. I see it first: there is a great blue heron ahead of us, her giant wings beating like a panicked heart. She is caught, with one long leg held tight in one of our traps.

"Daddy," I say. He winces when I call him that, as if — since the explosion — he doesn't want to be my father anymore. I move away from him and get up close to the bird. The pupil of its beady orange eye is huge and desperate.

"Jesus Christ." My father rubs his jaw, then rubs his hands together. I push towards the bird. My father strides from behind me and reaches the animal, which now stands paralyzed by our nearness.

"Shh," Daddy says to the heron as though it's a scared child. "Pass me that bag," he tells me and reaches out an arm without looking at me.

I wrangle off my shirt and use it to cradle the rabbits, tucking them into my waders to hold them in place. Then I hand over the sack to my father, who inches closer to the frozen heron. As he reaches for it, the bird flaps its wings, which must be longer than Daddy is tall, in one last attempt to fly, but real quick, my father drops the burlap over the eyes of the animal, and it falls completely still. Daddy nods to me and I press into the weight of the water, lean down and pull up the trap that bites into the bird's stick of a leg. My father tells me to hurry up. I wish I were the one holding the heron. I squeeze the spring to loosen the jaws of the trap, while Daddy holds the bird against his chest, as it beats its wings.

"Let me," I say.

My father hands me the heron, and I touch her feathers. She is light in my arms and smells like marsh.

"She's okay," my father says. In the morning sun, his face is soft as he looks at the bird.

I want to keep holding her. I stroke her neck, real careful not to harm her. All around us a thousand crickets sing.

"You got to let her go," my father says. He leans in to take off the heron's head-covering, counts to three in a real soft voice. I unwrap my arms from around her body and open them wide. The bird unpeels its wings, and without looking back, she flies. Daddy stands right up against me so I can feel his heat. He nudges my shoulder.

"You did good," he says. I nod and watch the arc of the bird over the trees. I rest my head against my father's shoulder, and he rests his hand on my head, ruffles my hair like he did when I was a kid. The heron croaks, and in the distance, from the other side of the bayou, we hear the sound of branches rustling. Daddy moves away from me, real sudden.

"But next time, just shoot the damn thing and save me the trouble," he says.

From the direction of the rustling, we hear gunfire. A single shot. My father's eyes dart and he waves at me to hurry through the water and into the truck. The whole way home he rubs his ear, and I can smell his rank breath fill up the air between us.

FOUR

WRAPPED AROUND YOUR FINGER

WHEN I SULK BACK into our house, still carrying a shirt full of rabbits, Mama's cigarette smoke spreads, a thick haze over the kitchen.

"Morning, cher," she says.

Mama smiles, but when she takes in the sight of the rabbits, she inhales too quickly and coughs until her face grows red. Rabbits in August are full of parasites and she knows it. She inhales again, this time real smooth and deep. My mama is still wearing her nightgown even though the full sun is in the kitchen now, and through the soft, yellowed fabric, the darkness of the triangle between her legs and her nipples that look like small purple grapes show. My cheeks are hot as Daddy barges in the door and Mama mutters, "Shit."

"We got rabbits," he says, pointing to my bundle.

"What do you want me to do with those?" Mama inhales once more and stubs out her smoke.

"Cook 'em" is my father's flat-as-a-pancake answer. "It'll burn the sickness out of them."

My mother leans back in her chair and lights another smoke, mouthing to herself the words my father has just said. She's silent, but I know the tone she'd have in her voice if she spoke out loud. I shoot Daddy a look as if to say, *See*?, but he doesn't care. He lowers himself heavy into his chair and asks Mama for some coffee. She tells him it's in the pot. "Fresh," she says to needle him that she didn't re-use old grounds. He pours himself a cup and slams the empty pot down. I bite my lip and imagine hitting my father in the teeth. When she's not feeling angry, Mama says we have to be patient, that he's hurting real bad about what happened on the rig, but he moved us to this dump and doesn't even care how it feels for us to have nothing. Mama pats my arm and tells me I should take the rabbits outside. My father slurps his coffee then cusses that he burnt the roof of his mouth. Mama calls him poor baby, but I catch her looking down to hide her smile as I go out back.

After my father got his job on the rig, we moved from a trailer to a blue house in Grand Isle at the end of a short street off the main road. We could run to the beach in minutes. Almost everyone I have ever known in my whole life lives in Grand Isle. Now we live north of Leeville in a house that's cranked up on cinder blocks. The floor is crooked, even rotten and soft in the corners of the kitchen, and the bathroom stinks of mildew. When it rains, water seeps in through the ceiling over the kitchen sink, and beneath the house a small lake forms, like the rain wants to get us from two directions. There are two other rotting houses near ours, but no one else is crazy enough to live in them, and the high grass and the trees hide us from the road. We're surrounded by cypress trees and marsh. Almost no one knows we're here. It's like my father wanted us all to disappear. The long bridge to Grand Isle looms in the sky near where we live, but since we moved, I've never crossed it, not even once. None of us has, as if Daddy's anger and sadness at what happened has created an invisible door we can't pass through.

Behind our house is a gravelly yard that is partly overgrown with weeds and grass. There's an ancient tin smokehouse that Daddy is determined to use like he thinks he's some kind of old-time trapper, and a shed with broken windows made of the same warped wood siding as the house, the greying paint peeling off. Chips of it lie on the ground, and no one bothers to pick them up.

In the yard there is a torn and bloodied towel with a blue flower pattern on it. It's still there from the last time we skinned animals — squirrels — so I lay the rabbits on the towel and then peel off my waders, rubbing my hands on my jeans to get rid of the scent of dead animal. Soon Mama comes outside and sits in one of the nearly busted lawn chairs behind the house. She sips her coffee and says, "Poor rabbits. Died for nothing."

"He's crazy," I say.

"Aw, cher," Mama says and squints against the sun. "Come on now."

"We should have stayed in Grand Isle." I plunk myself into the chair beside hers.

Mama sucks on her lips and strokes my cheek with the back of her hand, but I flinch away. She rubs the spot on my back between my shoulder blades. "You're a good trapper," she says and keeps rubbing round discs like Frisbees on my back, making me breathe deep. My eyelids grow heavy.

"At least I had friends in Grand Isle," I say.

"Should we run away then? You and me and Willow Rose? Get jobs and live on a fancy beach somewhere, drink pina coladas?" Mama asks.

"I wish," I say.

"Where to then?"

"Miami."

"Naw, not far enough," Mama smiles.

"California."

"I always thought I'd like France," Mama says.

"Your French is terrible," I say.

"Your *memere* would die to hear you talk like that," she says, even though Mama's mama is long dead. "And anyway, French is the language of love." She flutters her eyelashes and makes a kissy mouth.

"Mama!" I groan.

"Where then?" she asks me.

"Peru," I say.

"Uruguay!" she calls back.

When I was a kid, Mama and I used to play the geography game where you have to name a place that begins with the last letter of the place the other person named, and I can feel she's warming up for a round now, but I'm already stumped. When I can't think of anything that begins with Y, she tries again. "Uganda" she calls out.

"America," I say.

"Boring," she says, grinning and tsking at me.

"Australia, then, Austria, Amazonia."

"No such place as Amazonia," she says.

"You win."

"You give up too easy," she says and sinks back into her chair, pleased with herself.

Mama has the skinning knife with her, and she taps the butt on the arm of her chair, but neither of us makes a move. Instead, my mother lights a smoke, and exhaling to the side, she puts a finger to her lips. She smiles like Willow Rose does when she's about to get into trouble.

"Don't tell Daddy that you dumped them in the bayou," Mama says and gestures to the dead rabbits.

She puts her finger on her lips to shush me and motions for me to hurry up before she goes back inside, leaving me to get rid of the evidence. Daddy has likely gone back to bed like he usually does now, only getting up again in the evenings to eat and then drink into the night. Mama says he's afraid to sleep when it's dark because of the nightmares that make him wake up screaming like a baby, so when he does sleep, it's when the sun is full up, and he lays in his and Mama's room, which is darkened by the cardboard from moving boxes taped up against the window frames.

Mama will spend the rest of the day smoking her Pall Malls, and she'll watch game shows on the TV that she turns on while Daddy sleeps and then unplugs when he's up. When we first moved into this house, there was nothing — not even electricity — but Daddy's real smart about things like that, and he went out late one night carrying a ladder. When he came back home, he smiled like he was giddy or plastered, and he practically danced around Mama when she turned on the TV and light flickered from the screen. Minutes later he sniped at her to turn it off, but now the thing is always on during the day, with some game-show host announcing prizes like a new car or a dishwasher blaring into the living room where Mama sits around, smoking, watching and reading the same fashion magazines she bought way back in Grand Isle.

At first when we moved, Daddy grumbled to Mama that she should get a job. When Willow Rose and I were little, she worked as a waitress at the Blue Dolphin Cafe — I thought it was real fancy because they served steak and French fries with some kind of spicy mayonnaise, but when Daddy got the job on the rig, he picked her up in a hug that made her kick up her feet, and he told her she could quit. I remember her big grin when she tossed her blue waitress dress into the trash. Waitressing made her feet hurt, she said, and she told us that when you serve customers, they always treat you like you're a nobody, like they know you could never afford the steak they're eating right in front of you. Daddy says she can't get a job back in Grand Isle now because people would talk, and Mama's voice gets real tight when she tells him she can't get a job at all since we have no phone, and she doesn't know anyone in Golden Meadow, the nearest town, who would hire her, anyway. I think she is too angry at Daddy and at everything to go back to serving steak to tourists, and with Daddy so crazy and sad, watching game shows all day is the only way she can show it. And anyway, he got a payout from the oil company, so she says we can live okay for a little while. Daddy must know she won't budge because he doesn't bother her much about working these days. He lets her pass her days talking to the TV, answering game-show questions out loud and whooping when she gets them right. She tells us she'd clean up if only she could get on that quiz show for real.

The rabbits are heavy in my arms as I wrap them up again in my shirt and carry them all the way back to the swamp across the road and whisper them off to sleep for good in the dark water tinged with that gassy rainbow sheen.

Last night on the radio I heard that where Daddy's rig once stood, the oil still gushes into the Gulf. They say that more than two million barrels have spilled, and I can't even imagine what that means. On TV they tell stories about people from out of state, from far away places like California, who show up to help the animals, washing shorebirds, even dolphins, while the oil keeps on belching and my father carries on like a man on fire.

FIVE

OWNER OF A LONELY HEART

AFTER DUSK DADDY TAKES off. He doesn't have to tell us he's going to Lafitte Lodge, the Cajun bar in Leeville where the owner plays accordion and blasted men sing old-timey songs. I've never been, but even I know the rumour that the waitresses there wear short skirts and have short tempers. Willow Rose, Mama and I breathe easier when he's gone, and we eat smooth peanut butter sandwiches on white bread, cutting our sandwiches into fours to make them last longer. When we finish eating, I am still hungry.

"I'll get you some squirrel from the smokehouse," Willow Rose says, snickering.

Mama swats her arm, and they both crack up. "It's real good. Everyone knows that." Willow Rose keeps talking like she's on TV. "America's favourite food, yard squirrel! Come and get it."

We are hungry all the time but not hungry enough for the break-your-teeth strips of squirrel Daddy has dried out. He says the smokehouse will keep us from getting food stamps, but even though he's real proud of himself for that, the truth is that all he's fed us is jerky so tough it's like he's turned flesh into bone. Instead, Mama makes another peanut butter sandwich, carefully cuts it in two and then into four, and I share it with Willow Rose. "Mmmmm," Willow Rose says. "Would be even better with squirrel jam."

"Or rabbit parasites," I add.

Mama has brought the tape recorder back to the kitchen and makes us listen to her favourite tape for the hundredth time. She sings along with Janis Joplin, crooning real loud, asking the lord to buy her a Mercedes-Benz while me and Willow Rose groan at the way her voice wobbles and flattens. When the tape finally gets sucked into the machine and starts playing real fast like a cartoon voice, Willow Rose makes her voice high-pitched and keeps on speed-singing until Mama yanks the tape from the player and tosses it at my sister, cussing us out and then laughing at Willow Rose. She tells us she's going to feed us to the alligators like we deserve and that she should have been a hippie and gone to San Francisco or Woodstock but she missed her chance. When she says that, her voice is soft like she's fallen into a dream of herself with flowers in her hair right there in front of us. Willow Rose pipes up and says she should have been Madonna, before she breaks into the chorus of "Holiday." Over her singing, I say I should have been born rich so we could live somewhere real nice for once. I tell Mama that someday I'm going to buy her a house somewhere good like Hollywood or New York, and she tells me she'd settle for someplace nice in New Orleans, maybe the Garden District — one of those houses with the big old porches surrounded by a tidy lawn where she could grow old in peace, she says. I promise her I'll try, and she smiles in a way that feels like a little piece of glass in my heart. Out the window, the sky seeps from purple to black, and the frogs fill the air with their lonely bachelor songs. We are so far from any other light that soon we will be able to see the gleam of the stars from the kitchen window.

My belly wrenches with hunger long after we've finished our sandwiches, but in the icebox, we have a jar of mayonnaise, a half-eaten chicken leg, two onions so old they've shrivelled, and not much more. I wait until Mama and Willow Rose leave the kitchen before I tear into the chicken leg, but Willow Rose walks in on me just as I'm gulping the last of it down.

"That was mine," she says, her voice as irritable as my stomach feels.

"Tough," I say.

Willow Rose gets a glass from the sink, fills it with water and sits back down at the kitchen table.

“That’s some shit,” she says and puts her head on her folded arms on the table. I pat her head, stroke her hair, even though it makes me feel clumsy. I rub her back like Mama always does. She sticks her head up. “You think it’s always going to be like this?” she asks. I put my arm around her shoulders because it’s the only answer I have.

When we hear Daddy’s truck pull up in front of the house — the pebbles pinging off tires, the engine cutting off — we look at each other expectantly under the single light bulb that hangs in the kitchen. A door slams, feet crunch on gravel and then another door closes hard. There are two voices: Daddy’s and another man’s. Willow Rose gets a sly grin on her face like when she senses trouble’s coming, and for some reason my skin goes prickly.

“Anyone home?” Daddy never says that, never hollers when he comes in the door. I can tell by his voice that he is fucked-up drunk and whoever he is with thinks it’s hilarious: a loud laugh echoes all the way to the kitchen.

Mama peeks her head into the hallway. She’s in her nightgown, and when she sees what’s going on, she darts back to her room and shuts the door behind her. In a minute she’s back out dressed in jean shorts and an old blue T-shirt that used to be Daddy’s. It has a picture of a blonde cartoon woman with giant tits that make me think of watermelons pushed up into a small pink bikini. In one hand the woman holds a fishing rod with a fish at the end of it, and the faded white writing says ‘Hook, line, and sink ’er.’ When I was younger, that shirt gave me a boner.

Mama, Willow Rose and me stand in the corner of the kitchen like a pile of raccoon kits. Daddy brings in a man twice his size — he is tall and broad — and I swear he is missing two fingers on his right hand. On his chin there is a cleft like he’s a cartoon character. His green eyes are bloodshot and bright, but even though he looks both grizzled and drunk, he’s a good-looking man.

“Antoine,” is all Daddy says. And he gestures to the rest of us with his hand. Mama steps forward and reaches out her hand and says her name.

"Angeline."

"Nice to meet you, Angel baby," Antoine says. He brings her hand to his dry lips and kisses it. Mama lets him, but then rubs the back of her hand on her thigh when Antoine isn't looking. She hates being called Angel.

Me and Willow Rose shake his meaty hand next, and when it's my turn I want to run my fingers along Antoine's stumps to know what they feel like. He pulls his hand away and waves it at me.

"You like that, huh?"

I don't know what to say, but Antoine's face cracks into a grin and he bellows laughter at me.

"Come on," he says. "Y'all can touch them."

I don't, but he keeps shoving his hand into mine until I pass my fingers over his stumps. They feel like knuckles with a rubber eraser tip where the skin folds in on itself. A shiver bolts through me.

"Can I?" Willow Rose asks.

Mama gasps her name, but Willow Rose doesn't mind about manners, and neither does Antoine.

"Let her," he says.

Willow Rose traces the outline of Antoine's stumps and nods as though she's just learned something important.

"Cool," she says, and hums to herself.

Antoine raises an eyebrow, and looks at Mama, offering her a turn. She shakes her head.

"C'mon baby, that bad?" Antoine asks.

"It ain't that." Mama says.

"It's always the pretty ladies who make that face," Antoine says.

Daddy has set down two six-packs of beer on the counter. Michelob. He reaches for a can. Mama pulls her lips into a line thin as a whisker.

"It's light," Daddy says.

"Ain't no one getting drunk on this shit," Antoine says. He looks at Mama. "Excuse me, baby. This stuff. Want one?"

My father looks at Antoine with glazed eyes lit by the single bulb that hangs from the ceiling. "Naw — not Angeline." He snakes his arm around Mama's waist, draws her to him, kisses her close to her mouth. She straightens.

"I will," Mama says, and her fingers brush up against Antoine's stumps as she takes the silver can from him.

I drank my first beer when I was a kid. I sipped it before I even had grown-up teeth. Mama still has a picture of me sitting at the table of our first trailer; I'm grinning with no front teeth, and I'm wearing a Saints T-shirt that I loved to rags and am holding a can of Dixie. I remember it felt like a dare, when my father offered the can to me, so I sipped and then smacked my tongue against the roof of my mouth sorting out the bitter taste. It made Daddy smile and cheer me on as I drank more until Mama said "Emmett!" and took the can away.

My father, Antoine and Mama sit around the kitchen table. Mama kicks her feet up onto the fourth chair and tells Daddy to offer Antoine something to eat, which is funny because of what she must know is in our icebox. Antoine says he don't need nothing to eat, and Mama says, "That's good, 'cause all I got for you is squirrel jerky and peanut butter." They all laugh, even Daddy. When Mama isn't looking, I snatch one of the beers from the counter, and me and Willow Rose skulk out of the kitchen to the front room.

I stick the Michelob under the cushions of the sofa and press it open, quiet so Mama won't hear. Willow Rose whispers "*Canaille*!" I shrug and offer her the can. She pours the liquid down her throat in a long gulp, and then takes another. "Hey!" I say and grab the can back. We pass the beer back and forth and then we each lay on opposite sides of the brown, fuzzy sofa with the torn fabric and the nearly flat, but still soft pillows. We've had the same sofa for my whole life, and you can read our family history in the stain from when I spilled chocolate milk on it and Willow Rose screamed at me for wasting, and the tear in the back pillow that Willow Rose always picks at when she watches TV. Willow Rose's legs stretch out, and she kicks mine out of the way. I shove her legs over and whisper at her to shut her pie hole when she grumbles her protest.

By the time I was ten, Daddy would sneak me a Bud or a Miller when he came home from the store, and I'd drink up by myself and practise belching after, while I lay on my bed. When he worked on the rig, Daddy still drank, but instead of going between hamming it up and hollering at us when he was wasted, he talked and talked about rig life, telling me that getting an oil job was the only way sons-of-bitches like him — who grew up in Shitsville and never finished high school — could hope to be man enough to raise a decent family. You have to be a man, and oil is the only thing going in this place, he'd say, and he'd crack one open for me. I'd drink as much as he wanted me to. It made me feel like maybe my father thought I was okay.

From the other room Antoine asks what we're doing living in this nowhere place, and Daddy's voice snags as he tells the shortest version of the explosion followed by the quick move.

"Ain't that the way," Antoine says. "You think you got life by the balls, but it's always got you in the end."

The way he talks makes me think about his fingers and I wonder how they got like that. Another can hisses open in the other room.

"You got a family?" Daddy asks.

A can scrapes the table. "I don't know for sure. I got an ex who says I got a daughter, but I never met her. I just send money to the ex and hope it's true," Antoine says.

"You kidding?" Daddy asks.

"Nope," Antoine says.

"Shit," Daddy says.

"You're a good man to do that," Mama says.

"I figure maybe there is a daughter, and maybe there isn't, but it don't hurt to be generous." Antoine's quiet for a minute and then he says, "I must be some kind of sucker."

Everyone laughs.

Willow Rose and I watch TV on low until the sky grows dark, and I drift into sleep, only waking when Antoine is at the door with my father and Mama.

"I ain't so drunk I can't walk. I promise not to fall into the bayou," Antoine is saying. Daddy keeps saying he'll drive Antoine home, but Mama wrenches the keys from him, and Antoine tells Daddy he better listen to her. "Happy wife, happy life," he says. But then he adds, "Or is it, "Got no wife, happy life?" He winks and laughs along with Daddy.

I rise from the sofa to see Antoine off. Mama leans into Daddy like even she's tipsy. Antoine shakes my father's hand and says, "See you on Monday." Daddy nods and calls him boss, slapping him on the back and thanking him before opening the door. Antoine gets up real close to Mama then. He puts his face right next to hers and he kisses her on the cheek, right close to her lips. Mama is small beside him, and she shrinks away as he puts his hand on her backside and squeezes. Daddy doesn't notice as Mama flicks his hand away.

"Goodnight baby. It was nice to meet y'all," he says and slouches out the door.

Mama shakes her head at me, a caution to shut my mouth.

"What're you doing on Monday?" I ask my father.

"I got a job. He fixes cars — has a shop in Leeville." Daddy rubs his knuckles on my head. "See — we're back in business," he says to Mama, who smiles a tight-lipped smile. Even though he's still drunk, Daddy looks happy, like something in his face has come back to life.

I only pretend to go to bed when Mama tells me to. Instead, I stand in the shadows just outside the kitchen, listening to Daddy pop open another beer while Mama tells him he better not bring Antoine this way again. From the tightness in her voice, I can tell she is afraid to ruin Daddy's new job, but when Daddy says he'll bring over whoever he likes, she lays into him and says, "You keep your work friend at work, that's all I'm saying."

"You should be happy that man gave me a job," my father grunts.

"I'll be happy when I see him pay you."

"He'll pay."

"Fine, then," my Mama says and leaves the room, ignoring me as she passes but muttering so I can hear, "And tell him to keep his hands to his damn self."

SIX

SEND ME AN ANGEL

WEARING FILTHY BLUE JEANS and oil-blackened work shirts, my father goes to work every morning and comes home hands stained dark, hair puffed up like a bonfire in the heat and humidity. Most days he comes home with a six-pack or two of Bud or Miller, and Mama ignores him while he sits outside and pops open one can after another. We eat rice and hotdogs because Daddy has a job, and for now he doesn't yell that much. He even seems like he likes his work, smiling more like when we lived in Grand Isle. He tells us Antoine is lazy — he wants Daddy to do all the work while he watches, but Daddy likes to tell us about the crazy customers, like the three identical twin brothers — grown men — who came in wearing the exact same blue shirt and asking for a custom blue paint job on their shared sports car, which only had two seats. Antoine doesn't do paint jobs, but he convinced the men to let him check the oil just so he could see under the hood of their fancy European car. At least, he says, Antoine ain't causing no explosions, and he's easy with money. One day, Daddy comes home with bags of Cheetos for me and Willow Rose. "From Antoine," he says, passing them to us when Mama is out of the room. Another day he comes home with a roast chicken, and we gulp it down so quick that I have to stop myself from puking from eating so much.

One Friday, my father comes home with a six-pack of Bud, a bottle of Jack Daniel's that he hides in a plastic bag and a section of newspaper rolled into his back pocket. He goes from the front door straight to his bedroom, his bad mood come back for real this time.

I follow Mama into their room, and she asks "What's the matter, cher?" He says he's not feeling so good and closes his eyes, pushes her hand away.

That night me and Mama and Willow Rose sit around the table and eat potted meat on crackers when Daddy comes into the kitchen and turns his anger on me.

"Why don't you have a job?" he asks.

My spine tingles straight. "Where am I supposed to work?" I say.

"Y'all think I'm the only one who can earn money around here. Maybe I'm ready to retire for good," Daddy says, looking around the table.

Ever since we moved, I haven't done anything like we used to do in the summers on Grand Isle. I haven't gone swimming or ridden my bike with friends up and down the main street, looking for action or girls or something — anything — to do. Here, I wouldn't even know where to find a job. We are closest to Leeville, but practically no one lives there. I imagine myself walking along the side of the highway looking for cans or bottles for money — me and Willow Rose used to do that on the beach back home — but near our house now, there isn't even a place to bring cans, never mind somewhere to get a job.

"Maybe if you moved us somewhere normal, I could get a job," I say and bite into my cracker. "How about you drive me to New Orleans so I can get a job there?"

"You know I ain't driving you to New Orleans." My father's voice sounds like it might break. I bite into another cracker.

"Then I guess I ain't getting a job," I say.

"Goddamn it," my father says. "You don't know what it's like." His voice catches on something and sounds like it's about to tear.

He shoves the empty chair that he stands over, the force making it fall to the floor before he leaves the room. Willow Rose and I both look at Mama as if she will have answers, but Mama has pushed her plate away from her, and she offers it to Willow Rose, who stuffs her face with Mama's last cracker.

"He'll be okay," Mama says. She shakes her head at his mood and follows Daddy up to their room.

I snort and Willow Rose mimics me. I kick her leg. She laughs and says it didn't hurt, then grabs one of Mama's cigarettes and lights it, pretending to inhale until I make her stub it out before we get caught.

Mama's and Daddy's voices rise and drawers get opened and slammed shut behind their closed door. Willow Rose plonks down in front of the TV and blares some talk show full blast. I leave her there and creep into our room, using the time alone in our room to beat off as silent as I can while Mama and Daddy holler at each other.

One of my friends from school back in Grand Isle — his name was Adolphe after his great-grandfather, but Adolphe was such a terrible name that we all called him Dolphin, which became Fin for short — stole a *Playboy* magazine from his older brother for us to look at. The last time I saw Fin, he let me rip out the best page. I folded that picture into a tiny square and tucked it into my jeans pocket. I must have looked at it a thousand times in secret. It drove me wild. It had a girl with long dark hair wearing cutoff jean shorts that she pulled aside to show the pink of where she wasn't wearing panties. She sat directly in front of the camera pushing her thighs open, her hand touching herself. She had no shirt on. Her tits were round as if they'd been blown up like a balloon, with pink nipples that pointed up. Once, I'd walked in on Mama without her bra on and she looked more like she had two pancakes hanging off her, nothing like the girl in the picture. I would have done anything to touch tits like that girl had. The magazine said she was a college student, and it made me feel desperate — no one in my family ever went to college.

From inside Mama and Daddy's room, Daddy screams "I'm going," and Mama hollers back that he should go ahead and leave then. I freeze and do up my pants real quick, toss my hand across my forehead and pretend to be asleep. Two sets of footsteps bang down the hall, and in a minute Daddy's truck roars to life as he drives away.

Mama joins Willow Rose in front of the TV and I go back to thinking of my picture.

Before we moved, Mama washed my jeans without telling me, and the picture shredded, the pieces getting all over everything in the laundry. Mama cussed at me for not cleaning out my pockets, and I silently cussed at myself too. Still, even now all I can think about is how bad I want to climb on top of that college girl and get inside her and — I swear — two minutes would be enough.

SEVEN

GIRLS WITH GUNS

IN THE MORNING MY father leaves. He doesn't know how long he'll be gone. He puts a small bag of clothes and his thermos of coffee in his truck and tells me and Willow Rose he's going to visit his mama. He says she's old and sick and he's got to go be with her. I think he's cracking up because we don't even have a phone in our house, so I don't know how he'd know anything about his mama, or why he suddenly cares about her, but he's going, and Mama isn't even getting up to say goodbye.

Before he leaves, he sits me down on the crumbling front steps of the house. The sun has begun to heat the cement, warming my thighs. He shows me the revolver he keeps hidden in his night table. It's always been there. A Colt .22, a real old gun with a walnut grip that his own daddy gave to him. It's the only thing he has from his family. He passes it to me, and I take it in both hands.

"You know how to use this?"

The Colt isn't big, but it has heft. I finger the wood on the grip. It's smooth with age next to the cold metal of the trigger.

"Yes sir," I say. I crack open the cylinder to check if it's loaded. It's not.

"You're in charge now, you got that?" My father looks me right in the eyes and grabs me by the shoulder. He keeps staring at me like he's waiting for me to say something, but I don't know what.

"Yes sir," I say again. I click the cylinder back into place and look away from his gaze.

He wraps his long fingers around the grip of the gun. "Don't let nobody else touch this," he says, and his voice is at the edge of something that sounds like fear and anger.

"I won't," I say.

"Good." My father claps me on the shoulder and presses into it too long. "You keep that smokehouse full too. I'm relying on you," he says. And then he gets into his white truck — he bought it when he got his oil job — and the engine coughs to life. Before he drives down the gravel road, he raises his finger to me in a strange wave, his face wooden.

The tires of Daddy's truck raise a storm of dust and pebbles. I watch him drive away until the truck turns onto the main road and disappears. In the silence of the warm morning, I click the Colt open again and check the chamber one more time. Standing now, I point the gun way down the road and pull the trigger. The gun clicks and my imaginary bullet flies, following the direction of my arm. "Pow," I say and pull the trigger again.

From behind the house, the rooster crows, and when he stops making noise, I take a deep breath and sit alone on the front stoop, listening for the songbirds. They're the first thing I hear every morning where we live now, and if you pay attention, you can tell which birds are near. The coo of the mourning doves. The trill of the red-winged blackbirds. These are always there. And lately, I've been watching for a blue bird — real small — that's been winging high up in the cypress trees. Whenever I look for it, it's not there, but sometimes, I'll be outside just waiting for something to happen, and it appears. I know it by its call: *zhee-zhee-zizizizi-zeeet.* You can hardly see it because it's so small and blends in with the trees, but I'll hear it, and then it flits away, disappears into the sky. One time I was watching it, just standing there staring up at the trees outside the kitchen window, when Mama tiptoed outside. She whispered its name to me: "Cerulean Warbler." When I asked her how she knew, she pinched both my cheeks and said, "You think I never went to school?" And then she rubbed my face to take away the pinch. "I wanted to study birds someday," she said, but didn't finish her sentence. Mama came close to finishing high school, but then she had me, and I know this was what she was thinking when she lit up a cigarette, slowly exhaling smoke, smiling to make both of us feel better.

The front door creaks open and slams shut. Willow Rose sits down beside me on the steps. She's wearing jean shorts and a stained white T-shirt. The heels of her bare feet are cracked and dirty. I always wonder how her feet can be so dirty first thing in the morning. "You think he'll be back soon?" she asks. She's chewing pink bubble gum and I have no idea where it could have come from.

I show her that Daddy's left me his gun.

"No fair!" she says and wraps her hands around the grip. I pull it away.

"Daddy said I have to look after things now that he's gone."

Willow Rose snorts at that and digs into her pocket. "Look what I got," she says and shows me a bundle of worn dollar bills wrapped with a thin elastic.

"Where'd you get that?"

"None of your business." She snatches the money away and tucks it back into her pocket, the look of the devil on her face. She grins and blows a big pink bubble that pops in her face and hair. "Now we can buy real food," she says.

In our new life, Daddy likes to say, "Fuck the man!" and he keeps all his money from the payout in bundles that he hides in his room. Before we moved, he showed us how much he had, and he smiled, all gleeful like it would last forever, but his bundles now are thinner every time I catch sight of them. Sometimes I snitch a few dollars even though there's almost nothing for me to do with money around here. The nearest store in Leeville sells bait, ice, Cokes, Cheetos and not much more. Still, I keep stealing a few bills at a time and stockpiling them in the pages of the few books I brought with me from before that I keep hidden under my bed. I stole last year's geography textbook from school because of the pictures of deserts and oceans, and I have a copy of *The Old Man and the Sea* that the librarian gave to me because no one else had ever taken it out, and she watched me damn near cry when I read about Santiago dreaming of the lions. Nobody knows I have that book but her. Thinking of my secret stash, I tell Willow Rose she can keep her money, and I run my finger over the carved wood of the handle of the gun while she goes back inside leaving me to the quiet.

Now that Daddy is gone, I have to feed my family, but I don't feel like hunting. Even if Daddy says you can cook the parasites out of summer game, I still think it's gross, so instead I linger indoors. I lie on the brown couch and daydream. I stare at the map on my bedroom wall and imagine all the places I wish I could go, or I sit around with Willow Rose watching all the stupid shows on TV. I decide to read *The Old Man and The Sea* aloud to Willow Rose, following her around as she brushes her hair in the bathroom and then stares in the icebox looking for food, but she tells me to skip to the end so she knows what happens and that's that. Mama will eventually make groceries with bills from Daddy's bundles, but they won't last forever. Even if we're poor, all I want is real food from a grocery store and not the gamey taste of whatever animals Daddy's been bringing in. It would be easier to fish, but everyone around here knows that with the oil still oozing into the Gulf, the water and all the fish and everything else is full of sickness. Back home, no matter what lies the big oilmen and the politicians in their button-down shirts said about cleaning up, the shrimpers kept pulling up shrimp with no eyes or with heads full of tumours. We stopped eating shrimp and most fish then. Everyone did.

After about a week or more of boredom, Cup Noodles, and listening to Willow Rose complain about being hungry, I decide to teach my sister to hunt. Let her do something around the house for once. She's thirteen, old enough to use a gun, though Daddy never taught her. He says hunting is for men, even though I know Mama knows perfectly well how to shoot anything she wanted. I barely remember my *pepere* — my mother's father — but I know he had a mounted wild boar head that he shot up the bayou, and Mama says she learned to hunt from him. But even Mama has whispered to me that she doesn't trust Willow Rose with a gun — she's got too much fire in her already.

"Cock-a-doodle-doo!" I crow in Willow Rose's ear early one morning. She has to learn the best time for hunting is early, when everything is just stirring awake. She pulls her flat pillow with the yellow stains over her head, kicks out at me and misses. Next, I blast the radio with its morning talk show in her ear and she tells me to get lost. When I finally tell her I am taking her hunting she sticks her head out from under the pillow and practically pushes me over when she jumps up from her mattress. I know Willow Rose has always wished our father would take her hunting instead of me. She's like that — always looking for something to do that scares her or makes everyone notice her.

While I wait for Willow Rose, I do what Mama usually does and go outside to find the morning's eggs. Before we left Grand Isle, we had a coop full of chickens, but when we left, we only brought Mama's favourite two hens: one tawny brown and one brown and white, and the rooster. We plunked them in the back of Mama's old blue Chevy and drove up the highway with them shitting and squawking in the back seat. Now they mumble and cluck all day long in the yard, and Mama talks to them like they're her best friends. Most days Mama goes out to talk to the chickens in the morning and comes back inside with two eggs, like she's got a shiny present.

The hens lay in the same spots each night in their henhouse, and I find two gleaming eggs real quick. I scramble the eggs, making them stretch with powdered milk and some chopped up onion, cutting away the mouldy part. Thinking of Mama, I leave some egg in the pan, even though I am so hungry I could eat off my own arm, and Willow Rose pesters me for more. I tell her we have to be careful. I am in charge now.

I don't let Willow Rose hold the gun even though she asks about a dozen times. It's a .410 shotgun — the same one Daddy first taught me with before he let me use his other guns. Me and Willow

Rose walk through the tall grasses, the air heavy with heat and the sound of crickets. Willow Rose runs ahead and cartwheels so her white plastic sandals flip off her feet, the golden hairs on her legs lit up by the sun. She pulls a long blade of grass and pretends to smoke it, standing with her feet wide apart, one hand on her hips, like she thinks she's some movie star or something. Holding her grass cigarette away from her, she sings out in a crackly voice she must imagine is sexy that song that's been on the radio all summer long about love being nothing but a second-hand emotion. I tell her to stop fooling around. My shirt is damp on my back, and because I am not wearing underpants, the heat inside my jeans rubs at my groin. I keep thinking that if we were back home on a day like today, when the sun is scalding even before noon, we would have run for the Gulf and jumped in, but then I remember about the oil and tell myself that even the people who are there are probably still too afraid to go in the water. One time, after they used the chemicals that made the oil sink, I waded into the Gulf and the next day I had small, itchy, red dots on my skin from my feet to my knees.

Willow Rose is keen, but I haven't told her that I'll take credit for anything she puts in the smokehouse. Our father will whack me if he knows I'm teaching my sister to do my job. When we are close to the bayou, the spot where the cypress trees thicken into a knot, I crack open the gun to show Willow Rose. The sound makes my blood spark in my veins. I pull a black plastic shell from my jean pocket and remember the first time I used the same weapon with Daddy beside me telling me what to do. I must have been about seven or eight, and I thought my father could do anything. He taught me to load a gun and how to hold it. He taught me to be real patient, real quiet until you spy your prey and only then you raise your gun, cock it, aim and fire. He showed me everything, talked me through my first kill. Even now I can still hear his voice, gentle, sure, telling me what to do.

I show Willow Rose how to lead, aiming at the spot where you think your target is going to be, so that if it's a bird, it'll fly right into the BBs and meet them, not even aware death is coming for it. I show her how to load the gun, how to cock the hammer, pull the trigger and then to eject the shell. I tell her to always treat a gun like it's loaded, and she snickers at me like it's funny. I grab her wrist.

"A gun ain't no joke." I tell her. "Maybe you're too young."

She protests, purses her lips to stop herself grinning. "I can do it," she says.

I open the gun again and show her how to insert the shell. Willow Rose looks hard into the insides of the dark barrel. "Nice," she says. Once the gun is loaded, she reaches for it, but I pull it away, point to the grass. I tsk at her, telling her that things could go wrong real fast with a weapon. She straightens and clears her throat, tells me she's ready now. I remember everything Daddy taught me. I level the stock against my shoulder and whisper to Willow Rose how to hold a shotgun, how to gaze down the barrel at a target. I whisper to her that when you use a gun, you sometimes have to wait for a real long time before anything happens and then when you see something, you have to act real fast. Willow Rose nods at everything I say, suddenly all serious. We keep walking through the tall grass, scanning. Bored, Willow Rose plunks herself down and pulls up long grass and winds it around her wrist, making a bracelet then an arm band, and finally she exhales. "When're you going to shoot something?"

I don't bother to answer her. She crouches at my feet. The smell of marsh rises from the water like rot and mud and maybe shit. Mosquitoes buzz past and I rub my legs against each other trying to keep from getting bitten up. Willow Rose reaches out to catch a *mamzelle*, but it gets away, its blue wings vibrating.

"Willow Rose, watch this," I whisper.

A flock of crying gulls swoops onto a branch like a sudden storm gathering. I raise the shotgun, and pull back the hammer with my thumb until it clicks into place, a solid metallic noise, and I follow the path of the birds with the barrel of the gun. I press the trigger and unleash BBs that fly up to join the gulls. One grey-white bird comes down. Willow Rose calls out a joyous whoop and runs to find the gull in the tall grass. When we come upon it, its black eyes are open, staring. One of its wings beats lightly, and when I put my hand on it, I can feel the bird's heart pound. Willow Rose strokes the bird's head with her finger.

"It's still warm," she says.

"You got to break its neck, so it don't suffer." I tell her.

My sister takes a breath and picks up the animal in two hands. The bird's feathers are sleek, and she fits in the crook of Willow Rose's arm. My sister squinches up her face and twists the gull's neck until it snaps. She lets out her breath and murmurs, "We got one."

If my father were here, he'd get busy plucking and he'd roast the bird over a fire on a stick like it was the best barbecue he's ever had, but I have nothing to make a fire, and the thought of eating the oily, gritty meat of a gull makes me feel sick no matter how hungry I am. Half-hearted, I pluck one feather and then another, but then I look into the gull's eyes and think about how a minute ago, it too was alive. I dig a small hole in the soft ground with my hands where I leave the bird, covering her up with dirt, smoothing it over her still-warm body.

"My turn," Willow Rose says, and I let her take the weapon from me. I stand and we scan the tree branches for rustling leaves, a quiet scuttle. Willow Rose turns her head sharply in one direction and we catch sight of a squirrel that jitters up the trunk of a cypress. I hush Willow Rose as she lifts the gun to her shoulder real fast and I guide her aim. In an instant, the squirrel darts upwards and into the BBs that Willow Rose has sent in its direction. It falls to the grassy floor with a soft whump.

"I did it," she whispers, and her face cracks open like she has just learned life's most important secret.

When we pick up the squirrel from the grass another squirrel scampers up a nearby tree and shrieks out a warning.

"Jesse, I'm going to get real good at this," Willow Rose says. "I'm going to become a better hunter than you. I'm going to sell pelts and get rich enough that I can bust out of this place." She picks up her dead squirrel from the grass and holds it to her chest.

Back in Grand Isle, me and Daddy used to sometimes sell skins to an old guy, Armand, who would mount them and sell them mostly to tourists who wanted to pretend they'd shot some big game in the wilds of Louisiana, he'd say. I could hardly believe anyone would bother to come to where we lived for a holiday, but he paid us real good money, so he must have been telling the truth. I don't know where Armand is now, or even if he's still alive, but for some reason Willow Rose's big idea of how to make money makes me feel jealous that she'll find a way out of where we live now before I will. If I'm stuck here, she should be too.

"You going to help me skin it?" Willow Rose asks. Now she holds the animal up to my face like a prize, touching my cheek with a squirrel claw.

I push her way. "Later," I say, and I take the gun from Willow Rose. She mimics me in a squeaky girly voice.

"Doesn't matter. I can get Mama to help me," Willow Rose says, and she tosses the squirrel up, its limbs splaying open like life has re-entered its body for a second before she catches it again.

"Wait till Mama sees!" she crows and makes off for the house, her left arm swinging by her side in long strides.

EIGHT

COVER ME

SHIT. THAT'S WHAT I think the next morning when I wake and Willow Rose is gone. She never gets up before me, and I know right away she's gone for the .410.

I should go after her, but my groin swells with need, and I am alone, so I grab myself and in several fast strokes I'm done. I wipe myself with the soft pink sheet that covers my bed, then crumple it up so no one will see the wet spot.

By the time I get to the kitchen, Willow Rose bangs into the house with two dead birds, one in each hand, and the .410 tucked dangerously under arm. Her long hair is twined into two braids that are coming undone at the ends, and in the humid air, strands stick to her pink cheeks. She drops the two birds on the kitchen table where Mama sits smoking. Willow Rose is careless, like when Daddy tosses aside an empty beer can.

"Look what I got," Willow Rose says.

One of her birds is a mourning dove. The other is blue. My Cerulean Warbler.

"Damn it, Willow Rose," I say.

Mama looks at Willow Rose's kill, her eyebrows arched, and she tells her to get the birds off the table right now. I want Mama to get angry at Willow Rose, but instead she looks at me, waiting for an explanation.

"What'd you go and kill that blue one for?" I ask.

Willow Rose picks the birds up, one in each hand, and examines mangled feathers and congealed blood. She shrugs and admires her kills.

"I guess someone forgot to teach her not to kill beautiful things," my mother says, and then she sucks on her cigarette and tells Willow Rose to take the birds outside, but her gaze is on me. When the door slams behind my sister, Mama tsks at me for teaching Willow Rose to hunt, so I leave the kitchen and follow Willow Rose outside where she fusses over the two dead birds laying out beside yesterday's now-stiff squirrel like some kind of dead animal museum.

"I'm a good shot," my sister tells me, and she smiles like it is a secret or something good between us. I want to hit her between the eyes, but instead I tell her she's a real jerk killing that bird and then showing off to Mama about it. Willow Rose ignores me, instead plucking a feather from the dove and sticking it between her teeth. I tell her she's gross, and she tells me I'm a sucky baby.

Heat pricking at my skin, I pick up the Cerulean Warbler and hold it to my chest, wishing it back to life, while Willow Rose taunts me with coos. Inside, I find a soft T-shirt — blue with an outline of the state of Texas and the words Lone Star State on it. Daddy's only brother — they don't talk anymore, ever since Daddy told him he gave up on Jesus and Ronald Reagan — gave it to me when I was a kid. It grew tight around my shoulders years ago, but I could never bring myself to pass it on to Willow Rose because it made me feel like I could pretend I'd been to Texas, even though I'd barely ever left the bayou, never mind Louisiana. I wrap the warbler in the shirt and bring her to the biggest cypress trees, where I dig a shallow grave and leave her there. She will rest far from my sister and her gun.

When I get back to the house, Willow Rose sits in the passenger seat of Mama's Chevy. Her feet are kicked up on the dash, the door still open. When she sees me, she leans her head back, her eyes squinched shut, and starts singing that song about doves crying. I bang the passenger door shut so I don't have to hear her. When I go inside, my mother sits at the kitchen table counting the bills from one of Daddy's wads of cash. Most of the bills are singles worn soft. Mama's face is pinched up. She tells me she is going to make groceries up in Golden Meadow and for a second, I'm dying to jump in the car and go with her, just to be somewhere other than our cramped house even for an hour. As Mama's talking to me, she smooths the bills then folds them into the inside pocket of her torn red purse. The back pocket is held closed with a safety pin and I know, because I've snitched money from it, that the top zipper only works some of the time. My mama's look presses into me. "We can't keep doing this, Jesse," she says as she gets up to leave and presses her hand real heavy into my shoulder, making it clear that I'm not welcome on this trip.

I think of the bills that Willow Rose stole, and I'm bursting to tell, but instead I chew on the inside of my lips, then touch my tongue to the edges of my mouth to check for the hair there. Without a word, my mother puts her hand on my shoulder for just a second as if she is using me for balance, and then she leaves me alone in the house with the heavy heat spreading over my skin, slippery like melted butter.

NINE

TAKE ON ME

THE SHED SMELLS OF warmed-over mildew and is full of junk. Most of it is ours. There are unopened boxes: big ones with crushed corners, small heavy ones, all of them covered in a carpet of dust as if we left behind our old life and forgot all the things that were in it. But there is also junk that must be from someone else's left-behind life. To get my red bicycle, the one I rode all over Grand Isle, I wade into the mess, using my hands to read the shape of things ahead of me because there's no light in the shed except through the streaky window. I feel my way past a sink with no faucet, a mattress worn down to rough, rusted springs and two empty diesel canisters. I scratch my calf on the teeth of a rake that hangs by a nail on the wall. I grasp the leg of an overturned chair and draw my hand away from the writhing of termites.

I wrestle the bike from where it's wedged behind a ladder, and I fill the tires good and fat using a pump that sits, by some miracle, right near the bicycle. Getting the bike out of the garage and through the mess takes long minutes of awkward twisting and lifting. Finally pedalling down the road, the air whispers against the skin of my arms and I breathe in deep, riding the edges of the highway, bayou sitting murky on either side of it, all the way south to Leeville.

Cousin PJ's trailer sits at the bottom of everything, where Highway 1 runs out and dips into the grassy marsh like it's the end of the world. My mama calls PJ her cousin, but he looks much older than she is. His veiny hands make me think of the curled roots of oak trees, and his missing front teeth remind me of the old men in Grand Isle who gather in front of the grocery store and chatter to each other in Cajun. But PJ is skinny and strong, and his skin has been beaten thick by days out on his boat. When he used to visit us in Grand Isle, he'd show up sudden, like a rainstorm when the sun's out, and he'd sit in our kitchen telling us stories about wrestling an alligator in Mississippi after he lost a drunken bet, and the time he visited a *traiteur* who stole his teeth, he said, and took all the money in his wallet when he blacked out from the pain. My father hates PJ. He says it's because he don't work too much and because he's had three wives and five children without looking after any of them, but I know the real reason Daddy hates PJ is because he's jealous that PJ always has enough money and more fun than any other adult we know. He's travelled to New Orleans and all over Texas and Mississippi; he's even been to Washington, DC, to protest something about unmarked wells left behind by oil companies. Mama never invites him over anymore because all Daddy ever does is talk shit about him even while he's right there in our kitchen. I've been to PJ's trailer twice before, but this is the first time I come alone, unannounced. PJ is an oysterman, and even with the waters holding all that oil now, I know because he told us the last time we saw him, that what he brings in on his boat is worth more than he can eat. I know his haul is worth real cash.

PJ lies long on a green sofa outside his trailer, his arm hanging down, and he holds a lit cigarette between two fingers even as he dozes. His mouth is open, and he snores so heavy his eyelashes rattle. On the round wooden table nearby is a plate of French fries and an open bottle of Dixie. It's not yet noon. Catching him like that, I feel as though I've found out a secret. Stretched out on the couch at PJ's ankles is a ginger cat, paws to the sky and with matted hair that frames his jowly face in a knotted mane so that he looks like he's half lion and half sunflower. The cat breathes in almost the same rhythm as PJ, then, finally sensing my presence, he startles and bolts from the couch, running from me in a golden streak, and PJ wakes.

"Jesse, hey!"

PJ stretches upright, takes a short drag of the stub of his cigarette and then a longer one, trying to get the last of it, inhaling himself awake. The thing about PJ is that he doesn't even ask what I'm doing there, like he's used to people disappearing and reappearing again without warning. I gobble down the cold French fries he offers. They're tasteless and have the texture of boxboard, but they answer the angry demands of my stomach. Sometimes I imagine there's a mouth inside my belly, and it gapes open like a baby bird's and wails when I have nothing for it. I eat standing up and so fast that even PJ, whose eyes are unquestioning and as blue as the ocean in the pictures in the *National Geographic* magazines in my old school, tells me to slow down and then brings out more fries from his trailer, these ones rubbery, freshly warmed up. "Good breakfast," he says, and I swallow another fistful almost without chewing. PJ offers me a swig of beer that I gulp down while I flop onto his couch. When the ginger cat comes sauntering back, PJ yanks a huge bag of cat food from under the sofa and tosses fistfuls on the ground. The cat eats real fast and pretty soon two more — one calico with ginger, black and brown patches, and one white with a crooked neck — show up and join in the feast. PJ points out the patchy cat and tells me she just had kittens. He pops inside and then comes back out with an uncooked hotdog that he tosses to her. She runs off with it in her mouth, batting away the two other cats as she goes. PJ tells me she's off to feed her babies — a real good mom.

When the fries are finished, I'm still starving, and my belly rumbles, so PJ invites me in to eat more. Inside his trailer is full of odd knick-knacks: a clock he says he made that ticks backwards — his time-machine he says — several balls made out of rubber bands, some real old photos stuck with tape to his bare walls, but the thing I can't stop looking at is the jaws of an alligator that he has strung up above his narrow bed.

"That thing?" he says when I ask about it. "I shot it one day out on my boat. Must have been at least eight feet. I was drunk, and it came after me, so I killed it. Nearly tipped over trying to get it on board. An eight-footer!"

"What did you kill it with?" I ask.

"I had my AR with me. It comes in handy, you know, when there's trouble," he says.

I've never seen any kind of semi-automatic like that, and PJ must be able to tell by how I can't stop looking at the alligator jaws. "I'll show you," he says. He leans over his bed and fishes out the long gun. "I got some other stuff under there, maybe my AK," he says, and I don't know if he's joking, but I think he's not. He blows dust off the AR. "Chamber's empty and no magazine in this, so it's safe," he tells me and hands it over casual as if he's handing over a smoke or a can of beer.

The rifle is heavy. Heavier than any I've ever held. Heavy like fear and anger. I hold it to my shoulder as if I'm aiming. "Whoa there, don't get too excited," PJ says.

"Will you show me how to use it?" I ask. I imagine myself pulling the trigger and the noise it would let loose.

"Someday. I ain't got no ammo for it. These days it's just for decoration," he says. I hand it back to PJ.

"Without ammo, It won't scare no alligator, but the sight of it'll make any man run like hell." PJ holds the gun to his shoulder now and pretends to pull the trigger. "Whoo hoo!" he calls out, holding the gun in the air before he shoves it back under his bed. "Lots of fun in that thing. Sometime I'll show you how it works," he says and makes his way into his tiny kitchen where he offers to make me some toast. It's all he's got, he says. Toast and mayonnaise — a real bayou delight, he jokes. I'm hungry enough to eat all the plain toast in the world if that's what he's serving, so we crowd together at his table and keep eating.

I'm close to full, but my belly tightens all nervous when I finally blurt out that I want to work with him sometime. I tell him I need money real bad, but there's nowhere for a kid like me to get a job. PJ stuffs the last piece of toast into his mouth, asks if I want to come out on his boat with him. I nod and tell him I'll do anything — I just need to get out of our house and bring some food home.

"You know your daddy don't like me so much," he says.

"He likes you fine," I say.

"Now that's a fat lie," PJ says. "Your daddy hates me, and if you work with me, he's going to be real mad."

"I don't care what he thinks. I need to make some money. Buy food," I say. "And anyway, he's gone away for a while, so I can do what I want."

PJ chews and thinks for a minute. Then he nods his head and makes me promise I won't tell my father anything about working with him. I agree. He makes me swear on a full can of Dixie and then he says, "And if he do find out, I ain't admitting nothing," I nod, excited to make money, but maybe even more excited to go behind Daddy's back to do it.

"You show up early and you can come out with me. Make a little cash for you and your mama," he says. I thank him so many times he tells me to cut it out, and then he shows me a notebook that he keeps under the bed with his gun. He says he's writing his life story and he tells me, "Ain't nobody ever going to read this, but at least I'll know where I've been when I'm too old to remember, and this place is long gone. At least my memories won't be gone." From inside his notebook, he tears out a piece of paper and makes me sign an oath he writes saying that I won't tell my daddy about working for him. I sign and we shake on it. I have a job.

Before I leave, PJ pours a small bucket worth of oysters into a plastic bag that I hang over the handlebars of my bike. I make my way back up the highway, feeling victory burning in my chest.

Outside the back door at home, there's a package: a plastic bag with Cokes, Cheetos and a note that I read under the kitchen bulb. Two words — From Antoine — are scrawled in pencil on a scrap of paper, the back of a cash register bill. He has taped a twenty-dollar bill to each of two bags of Cheetos, and Mama comes into the kitchen right in time to catch me peeling off the bills, about to stick them in my pocket. I suck in my breath and Mama's face turns sharp like a knife.

"What's all this?" she asks.

My skin feels hot, but I don't know if it's because I've been caught or because of the look on Mama's face when she examines the note from Antoine. She tears up the flimsy paper with Antoine's large, uneven handwriting on it, but she demands the money, holding out a flat palm.

"I'll give it back to him," she says and tucks the cash into the pocket at her hip. When I protest, she stands in the kitchen doorway and blocks me. "This is no good," she says. After she leaves, I crack open a Coke anyway, swallow down the warm sugary drink like the way my father puts back his beer before I crawl into my bed for a nap.

I dream I am sucking on a cigarette and my irritated throat wakes me. Coughing, I race to the kitchen where black smoke rises over the stove and forms a dark halo around the light bulb. Willow Rose cries my name, and then swoops a heavy pan into the sink, turning on the water in a hurry, making the pan sizzle and steam.

"What in hell?" I side-check her, feel her elbow in my rib as I shove her away to sigh over what she has done. In the pan are eight charred oysters, still smoking, heat rising from them like coals.

"I was hungry," my sister says, and in the roundness of her eyes there is an apology but also the shine of need. My own stomach pulses, and even though there are plenty more oysters, I say all the curses I know from my father.

Before my father got his job with the oil company we lived poor, but never like this. We lived in cramped trailers tucked in dishevelled camps where the shrimpers and oystermen set up alone or with their wives and a bunch of kids. We'd cook over an open fire sometimes, and we'd run around outdoors as much as we could. Daddy fixed cars, boats, anything that needed fixing, or he'd rent himself out with his truck to haul things or build things for the people on

Grand Isle who could afford a bigger porch or even extra rooms added on to their houses. My father could learn anything real fast, so no matter what job came up, he'd take it and he'd do it better than anyone else could. We'd drive around Grand Isle and he'd point out the nice things he'd made, and I'd feel like Daddy was the secret behind everything good in town. Once when he needed his truck for a job out near Port Fourchon, he'd run out of gas, so he hotwired a neighbour's car and stepped on it, driving fast like a lightning streak to the gas station where he filled up a fuel can just in time for our neighbour's wife to pull into the parking lot of the grocery store next door. He got into the car he'd taken and sped back so fast that by time she was home the car was parked and he was inside our trailer drinking a can of Bud, feet up on the table, all calm and cool like he was a hero in a movie. Later he said he even went back to the gas station and paid for the fuel he took, telling them he clean forgot to pay. He used to be good crazy like that, and even when it was only a little, we always had something to eat.

"Damn shame," I say and dump the oysters in the trash. Willow Rose stands in the middle of the smoky kitchen; around her neck she wears a gold-coloured chain with a red glittery heart pendant. She puts one hand on her hip and with the other hand she holds up her middle finger. Then she slinks down in a kitchen chair and says, "I'm still hungry."

"Where's Mama at?" I ask.

"Talking to the chickens." Willow Rose props open the back door to air out the kitchen. Then as if suddenly possessed she runs out into the yard singing about not needing a heart if it can be broken. I follow her out but she skips her way to the shed and yells back to me, "I'm going hunting!" Mama watches her like Willow Rose is a stranger and then shakes her head in my direction. She is wearing a wide red skirt with knit flowers on it, and a hem that's come undone and sags around her calves.

When I was much younger, I used to think Mama liked me better than Willow Rose. She'd read books to me at the beach while

Willow Rose would make mud pies and kick up sand. Willow Rose's grades were plenty good, but I was the one who liked school and who paid attention to what Mama said when she taught us to mind our manners. Willow Rose used to call me Mama's boy, and she was right. But now Mama looks at me like she doesn't like my face. She has nothing to say to me when I follow her back into the kitchen.

"Is there anything for dinner?" I blurt out.

Mama shakes her head and snorts at me. "What did you go teaching Willow Rose to use that gun for?"

"I thought she could help out. She's old enough."

"Daddy better not catch her with that gun when he's back home. You know how he is."

"I'm glad he's gone," I say.

"I could have guessed that," Mama says, and she pops open a bag of Cheetos. The powdered dust leaves streaks on her fingers that she licks off. I reach into the bag and she teases me, pulling the bag away but then offering it to me so that we stuff our faces, crunching the Cheetos down, washing them back with the remaining Coke.

"Yemen," she says.

"What?" I ask her.

"Yemen. It starts with a *Y*. You should know it."

When I was a kid, me and Mama kept a list of place names, and I would study it so that I could beat her at our geography game and also so that I'd know where to go when I got old enough. Mama used to tell me that even people with no money can have dreams. We lost that list a long time ago, but I never forgot about wanting to go to all the places on it, starting with Australia and ending with Zanzibar.

TEN

STATE OF SHOCK

A DAY LATER MAMA tells me and Willow Rose it's time to eat a proper dinner for once. Tonight we'll eat steamed oysters and roux: our first real meal in ages. Mama acts like she feels rich; she has put the twenties from Antoine in a drawer in the kitchen and tells me she'll leave them there just in case, and we don't discuss what the "in case" means, but she looks happy to have a little extra. Mama says Daddy should be back any day now, but if she's worried by his absence, she doesn't show it. With the heat so thick, we wait until late to start cooking.

"Stop it," Mama says and slaps my hand as I pinch a slice of pepper from the pot. My fingers singed, I put them in my mouth to lick off the sauce, all buttery and thick, and my stomach growls.

In the evening, after we've cooked, Mama and I sit in the kitchen and fan ourselves with our hands; her cheeks are red, forehead moist. I sit beside her and gulp down the last of the Cokes that Antoine left. Willow Rose, who has been out, pops her head into the kitchen, her eyes darting.

"Antoine's here," she whispers and points to the front of the house from where I hear a car come to a stop and a door slam. Mama's forehead wrinkles up like a soaked lima bean, and she runs her hands through her tangled hair.

"What's he doing here? Put those outside," she says to Willow Rose, waving her hand at the squirrels she holds. Willow Rose sighs.

"When will you teach me to skin?"

"Never ever ever," Mama says and shakes her head. Willow Rose stomps outside and comes back in just as Antoine thumps on the door and then barges in, calling to us. Mama hurries to the front of the house.

"Antoine!"

"Angel, baby. I thought I'd better check how y'all doing with Emmett gone so long." Willow Rose sneaks a look at me and mouths *Angel.*

"We're doing just fine," my Mama says and stands at the door, blocking it.

"You going to keep me standing here?" Antoine asks, laughing from his belly.

"We were just making dinner," Mama says.

"I don't mind if I join you if you don't," Antoine says, and if you didn't know anything about him, you'd think he was real charming. Even I want to laugh when he does.

"It's just a simple dinner," Mama says.

"Aw come on, baby, I'm a simple man, a simple boss man. Can't you tell? And a dainty eater. I just want to make sure y'all are doing okay. I won't stay late. I promise."

"All right," my Mama says and steps aside with a sigh and quick look at me.

Mama frowns as Antoine talks on about how now that Emmett is like family to him, he feels right at home with us. Antoine carries another plastic bag like yesterday's, filled with Cokes and Cheetos, and in his other hand he carries a six-pack of Old Milwaukee. When he leans in and grabs me in a sweaty embrace, I smell that he is already drunk.

"You got my things from yesterday?" Antoine asks. He winks.

Mama goes to the just-in-case drawer and pulls out the two twenties and holds them out to Antoine, saying we don't need any money. She smiles, but tight like it makes her cheeks hurt.

"Come on now, it don't mean nothing. Just to help you out while Emmett's gone. He'll have to work extra to make it up when he's back." Antoine puts a hand on Mama's arm, smiles big, and he lets the bills fall to the table, where they stay. "Smells like you got something good on the stove."

Mama closes her eyes and then nods her head, lips stretched across her face in a fake smile. I go to open a bag of Cheetos and smile at Antoine in thanks, crunching them in my mouth, feeling the hunger in my belly surge. Antoine breaks into a beer. He puts the rest of them in the icebox.

"Good to see y'all," he says. "Nice to be with folks for dinner."

Mama stirs the roux on the stove, warming it up real slow. "No one should eat alone," she says and I can't tell if she means it.

"I see your girl out there with that gun. She out hunting?" Antoine says.

Mama says that Willow Rose is just fooling around. I stuff my mouth with more Cheetos, swallow fast and say, "I taught her."

"Jesse," Mama says like a warning.

"But you ain't hunting today?" Antoine asks.

"Jesse's been cooking oysters," my mother tells him.

"You got your girl out there with a gun and your boy in here with the stove?" Antoine lets out a laugh that lands like a punch on my chest.

"It ain't like that," I say.

"Sure looks like it is," he says, slurping beer. "Don't worry," Antoine tells me. "I won't tell your Daddy nothing." He winks at me and like a baby, I say nothing, but the words stuck in my throat make me feel like I've swallowed a chicken bone. Antoine turns to my mother.

"Baby, you want me to set this table?" It's a strange question, like he is speaking some foreign language, but Mama twirls around and hands Antoine a stack of plates that he sets down, each one in the right place like he's been practising. I've never seen my own father set a table in my life. Antoine catches me staring at him and my Mama is watching too, a smile growing over her face.

"See now, you're not the only man who can find his way in the kitchen," he says to me.

When Mama offers the knives and forks, he cups her wrists like baby birds in his hands just for a second before he takes the cutlery from her and sets them on the table. Mama doesn't pull away. "I never would have guessed you were so domestic," she says.

"I told you I was full of surprises," Antoine says.

At dinner, he sits up straight in his chair and looks real happy. Mama serves white rice, roux and oysters freshly steamed open, hot enough to burn the tips of your fingers right off. Though he eats and eats, Antoine wipes his mouth all delicate between each bite, and he holds his knife and fork like someone taught him in a class on manners. Even when he gulps down one beer and then another, he chews with his mouth closed. When his plate is clean, he thanks my Mama for feeding him before he cracks open another Old Milwaukee. Mama murmurs that he's always welcome, and Willow Rose and I exchange a shocked look.

"All manners over here — admit it!" Antoine says.

"You are a very polite man. It's true," Mama says and grins like everything is okay.

"I told you I was. It's been a long time since I had a meal like that," Antoine says to Mama. He looks up at her through his short eyelashes. "Thank you again, baby."

I know there's only a little left in the pans, but when Antoine asks for more, Mama takes his plate and scrapes the crust of rice with thickened roux, and Antoine covers his mouth with his hand that is missing fingers and belches and then says "Excuse me, y'all. That means the food was good, you understand." Willow Rose snickers, and Antoine turns to her.

"You want to know how I lost these fingers?" he asks.

Willow Rose nods.

"It was an alligator made a meal of them."

"I don't believe you," I say.

Surprise brightens Antoine's face like he likes me better now. "You never hunted one of them gators? You got to be careful. Sometimes they hunt you right back," he says, and Willow Rose raises her eyebrows. Antoine turns to her.

"If you want, someday I'll take you out gator hunting."

"I'll go too," I say.

"Got to get you out of the kitchen." Antoine nods my way and then at Mama. "You come too. Gators won't eat no pretty lady like you."

Mama starts to clear the table, but Antoine puts a hand on her wrist again.

"You got more of them oysters?"

Mama keeps clearing and apologizes, but Antoine grabs her by the arm and tells her to stop, urging her to sit back down.

"Let me get another beer. Then I'll help clean up," Antoine says.

"*You're* going to help clean up?" Willow Rose asks.

"How else am I going to express my gratitude to your Mama for this meal?" Antoine replies and Willow Rose looks at me in wonder, like an alien has made himself at home in our kitchen.

Almost all the dishes we have are piled into the sink when Antoine asks if Daddy's been in touch. Mama turns on the water and pours just a dab of diluted soap in and lets the sink fill.

"He should be back anytime," Mama says, her voice sure.

Antoine picks up the stained dishtowel and passes it between his hands real slow.

"He better hurry back. I already paid him for work he ain't done yet."

Antoine looks right at Mama. She shuts off the water and begins to scrub the plates. She scrubs them extra hard and keeps her back to Antoine and us.

"He okay?" Antoine asks. He leans against the counter, right up close to Mama.

"He's just fine. He'll be back real soon," Mama says, still focused on the dishes.

"I wish that for you, baby," Antoine says and he dries all the plates, standing right next to Mama, so tall and wide beside her small frame. While he dries, he tells Mama that what happened to Daddy in that explosion must have been real bad. He says he can't imagine what it must have been like to feel that fire on you and to lose so many men, and when he says that, I realize I've barely thought about anything except how Daddy's acted since that night, and not about what he saw or felt. Mama sits down real sudden like maybe she's thinking the same. When Antoine says he's going to go out to his truck to get some more beer Mama turns to me and Willow Rose.

"You must be tired from the heat," she says, and gets back up to clatter the last of the forks and knives in the sink, scrubbing them real hard. When Antoine comes back in, he puts another six-pack in the icebox and goes right back to drying cutlery and putting it away. Me and Willow Rose stare at him until he shakes his head at us.

"You never seen a man help out a lady before?" he asks.

"Emmett's not much use in the kitchen, but he's real good at everything else," Mama says.

Antoine turns to me and says, "Impressing a lady is all about being a gentleman. You may not be the richest or the best looking, but you can always dry dishes. Ain't that right, baby?"

Mama nods and says, "It's nice to see a man willing to help out."

"See? You learned something tonight," he says to me.

"But it's not everything," Mama adds.

Pretending to be hurt, Antoine tosses the end of the ragged blue dishcloth to Mama and, each of them holding a corner of it, he twirls her around in a dance that makes my Mama laugh.

After the dishes are done, me and Willow Rose get sick of listening to Antoine carry on about how it's some strange coincidence that Janis Joplin, Jimi Hendrix and Jim Morrison all died at only twenty-seven years old, which, I realize, is only twelve years older than me, and I haven't done anything yet. He keeps talking and talking and Mama nods her head, listening, chiming in only a little. Finally, instead of listening to Antoine say another word about Jimi Hendrix choking on barf, I excuse myself to go to our room and Mama nods like she wishes she could leave too. Willow Rose follows me.

My sister takes a shower and I sprawl on the bed. I'm hot like I've been roasted from the inside out, and the weight of the heat and all that time in the kitchen seeps into me. At first, I try to read from my geography book, but Willow Rose turns on the radio and we listen to Bruce Springsteen singing about dancing in the dark — it's the number seven song on the Top 10 that Willow Rose and I like to listen to each week. We listen in silence, until the song changes and my sister whispers, "Mama thought Antoine was real funny."

"She's too nice to kick him out," I say.

"He was real drunk."

"Real drunk," I agree.

"More drunk than I've seen Daddy."

"Naw. Daddy gets blitzed all the time."

From her mattress on the floor, Willow Rose reminds me of the time Daddy got drunk and climbed a ladder up a tree to chase the neighbour's cat. I remind her of one drunken Christmas when Daddy shot squirrels from his chair outside the trailer and tried to put one on top of the Christmas tree like it was an angel. Willow Rose laughs so hard she tells me she's going to pee herself, and I tell her she better not or it'll be the last time she ever laughs like that. We hear Mama and Antoine move from the kitchen to the chairs out back, and from our window we listen to their voices, straining to hear every word until it becomes boring. We turn up the radio and listen to the rest of the Top 10, trying to predict which song will be in what spot. Willow Rose loves the one called "Sad Songs," but I think it's only for girls. The top song is from that movie *Ghostbusters*, which I bet all my friends in Grand Isle have seen by now. Even on Grand Isle, there is a movie theatre. Finally, I drift off to sleep thinking of all the streets where all my friends live, remembering so that I won't forget.

I dream a jumble of things and then I dream that I am awake, that I hear Mama's voice from outside, and then I am awake, but the heat and the weight of the dream make me feel like I am wrapped in a cocoon that suffocates me as I try to fight it off. The radio is still on, droning music with a fast beat, a song I don't know. For seconds or maybe minutes, I strain my ears, unsure if I hear what I think I hear — a scream? a call? — from outside. I am paralyzed, plastered to the bed. Then, like I am a ghost, I watch myself rise. I am only wearing underpants when I float into the kitchen, out the back door.

Mama. She is real and she is pressed against the wall of the house. Antoine pushes up against her and blocks me from seeing my mother's face. Her right elbow is pressed into Antoine's chest, shoving him but useless against his weight. She tries to push his huge face away from hers and he buries his mouth in her chest, puts a hand up against her throat.

I don't feel myself do it, but there is a scream and it is mine.

Mama's eyes are wild and darting like she is an animal caught down the barrel of a gun.

"Get inside!" I do not know the voice that comes from my mother's throat.

The backdoor slams open and shut. Willow Rose stands there in her oversized T-shirt, staring.

"Mama!"

"Jesse — get her inside."

Their voices penetrate the thing that paralyzes me, and I scoop up Willow Rose in my arms and run. "It's okay," I keep repeating as I hold my sister's head to my chest. She claws at my hands and hollers to put her down. I bring her to our bedroom and tell her to stay there. I close the door to our room, and I go for the Colt.

Back outside, Mama huddles in one of the wrecked chairs like she is broken, her knees to her chest, head hanging to the side like she's going to puke. Antoine puts a hand on her back, and I swear he smiles when I point the gun. He takes a step towards me. My knees tremble.

He steps closer and wraps a thick hand around my wrist. He pries the gun from my fingers with his thick ones.

"It ain't like that, see?" he says.

When he leaves around the side of the house, he takes the gun with him and waves at me with the hand with the missing fingers, calling out goodnight as he disappears.

My mother won't move. I fling my arms around her and I can feel her heart, her fast breath pressed into my neck. When she looks up, her whole face is a scream.

ELEVEN

EMMETT - OUT OF TOUCH

WHAT DID I WANT? Forgiveness? A hero's welcome? Or just to disappear? You have to be a dumbass motherfucker to think the wife of your dead friend owes you something. Or that she wants to see your face.

Finding her was easy. With a name like Allmendinger — Frank Allmendinger — there weren't too many in the whole state of Mississippi and only one in New Albany. When I met Frank, I thought he was joking about his name, but he said it was German and acted like having a name like that made him something, all fancy-like. Allmendinger. What a name.

It was the newspaper article that made me go. Antoine — that bitch — he handed it to me, then pretended he didn't know anything, like I hadn't near cried to him like a pussy when I told him everything including how I tried to save a man and failed. I even told him about the whisky, like the dumbfuck that I am. The multi-page spread told all about the blowout and how it started with oil executives who didn't know shit about what was going on everyday on the rig, about whether or not the blowout preventers worked or didn't, about how dangerous it was to bore through the ocean floor so quickly. The article said that the dead — mostly drillers and one floorhand — were all taken out by the first explosion with its debris and its fireballs on the drilling floor. It said nothing about anyone going overboard and drowning. None of the bodies were ever recovered. All those other men cooked in that fire. If they were lucky, they would have died before they knew what hit them. But not

Frank. He wasn't even on shift. He should have made it out. But there was his name on the list with all the other men. And then there were the pictures. Photos of the widows and children. When I saw her face, and her daughters, I wanted to take a gun and put it to my head.

Seven hours. That's how long it takes to drive to New Albany. Longer if you stop to piss. The whole time, up the highway, past the state line, I told myself to turn back. But I'd already failed at everything else. Someone should have stopped me, arrested me for drinking behind the wheel. Anything to make it so that I didn't turn up on that woman's doorstep like the pussy ass I am.

But I did. Their house — I would have known it anywhere. Frank told me that when his girls were little, he'd let them choose the paint colours for their front porch, and they'd picked rainbow. When I pulled up, there it was: the steps leading to the porch were yellow, orange and red, and the patio had a purple floor and a turquoise ceiling with three childishly drawn yellow butterflies. Any kid would have loved that porch, even with the peeling paint and the third step having a loose board. I stepped up to the front door and saw a little sign that said Allmendinger, with a hummingbird beside the name. What right did I have to be there? I began to feel like you do when you wake from a nightmare, and you can't tell if the thing chasing you is real. I got back in my truck and sobbed into the steering wheel right there on Frank's street.

I had nowhere to go, so I drove to a dingy grocery store looking to get loaded, but the cashier told me I'd have to drive to the next county if I wanted beer, and I'd be lucky to find some that wasn't warm. He gave me directions and I drove all the way to the One Stop past the county line and stocked up along with a half dozen other men with Union County license plates. Back in New Albany I found a Walmart and pulled into the parking lot. Good and drunk, I lay across the seat of my truck, and I fell into a raw sleep. No one bothered me. When I got hungry, I went into the store and bought cheese puffs and ramen noodles that I ate raw, and a Coke. I ate shit and I felt like shit. I slept in my truck that night with a cramped neck and an aching head.

It took me two more drunken nights and a return trip to the One Stop to go back to the house with the rainbow porch. All I knew was that I was sick of that Walmart parking lot, but my plan was no better than the first time. I bought a package of two white T-shirts for four dollars at Walmart. I figured the least I could do was wear a clean shirt. I only drank one beer. I went back to the house at five o'clock.

The sound of the doorbell rang clear into the house. A dog barked, and then another dog responded, and a woman's voice shushed them as footsteps came closer. When she opened the door and I saw her through the screen, I recognized her instantly from everything Frank had said. Kathy. Her blonde hair was pulled back in a medium-length ponytail and she looked older than I'd imagined, pretty. She had the dimples in both cheeks that Frank had gone on about. She wore a clean blue shirt and jeans that came just below her knees. Her toenails were painted bright pink, and I tried not to stare at her feet. She wore glasses that made her look smart, and everything about her made me think she didn't need me, would probably hate someone like me. Frank told me she worked at a bank. She didn't unlock the screen door when she saw me. She stood behind it and waited for me to say who I was.

"Mrs. Allmendinger?" I asked. She told me yes and kept the screen door closed.

I began to sweat all cold even though the sun burned hot. My voice quivered.

"I was on the Omega Deep." Her eyes widened. "I was with Frank."

Her face clenched into the look like when you stub your toe, like she wanted to howl, but she didn't. She stood there, behind the screen door, completely still except for her chest rising and falling. I reached out and put my hand on the door, wishing I could comfort her through the mesh.

"Oh Jesus," she said and covered her face with her hands.

"I'm sorry, Ma'am," I said. She opened the door, hand over her heart, she showed me into the sunny kitchen while the two small white dogs trotted behind us.

"The girls will be home soon," she said.

"I won't stay," I said.

Silence draped the kitchen. Finally, Kathy excused herself, and I could hear her blow her nose from the other room.

"Were you a driller?" she asked when she sat down next to me at the table, her eyes red.

"No ma'am. I was a roughneck. A roustabout."

"When did you last see Frank?" she asked.

"Ma'am… I was with him at the end."

And then I told her everything, about how I found him injured and how I tried to get us to the lifeboats, how I made him jump to try to save him. That I never meant any harm to come to him.

"You're saying my husband jumped?" Her eyes grew round and wild.

"We had no choice. The boats were gone," I said.

"My husband drowned," she said, and her face crumpled.

"I'm so sorry," I said.

"He couldn't swim," she said.

"I know."

"I don't know if I believe you. They told me he must have gone to help out on the rig floor or in the engine room when they first saw all that mud come up. It wasn't even his shift." She began to bawl for real.

"It never should have happened," I said.

"Who would leave him like that? What kind of men?"

"Ma'am, I'm real sorry. I tried."

"He was scared of water. He must have been… the terror he must have felt."

She cried like a baby then, red face in her arms, the kind of crying I wished I could do. I patted her back real awkward for as long as she sobbed, and when she stopped she told me she needed to be alone, and I understood.

I drove away so fast I blew through a stop sign, barely missing a shiny white car, but I kept driving until I got back to my parking lot, where I cracked open one Bud after another and drank myself into a fit, the kind that made me yell at the woman who parked too close to my truck and then cuss out the poor kid collecting carts from the lot because he was making so much noise. When another kid — a store manager, I guessed from his shirt and tie — came to bang on my window, I pretended to be asleep and ignored him until he walked away. I spent the night there stewing in my rage, banging a fist against my chest until sleep finally came over me.

My first days on the rig, before I knew they'd keep me on, I worked on a crew with Frank, tripping pipe. Half the time I was afraid I'd lose a hand, we were going so fast, but Frank saw the fear in my eyes, and he told me not to worry, that no man had lost a hand on his watch so far. I laughed and worked faster to prove myself, and at the end of the shift Frank told me it was true what he said about no one losing a hand, but if I wanted to hear about the man who lost a foot, he'd be happy to tell me. If he had worked like we did, I said, he was lucky he didn't lose his head, and Frank laughed like maybe that had happened too. I wouldn't have doubted it. We kept up the pace so hard sending the pipe down into the well — Frank said we broke a record. I said I damn near broke my back, but it was soon after that that I stopped being a worm and made roustabout. Frank recommended me. He even gave me an engraved flask to celebrate. "For your days off," he said. The flask said Skinny Mother Fucker, and Frank elbowed me in the ribs and told me to put something on them when he handed it over. "You gotta have meat on you for this job," he said and grabbed his own gut, as if to show it off. I never even brought that flask home, just kept it with me on board as a reminder of who I wanted to be and didn't want to be.

I spent three more days in the parking lot, considering what I really knew about Frank anyway. He went to college — Ole Miss — with the guy who was my roommate when I was a worm. He'd studied something in science that I could never remember. He met his wife at college. When we ate together, Frank ate everything fast, like he was starving, but always polite, always covering his lap with a napkin like he was dining with the queen. We played cards, watched TV. I beat him in pool, sometimes in poker, and even though he had big, thick arms, I could lift heavier weights than he could in the musty weight room on the rig. But Frank never minded anything I did or said; he made me feel like a bloody comedy routine. I was always cracking him up, but eventually I got the drift that that was just the kind of guy Frank was — he let everyone make him laugh like that. I wasn't special. In his room he had pictures up of his family: his wife, two blonde daughters and those dogs. When I'd been in his house, I recognized a photo in a silver frame on the table in the front hallway. It's a sunny day and they're all outside, and his wife holds one of the dogs, and the younger daughter looks directly at it, making a funny face. Her expression reminds me of Willow Rose. The other daughter is holding a dog that must have stuck its tongue out and licked her nose just as the camera clicked, like it was trained to be a clown. In the picture everyone looks happy, and Frank is smiling the biggest of them all, arms wrapped around everyone from behind.

For days my truck filled with cigarette butts, cans of beer and Coke, bags of chips and boxes of crackers. I stank sour, like piss, so on the third day I bought a bar of soap and washed myself in the restroom at Walmart and then wandered around the store pretending to be a regular customer. On a whim I swiped some stuff from someone else's cart — a pair of binoculars, a knife — and brought it back to my truck where I finally cleared out the trash I'd collected. I bought more beer.

I'd parked at the far end of the lot, and from there I noticed that mine wasn't the only vehicle that never left. I noticed other things too. Like how much crap people buy and how all their crap — or maybe not having enough crap — makes them angry. All those families fighting with each other in the parking lot. Women yelling at children, men and women glaring at each other. It makes you wonder why anyone has a family and if buying all that shit makes anything better, or if it just distracts you from your misery for a few minutes. Maybe the only happy families are the ones who feel important because they can afford to buy high-class garbage somewhere else.

After I washed myself, I spent one more night in my truck, and then I decided I wasn't done feeling sorry for myself. I went back. I didn't know if it was a weekend or a weekday: I'd lost track of everything. I hadn't shaved in days. I knew what I looked like.

I stopped the truck a few houses away and watched. Kathy was out front, mowing the lawn. She wore green shorts, a white tank top, and her white sneakers had turned the colour of the grass as she made clean lines back and forth in front of her house. I saw one of her daughters — must have been the younger one — come outside wearing soccer shorts and a team shirt, kiss her mama and then walk down the street, her long ponytail swooshing behind her. How could they be so normal, as if they were okay? Maybe their break was cleaner; they didn't have to carry around a dead weight with them. I sat there like I was watching a movie, fixated until I noticed I was covered in sweat. I saw Frank's face — those eyes flashing in terror — and in my chest I felt that feeling of hitting the water. I should have been the one to die.

When I lumbered up to her house, Kathy saw me and turned off the mower.

"You're back." Her voice sounded so brittle I thought it might break, her breath heavy like she'd been running.

I lost track of what I came to say. Instead, I put a hand on her arm. She pulled away from me.

A neighbour across the street came outside, waved and then got into her station wagon and drove off.

"I'm real sorry. Frank deserved better."

"It was better when I thought he'd died with all the others. On the floor, helping out. At least maybe that would have been fast. He wouldn't have been alone in the water."

"He would have burned alive if he'd been on the drilling floor." I noticed how thick and lush the grass was at my feet.

"Why didn't they come for him? Carry him to the lifeboat?"

"I wish I knew, Ma'am."

"I can't stand to think of him in the water. I keep having nightmares, like it's all fresh again," she said. "Why did you come here? Couldn't you have left me in peace?"

"I thought you should know," I said, staring at my feet.

"I wish I didn't," she said.

Like a sissy, I began to cry right there thinking about Frank's face, and the fire, and how it felt to fall through air. I wished I could remember letting go of his hand. I hadn't even seen him enter the water. I sobbed loud on Frank's widow's lawn, howling like the animal I was.

"Stop it," Kathy said. She turned on the motor. "Stop it before Violet hears you. You think you're the only one who wants to cry?"

I put my head in my hands and hiccupped in that terrible way when you're trying not to cry and you can't catch your breath. "I'm sorry," I whispered into my stupid hand.

I felt her palm on my shoulder. "Shhh," she said and kept patting my shoulder.

"I'm going to leave now," I said.

"Goddamn I miss Frank," she said, and she clutched my arm as if to steady herself. I kept right on bawling until I took a deep breath, looked up at that rainbow patio and started to hiccup all over again. Kathy left me standing on the lawn while she got me a glass of water, which I gulped down while trying to keep from crying more.

"Have you got a family?" she asked. I nodded. "They're lucky to still have you. Go back to them. Get yourself together," she said.

I managed to stop crying and I tried to hug Kathy or shake her hand or something, but she stepped aside and said, "You need to go home, Emmett, and don't come back here. If my daughters hear how their father died — just don't come back here."

I ran stop signs until I got back to my parking lot, and the sobs became fists on the steering wheel. What kind of a man bawls on his friend's widow's front lawn, asks her to comfort him? What kind of a man?

In the Walmart, the headline on the newspaper tells me that the cap they tried to put on the oil well failed. No one knows for sure how much oil has filled the Gulf.

TWELVE

JESSE – BORDERLINE

I KICK TWISTED SHEETS from around my legs and get up with the sound of birds. My chest feels like I've been clubbed, and an electric surge rises beneath my skin reminding me of what happened last night. I'd let Willow Rose stay in my bed, and now, at dawn, she sprawls there, breath heavy with sleep.

After Antoine left, Mama curled into herself and went silent. When I put my arm around her and tried to help her inside, she told me to go away, to forget I'd seen anything. I knew if Daddy knew, he'd want to kill someone. Antoine, me. Definitely me. He'd left me in charge.

All my muscles ache and my head feels like someone wrapped it in a thick towel and I can't think properly. Did Antoine really do that to Mama? Did he really take the Colt? Maybe he was telling the truth that it wasn't how I thought it was. Maybe I got it wrong. Maybe I didn't understand Mama's face.

An hour or more into the still-early morning, I'm alone pacing, waiting. Waiting for the hens to lay, waiting for Mama to come to the kitchen and be okay, but the door to her room stays shut. There is silence behind it.

If I could kick myself in the head, I would. Mama knew she didn't want Antoine over, but she let him in, and I was there and said nothing. And then he was all polite, convincing everyone that he was okay. Today the house feels smaller than ever.

In a flurry, I pull my bike from the garage and pedal down the highway. My breath is fast, and my skin is red-hot; I pedal so fast my thighs burn. I clench the handlebars of my bike in tight fists and all I can think of is that I am going to kill Antoine. I have to make things right before Daddy finds out. It's what a man would do.

You can't miss Antoine's shop at the edge of Leeville before the turnoff to the bridge to Grand Isle. You can't miss it because it has a huge sign with red writing that says "Fat Antoine ~ Car Mechanic ~ We Do EVERYTHING For You!!" Next to the garage is a house that I guess belongs to Antoine. I practically skid off the road, my brakes squealing, and I tumble to the ground, bike landing beside me. I hoist myself up and notice the smile drawn under the two exclamation marks on Antoine's sign. I want to strangle him. I imagine my hands grabbing him by his thick neck, his eyes bulging, then closing. I don't wait. I leave my bike on his scrubby lawn and bang on the door of his house with one fist, then two. When he doesn't answer, I turn the knob, but it's locked. Without thinking, I pound the window right beside the door with all the force I've got and, to my surprise, it shatters under my fist. I smile at the broken glass, pull away my hand to see bloody streaks form.

"Jesus Christ," Antoine says, and then his hand with the missing fingers sticks through the broken window.

"I did it," I say through the hole in the glass.

Antoine opens the door. He's wearing the same blue T-shirt and jeans as yesterday. His feet are bare, beard grown in stubbly, and when he says my name, I lunge at him, two fists on his wide chest. He throws me down. My open palm lands on shards of glass.

"You little shit, what do you think you're doing?"

I examine my hand. "I'm bleeding," I say, looking at the cut flesh of my palm, then the cut-up knuckles.

"Get inside," Antoine says.

My hand is really gushing now, so I follow him in, and he thrusts me a dirty dishtowel that I bleed through, then ball up and keep holding to my palm. He tells me to keep putting pressure on my cuts. We stand in his kitchen. There are dirty dishes in the sink, and the yellow walls look like a layer of thick dust settled over them years ago. It smells like coffee and old milk. Both of us breathe heavily.

"I guess y'all are going to have to pay for that window."

"You hurt my mother."

"What makes you so sure about what you saw?"

I lunge at him again, leaving a bloody mark on his shirt. He grabs me by both wrists and holds them so tight I can't feel my hands.

"You come here to accuse me? Ain't you the one pulled a gun on me last night? I should call the cops on you," he says. He is still holding my wrists. I struggle, but even without all his fingers, his hands are strong. My left hand bleeds so that blood trickles onto his hand, and he finally pulls away and says "Shit. Fuck." He lets go of me and thrusts his hand under running water.

"I want my gun back."

"Funny thing is, that thing wasn't even loaded. You tried to kill a man with an unloaded gun," he says.

"Give it to me."

"I like it," he says.

"It's my father's," I say.

"Your father ain't been at work in a long time. I was good to him. Even set aside an old car for him to work on for himself. Paid him for his time. He's missing some screws, you know," Antoine says.

I ball up my fists and lunge at him from behind. He holds me away from him like I'm a dead rat.

"I'm going to kill you," I tell him.

"No you ain't," he says and pushes me into a kitchen chair. "Would you take care of that fucking hand?" Antoine pulls another dishrag from a drawer and tells me to quit bleeding all over everything. Maybe it's all the blood, but suddenly I feel faint, or like I might cry. I whisper again that I should kill him.

"Grow up. Your father's gone," he says.

"Shut up," I mumble.

"Maybe you should take his job while he's away. Make some real money so you can help your mama, or at least pay for that window."

"Fuck you." I pound my fist and make my hand bleed more.

"Suit yourself," he says and watches me press on my wound.

"When my father gets back," I begin to say.

"You ask your mother what you saw," he says.

"He'll beat your ass," I say.

Antoine leaves the room. When he comes back, he hands me two twenties.

"Take that. I saw what was in your mama's icebox."

"Go to hell," I say.

"Take the money," he tells me and lays it on the table beside where I sit. For long seconds we stare at each other. I check my hand. The bleeding has lessened, but my hand has cuts all over. I wrap the rag back around my hand as little balls of blood start to form again. I want the money. The thought of taking it makes me feel sick.

"Take it," Antoine says. I snake my good hand around the bills and rub them between my fingers.

"Don't think…" I start to say.

"Get the fuck out of here before I call the cops on you for destroying my property," Antoine says, and he pushes against my shoulders with both hands before I back away, my hands in the air. Inside I am buzzing with anger at Antoine and myself, but I am out of words.

"I'll see you again." Antoine calls after me, his voice mocking.

"Fuck you," I say before I make it through his door.

"Fuck you, too," he says, and he locks the door behind me. As I get on my bike, he flicks out the rest of the broken glass from the window, and I hear the pieces fall to the ground.

On the bike ride home my hand begins to bleed again, and I'm eaten up with my failure and by wondering what did I really know about sex, anyway? Back in Grand Isle, Fin told me that his brother told him that lots of girls act like they don't want it even when they do. No one else ever told me anything. At home, before things changed, sometimes Daddy would grab Mama's backside in front of me and Willow Rose, and she'd push him away like he was embarrassing her, but then sometimes she'd laugh and let him grab her, even in public. Maybe Fin was right about some things, but even if

I wanted to think it was like that with Antoine, I could see the truth. Antoine was a monster and I let him into our house.

My hand starts bleeding hard before I get anywhere, so instead of going home, I turn back to PJ's trailer. The morning is still young, and I figure maybe he hasn't gone out on his boat yet. I find PJ and two of the cats — the ginger one and the white one — on the green couch. PJ smokes a Marlboro and drinks coffee from a giant mug with a picture of Ronald Reagan's and George Bush's faces on it. The caption says "Let's Make America Great Again."

"Hey, Jesse! You come to work?" he asks when I skid up on my bike. When I tell him yes, he pats the seat beside him on the couch and tells me he's taking it slow this morning. "You hungry?" he asks.

For some reason I nearly cry when he asks me that, but I stop myself, nod and fall into the couch beside PJ and the cats, who both startle, but this time they stay. The white one frantically cleans the ginger's ear until the ginger swats her away.

"What's up with you? You hurt your hand?" PJ wants to know. I don't feel like talking about it — I'm too tired, and all I can think about is how bad I want to fall into a sleep that will erase everything, rewind to yesterday so that I can make it different, send Antoine away like I should have. Get back Daddy's gun. Undo this morning. Instead of telling PJ anything I blurt out a question, asking if he has a girlfriend.

"Naw. Not me. Too much trouble. You know I already got too many exes and too many kids running around with my genes. Why — you got girl trouble?"

I shake my head and PJ keeps talking. "That's good, 'cause I'm sure I can't help you with that. I'm good at oysters and maybe some other things, but I don't know shit about women," he says and slurps his coffee. "Let's take care of that hand," he adds.

PJ takes me inside and makes me wash my hand and, to my surprise, he pulls out a dusty box of gauze from inside a kitchen cupboard and he wraps it around my hand, then tapes it over with duct tape, saying it's all he's got. He jokes that he's a nurse in training, then he asks me if I want some toast. This time he's even got some peanut butter to put on it. Real luxury, he tells me.

When PJ's friend Andy shows up, he's all round cheeks and stubble and, unlike most adults around here, he has straight white teeth that gleam when he smiles. He has one brown eye and one green one and a real gravelly voice. PJ introduces me, says I'm going oystering with them today, and Andy asks if I'm coonass. When PJ says my mama's Cajun, but not my daddy, Andy slaps his thick thigh and says, "We'll call him Halfass."

PJ says we're late to get out on the water, so we won't go all the way out to the Gulf, but we'll go to the oyster beds in the bayou, the ones that haven't yet been shut down by the oil. From PJ's small skiff — the Miss America — the water looks dark, and if you stick your finger in it, you can lick off the light salty flavour, the brine that grows the oysters just right. I ignore the rainbow slicks that sit on the water. Some people don't like summer oysters, but PJ says that especially after the explosion, the money is real good for a big haul, no matter the season. He tells me the tourists up in New Orleans will eat anything for any price so long as you tell them it's the real thing, and since shrimp are scarce now, he's hit the jackpot.

We glide out past the tall grasses, watching for the alligators whose cold eyes peer above the surface of the water like waiting death. We sail beneath the lace of the Spanish moss, pushing through duckweed that bakes in the hot sun and smells like warmth and decay, and I breathe it all in and tell myself to relax, but my brain keeps skipping back to what I saw last night. PJ and Andy drink cans of Dixie and share a bag of chips with me. When we pass a stand of brown trees that look like skeletons that raised themselves up from the dead right in the middle of the swampy water, I comment on how strange they look out there.

"Used to be land there. And there." Andy points to a row of telephone poles, still with wires between them, planted too far from land to make sense.

PJ barely looks up from steering the boat. "You seen my stick?" he asks.

Andy nods and says, "Now that's something. Tell him."

"Out near my trailer, I hammered it into the ground not five or six years ago. Now the damn thing is part drowned, more and more waterlogged every year and the water keeps creeping closer to my trailer."

"Everything's going to drown here someday," Andy says.

"It's all that dredging for oil. Now they know it's out there, ain't no going back." PJ rubs his fingers together and mouths *Money, money, money.* "His Daddy was in that explosion." PJ looks over his shoulder at me. Andy's eyes get real big, and he nods his head slow like he knows what that means.

"I'm real sorry," Andy says.

I nod back at Andy, like we share something but I'm not sure what.

"They never found any of the bodies, you know, all burned up," Andy says.

"My daddy went overboard. He jumped because the lifeboats left without him," I say, and when I see the look on Andy's face, I keep on. "He tried to save another man — he was hurt and he jumped too, but he didn't make it."

"I thought all the men who died were working on the rig floor when the explosion happened," Andy says.

I shake my head and Andy looks surprised.

"My friend's brother — his nephew was there — he said it was all men from the same crew working the rig floor who were gone, wiped out together. He said as soon as the gas came up the well, it sparked up like the devil's fireworks and took them out just like that." Andy snaps his fingers and keeps talking. "He ain't said nothing about men jumping."

I shrug and say that all I know is that Daddy hasn't been right since he lost his friend in the Gulf.

"I'm not much for praying, but next time I do, I'm going to pray for your Daddy's friend. That's a terrible way to die," Andy says.

"Hey, Halfass — you want a beer?" PJ asks. I accept, glad for the distraction.

Andy keeps talking, "That blast — it never should have happened. The big men got greedy. Now — the shrimp, the birds, all those men — everyone's paid a real big price," he says.

"And the oil ain't done spilling. It could still come for the oysters," PJ says.

In silence, we sail past more ghost trees.

Something scurries in the water. "Oil ain't the only problem — you seen them nutria?" Andy asks.

I had seen them before. They look cute, like giant mice.

"I'm telling you, you bring me the tail of one of those marsh rats, I'll give you five bucks. Maybe even ten. Those things eat up all the grass — they're miserable little fuckers."

PJ laughs at Andy. "He's racist against marsh rats, says they ain't from here."

"They ain't!" Andy swigs his beer and tosses the can overboard.

"If we ain't got one problem around here we got another. Goddamn oil companies leave unmarked wells out on the Gulf — those could kill a man, and don't even get me started on them diseased shrimp," PJ says. But he leans against the steering wheel of his boat, and the sun glints off his face and glitters on the water. In the distance a rare roseate spoonbill lifts itself up from a tree and flies, and everyone is quiet until a pelican dives like a bomb hitting the water.

"Now that's what," PJ says and grins like he thinks he's in the most beautiful place on earth.

The dredge pulls up a massive load of oysters that PJ dumps on the floor of the boat. Andy teaches me to sort them, lets me crack some open right there and eat them raw, salty juices creeping down the side of my mouth as I swallow the smooth jelly-like creatures, filling my belly.

"Lots of money in this catch. Maybe a thousand or more," Andy says and smiles real big. I put my hand over my heart so that Andy will not hear how fast it beats, how hungry I am for a piece of that.

Back in PJ's trailer, he tosses back another Dixie and offers me oysters for my family. I stand there wordless until he thrusts a ten-dollar bill in my hand, and I damn near start crying, but instead I thank him for the great day and slip into the early evening where I can hide the look on my face. I tie the plastic bag of oysters to the handlebars of my bike and race up the highway, feeling the dread creep into my throat with every stroke of the pedals.

THIRTEEN

NOBODY TOLD ME

WILLOW ROSE'S COLLECTION OF dead squirrels is gone from the yard. This is the first thing I notice when I come home from PJ's. The second thing I notice is the weight of the silence inside.

Mama won't come out of her room. Willow Rose lies on her mattress with her eyes closed, one arm flung over her forehead. Her stomach grumbles, telling me she's hungry, but she won't get herself anything to eat. I bring her bread and peanut butter, and she tells me that Mama has not come out of her room all day.

In the kitchen I pour a glass of water then knock on Mama's door. She won't answer. Nausea settles in my gut and burns. I'm only pretending I know what to do as I turn the knob and let myself in. I expect to find my mother lying in her unmade bed. I expect her face to be streaked with tears. When I find her, my mama is dressed, and she stands in front of the mirror and braids her hair. Her face is stony. I hand her the water.

"What happened to you?" she asks, looking at my hand.

"Nothing. Are you... ?" I start to ask as I try to put my arm around her shoulders. She shifts away from me, hands back the glass of water after only a sip.

"I'm going to cook dinner," she says. It is late — way past dinner — and Mama won't look at me. I trot after her to the kitchen and show her the oysters. Even then she says nothing to me except things like, "Could you pass me a knife." When the oysters are steaming, she says, with her face to the pot, "There's no point telling Daddy anything." It is an announcement and a warning, not a conversation.

After she says it, she keeps staring at the stove, like I am not even there.

That night me and Willow Rose and Mama gather around the table, each of us mute like we don't know the lines we are supposed to say. We pick at our food. We dodge each other's eyes, and Willow Rose begins to clear the dishes before we are even done. I stand next to her drying dishes as fast as she washes them and I begin to talk. "Did you know that all the other men who died on the rig were together? Working the rig floor? No one even knew about anyone jumping or drowning," I say.

"Who told you that?" Mama asks.

"PJ's friend," I say.

"Was he there when it happened?" Mama asks. I shake my head. "Not everything an oysterman says is God's truth. Must have been others who missed the lifeboats and went overboard like that."

"They should have waited for them. Then maybe Daddy wouldn't be so crazy now," I say.

"You should be grateful he's alive," Mama says.

Willow Rose drops a plate into the sink and the splash of water hits my face. She snorts.

"And don't you go repeating what you heard to Daddy," Mama says and then she gets up to leave the kitchen.

"Grateful," Willow Rose murmurs and grins a real crazy pretend-grin as she hands me one more plate to dry.

FOURTEEN

REBEL YELL

I STAND IN THE kitchen the very next day, fussing over oysters that no one wants to eat, feeling like the time I rode my bike with a flat tire, wrecked the wheel, and Daddy told me I was more useless than two titties on a bull. Got to learn to do things right, he told me, and he found the hole in my tire and mended it with a patch, real quick, like it was nothing.

Mama is in her room and Willow Rose took off with the .410 and hasn't come back all afternoon. I am staring inside the icebox when I hear tires on the gravel road. Like a jackrabbit, I sprint to Mama's room as the front door opens and heavy footsteps come towards us.

"I'll go," I say, feeling suddenly sick, but Mama shakes her head, pushes her lips together and beats me out of the room to the front door.

"Emmett!" she sounds surprised.

My father looks like he's been puked up by a dog. He has lines on his face that I don't remember from before, and he has the thickest stubble I've ever seen him wear.

My father, who no longer looks like my father, pushes past me into the bedroom. My mother looks at me, her face a question mark, and follows Daddy, closing the door behind the two of them. I grasp my still aching hand, slink away and wonder — will he be able to tell what happened to Mama?

In the kitchen, I finish washing plates, dry them and go to set the table pretending everything's normal. I sneak up to Mama and

Daddy's door listening for what's happening. Daddy emerges from the bedroom, steps around me and goes into the shower. I wander back to the kitchen. Not much later, Daddy joins me, hair wet and slicked to his head, his beard gone, making his cheeks look raw and hollow. Mama follows, her hair now ruffled like the way chickens look when they bathe in the dirt.

"Daddy," I say and go to him as if to hug him or maybe shake his hand, but he stands there totally stiff, so I back off, sit in a chair and pick at my nails. "How's Nana?" I ask, but the question feels strange in my mouth. I haven't seen his family since I was a kid. I don't know what my own grandmother's face looks like.

"She's fine. Real good," my father says. I wait for more, but instead he opens the icebox and sticks his head inside.

"She better then?" I keep on, trying to fill the air.

"I said she's real good," my father says, voice sharp.

"Maybe she'll come visit us someday," I say.

"There anything to eat around here?" Daddy says ignoring me.

"How come we never visit Nana all together?" I ask.

"Since when do you care about your grandmother so much?" my father asks.

I'm about to protest, but my mother puts her hand on my arm, willing me to stop.

"Where're these from?" my father asks, peering into the oyster bowl.

Mama darts a harsh look at me, and I open up my mouth.

"I got 'em cheap in Golden Meadow."

"Ain't no cheap oysters no more. Y'all spending my money on this crap?"

"Naw, I told you. They were cheap. Some kid was selling them at a stand."

I chew on a hangnail until it bleeds. I can sense Daddy's temper flaring.

"You ain't bought no oysters from no kid," Daddy tugs at his ear. "Did you?"

"I did," I say, but my voice falters. Mama closes her eyes.

"Bullshit," Daddy spits out the word. "I told you to look after things around here, and this is what you come up with."

He reaches into the icebox and pulls out the bowl with the oysters in it.

"I know where you got these," he says and he dumps the oysters on the floor and then hurls the green bowl, breaking it into three big pieces. He steps on an oyster good and slow, cracking it, making it leak from under his shoe.

"Those were for dinner," I say, but my voice is quiet now.

Daddy reaches for me. He grabs me by the shirt and pulls me to him so that I can look up his nostrils and into the back of his mouth where his black fillings are.

"Y'all better learn to look after things when I tell you to, not go running for handouts from that son of a bitch."

My father shakes me. He shakes me from side to side like a dog shakes a squirrel in its mouth, and then he slaps my face. I grab his wrist and push him away, but he is stronger and leans his weight against me, pressing me against the kitchen counter.

"You got anything to show for yourself besides this?" My father's arm lies heavy across my chest.

"At least I fed my family," I say.

My father grabs the back of my hair.

"Stop it!" my mother yells.

The .410 in her hands, Willow Rose bursts into the kitchen. My father's head swivels in her direction and his eyes flame. While I take in Willow Rose's raised eyebrows and open mouth, my father clocks me in the jaw, and I tumble to the floor.

"Jesse!" Mama comes to me, but I shrug her off, standing up on my own. She holds my elbow and then backs off. Willow Rose has skittered out of the kitchen.

"This what I come home to? My God, I leave here, and everything's gone to shit."

"That's enough," Mama says. She bends down and picks up the large pieces of the broken bowl. "Nothing's gone to shit while you were away. Willow Rose's just playing around." She looks at me and shakes her head as she holds the bowl in front of her, runs her fingers over the edges where it split apart.

"At least I got a daughter willing to help out around here," he says, and he crunches more oysters under his feet. From the floor I can smell the faint odour of brine, of bayou, and my stomach clenches at the sight of our dinner ruined. "Now clean up this mess, goddammit," he tells me, and then he heaves himself out of the kitchen and to his room, leaving a trail of oyster juice footprints behind him.

"You never should have given Willow Rose that thing," Mama mutters, and she bends down to gather slippery oysters from the floor, shaking her head at me. I pull out the trash and help Mama toss the oozing pieces, and when they are all gone, she brushes off her knees and gives me a sad look before she leaves me alone to pass a soapy rag over the floor, as if doing it enough will scrub away the traces of Daddy's rage.

FIFTEEN

WHEN DOVES CRY

THE PULSING ACHE IN my jaw and the sting of my hand brings me out of my dreams before it is even dawn. From my bed, I turn my back on Willow Rose and face the wall where my map hangs. My father has never hit me so hard before. I wish I knew if Mama told him after all or if he guessed. Those oysters made him madder than he should have been if it was just the oysters. While my mind spins, I trace the line around the bottom of the United States. Louisiana. Mississippi. Alabama. Georgia. How many oil rigs in the Gulf, I wonder, still pumping oil from deep, deep down? What are the chances that any one man will be on the one platform that explodes like that?

From the hall I hear my parents' bedroom door open and close. My spine prickles as the door to our room clicks open. I ball up a fist and curl into myself.

"Willow Rose," my father says. I won't look at him, but my sister rustles into wakefulness.

"I'm taking you hunting," he says.

I hold my breath, pretend I am underwater, try to drown out my father's voice. I won't let him know I am awake. Our door clicks closed again, and Willow Rose scrambles up from her mattress. I sit up.

"It's not fair," I say.

Willow Rose buttons her jeans, her hair falls over her face. She says nothing.

"I should get to go," I say. I know the meanness in my voice is unfair, but I can't stop the feeling that something inside of me is broiling over, looking for someone to whip. I slip out of bed and grab Willow Rose by the arm.

"Let go." She twists her arm to get away, but I hold on.

"You going to tell him I taught you everything? That I showed you how to use that gun?"

Willow Rose shoves me now with her other elbow, and I let go.

"It's not my fault he wants to take me and not you," she says and rubs her arm on her shirt.

"He hates me," I say and fling myself back down on my bed.

"No he doesn't. He's just crazy sometimes," Willow Rose says.

"Totally crazy. You shouldn't go with him. It's my job," I say.

"I want him to know I'm good at something too," Willow Rose says. She looks at herself in our tiny, dark mirror as she sweeps her hair into a ponytail. From old pictures I know that when Willow Rose was a baby, she didn't get hair until she was almost two years old, and now she won't let anyone cut it; only she can trim the ends, which she does with the kitchen scissors. She looks at me sitting on the bed, and I stare back like I want my stare to burn her. I imagine for a second this must be how it feels to be the younger one. She opens the door, then half closes it and looks at me. "I'm not the one who got you in trouble," she says, and then she slides out the door and shuts it behind her.

I lie there wishing for sleep to return, but everything inside me is too hot. I pick at the tape around my hand while I think of what to do next. Daddy taught me that when you go hunting, you should always come back with something, it don't even matter what. When I remember this, I make a decision. I tiptoe out of my room — I don't want Mama to hear me — and I take the rifle, the .22 from behind the back door. I am still a better hunter than Willow Rose, and she needs to know — Daddy needs to know — the truth.

The stock of the .22 is smooth, polished wood that shines like dark honey. It's Daddy's favourite gun; light and quick he says. Accurate. My father told me he once shot a cottonmouth with it; he told me that snake was coming at him so fast he thought he was a dead man, so he shot the monster with a single bullet, and even though it's better to shoot at snakes with a BB gun, Daddy saved himself from the snake and threw it into an alligator's mouth in the bayou. I sling the rifle across my back and shove way more ammunition in my pockets than I need. You'd think I was planning a bloodbath.

I pump the pedals of my bike into the air, thick with the smell of swamp, and head north, standing as I ride, feeling the burn in my thighs. I want to have muscular legs like my father used to. I ride until I come to one of the ancient drawbridges and cross over and keep riding up the other side of the bayou until I find a quiet road into the woods.

Surrounded by trees and with blood throbbing beneath my skin, I feel like I have a scream caught in my throat that I can't let out. I do something I have never done. I release a single bullet into the sky, aiming at nothing, just to hear the crack and bang. Relieved, I slump down against a tree and feel the breath move through me fast, heavy. Antoine. Daddy's Colt. Mama. Willow Rose. Daddy. I won't let myself cry. I remember my father's words. I wait.

Finally, a raccoon — a family of them — lumbers by. As a kid, I wanted nothing more than a pet raccoon: their masks, the way they look so smart. I wanted one so bad. Raccoon meat is dark and greasy, but sometimes Daddy used to barbecue them, and we'd eat them with potatoes or whatever else we had. I think of this now and my stomach bunches up, making me near sick right there. I take a deep breath and think of my father's face. The kits — three of them — are still little. They make their way towards the water, frisking with each other, one running ahead, another lagging. The mother watches over them with a serious face.

I breathe in hard and then again before I look down the barrel of my gun. I aim it at a kit, then change my mind, hands shaking, and aim at the mother. I follow her down her path for seconds before I pull back the trigger, hold it and release. When the bullet sails from the .22, the raccoon babies scatter, but the mama is hit and instantly slumps to the ground. A lump in my throat becomes a wail so loud

I'm sure the leaves on the trees shake. I throw down the rifle and let the tears rip. The raccoon's eyes are open, and when I touch her, I tell myself I have no right to cry like that. It's my fault she's dead.

As if under a spell, I collect the raccoon in a bag. I feel her weight knock against me the whole way home, a shameful trophy that I lay out in the yard for everyone to see once I am home. It is a large, meaty animal.

Mama steps outside, and when she grasps what I've done, she draws in her breath and gasps my name. Mama lights a smoke and inhales, plunking herself down in a chair. I sit down beside her, and she looks at me, disgust on her face. "You better go wash up," she says. But I stay sitting, picking at a small bloodstain on my hands. Finally, I break the quiet.

"What happened to Daddy when he was gone?" I ask.

My mother takes an extra-long drag. "I wish I knew," she says.

"He seems terrible now," I say.

She shifts position and pulls her hair from her face, and then lets it fall back over her shoulders. Beneath her eyes are shadows that sit on her cheeks. She finishes her smoke and then lights another. "You remember what I said about not telling?" she asks.

"Yes ma'am." I feel better knowing she hasn't told.

"He's got it real bad," Mama says and looks at my raccoon. "Full of parasites," she says.

"It's almost September," I say, imitating something I've heard Daddy say about late summer game.

"Bullshit," Mama says and snorts.

We glare at each other until Mama inhales too hard and chokes. I swallow back my words for so long my throat aches until I finally blurt them out. "Are you okay?"

My mother looks at me with eyes so sad and tired I want to duck so that I don't have to look at them. She draws on her smoke and takes a real deep breath in and then pushes the smoke out her mouth into the still air. "Is anyone around here okay?" she asks, stubs out her cigarette, inhales hard and says, "Anyone?"

I want my father to take in the size of the raccoon before I skin it, so I let it sit in the yard long after Mama goes inside. The black-feathered rooster comes around, crowing over my kill, while I feed the bird grain from my hand, rub the softness of its crown between my fingers. That is how Daddy finds me when he and Willow Rose clatter into the yard with the .410 and a burlap bag full of game.

The rooster crows.

"I got a raccoon," I say.

My father looks at the animal, nods and says, "Nice and big. Good."

"Biggest one I saw," I tell him, and my father nods and then lays down his own bag and gestures at Willow Rose, who pulls two animals from inside the bag.

"Possums!" she says and holds up the animals to show me.

"I used the .22. Saw a whole family of raccoons," I say.

My father claps a hand on my shoulder and inspects my raccoon, admires its weight. The rooster calls out again and Daddy rubs his head, wincing at the noise.

"Why is that goddamn bird making noise at this hour?" my father asks me.

"I don't know," I say and take a step in front of the rooster, putting myself between the bird and my father.

"It ain't early," my father says and rubs his fingers to his temples where, on the left side, a blue vein shows itself big and thick.

"Maybe it's hungry," I say.

"Hungry, my ass," my father says.

"I'm hungry," Willow Rose says.

"I'll go get the skinning knife," I say.

One of the hens, the brown one, crosses the path of the rooster cackling away, and the rooster kicks up a fuss, cawing and chasing her in circles, pecking after her. My father kicks at the big bird and it flaps harder.

"You going to do something about that noise?" my father asks me.

"What'm I supposed to do?" I begin to back into the house.

Willow Rose tells the rooster to hush.

"Maybe someone needs to make that thing shut up for good."

"I'm going inside," I say.

"You got the .22. You do it," my father says.

I hold the rifle by the barrel and do nothing.

"That thing loaded?" my father asks.

I shake my head. The rooster struts away from where we stand and then crows. Willow Rose chews on a strand of her hair.

"You got ammo?" my father asks me.

I don't answer, just dig my toes into the dusty ground.

"You do," my father says.

I shake my head.

"Do it," he says.

"No," I say.

"No?" My father nods his head and inhales all loud like he means something by it. "No?" He repeats himself.

"I won't do it," I say. I fix my eyes on my father's face and concentrate hard. My skin prickles with heat, and I feel it pool in my groin, trickle down the backs of my legs. The moisture sits above my father's lip.

"I didn't raise you to be chickenshit." He pinches his earlobe between two fingers.

I ball up a fist. "Ain't no reason to kill it," I say. My father glares at me. "Ain't no reason to kill things we can't even eat." I gesture to all the dead animals surrounding us, knowing that Mama is right and that we could all get real sick.

"Ain't nothing wrong with getting some target practice," Daddy says. He points his chin at Willow Rose and says, "She'll do it."

Willow Rose tightens her grip on her gun.

I bite the inside of my lip. "No she won't," I say.

"She will." My father nods at my sister. She looks at each of us in turn. "Do it," my father says.

Willow Rose loads the .410 real quick. She looks down the barrel like I taught her, and she follows the rooster with her gun. Then she pauses, lowers the gun.

"You don't have to," I tell Willow Rose.

"Sissy," my father says.

"Son of a bitch," I hiss.

Willow Rose lifts the gun back up to where it was, pressing it against her shoulder. She watches the rooster strut away from her. "Don't," I whisper to her. But she watches the bird and releases an explosion of BBs that knocks it to the ground as it cries out. Willow Rose lets out a yelp that sounds like she has just shocked herself.

"Maybe now I can get some quiet around here," my father says, and he claps my sister's shoulder. Willow Rose looks back and forth between me and my father.

"Murderer." I spit the word at her and leave the two of them outside, looking at their kills and mine.

PART TWO

SIXTEEN

JESSE – BOYS DO FALL IN LOVE

VANILLA ICE CREAM CONES. I'm in my new homeroom class on the first day of school in Golden Meadow, and the girl sitting next to me — she's wearing a Rolling Stones T-shirt with the sleeves cut off — has tits that make me think of two soft serve cones. It's the only thing I think of all day.

Yesterday Willow Rose shrieked at whoever would listen that she had nothing to wear to school, so Daddy took her to Dollar General up in Galliano, and she came back with a bag full of things she wouldn't show me, except for the flimsy notebook she tossed my way as if that made her real generous. Mama cussed and said we don't have money for Willow Rose to have new clothes, but Daddy said he can do what he wants with his money, and then he opened two cans of Bud at once and drank them down one after the other. I don't care much about new clothes, but I threw a fork at my father when he said we'd have to get to school on our own. In Grand Isle we always rode our bikes, and I knew everyone in my grade from when I was a kid, but now I don't know anyone, and I have to show up with my kid sister doubled on my bike because no one bothered to take hers when we left Grand Isle. Back home, I was good at school — not so good that anyone bugged me about it — but I always knew that if I could find a way to get my work done, I'd be fine, but that was before we lived in a house in the middle of nowhere, before my father turned crazy.

By the end of homeroom, I know that her name is Lisette and that I need to find a way to touch her thick brown hair and her tits.

Before first period, I duck into the bathroom to tuck my boner into the waistband of my jeans and then find her again in my first period science class, where she waits for the teacher, headphones covering her ears, slouched in her seat, doodling in a fresh notebook. Like most girls, she wears real short shorts, and her tanned legs are stuck out into the aisle so that I nearly trip over her pink high-tops. If she knows anyone else in the classroom, she doesn't care. Since I already know that I want to put my hand up her shirt and down her pants, I ask her to be my lab partner, and she says no — she already promised her best friend who she says is still on holiday — but I think about Fin telling me that sometimes girls say no when they mean yes, and I decide this is a good start.

In civics class our teacher talks about the miracle of space travel. She tells us that the Space Shuttle *Discovery* will land tomorrow in California, and she shows us a short video of its launch from Cape Canaveral in Florida. As our teacher talks about American brilliance and how even if the Soviets were the first in space we were first to the moon and that counts for more, Lisette leans over to me and whispers that she once saw a rocket launch for real, and I can't think of a thing to tell her in return. I decide right then that one day, I will drive to Florida to see a rocket launch, like Lisette has seen. When we leave class, I think fast and remember my father telling me about how he got Mama's attention the first time. They were at Mardi Gras in Houma. Daddy was working at odd jobs, and Mama was a senior visiting town with her friends, and he saw her. He tossed her a beaded necklace, and — my mama always jokes that she's been paying for it ever since — she grabbed the beads and then lifted up her shirt like they do in New Orleans. My father says if your balls are big enough, pretty words are as good as fancy jewellry, so I take a deep breath and tell Lisette that I love her shirt. Daddy says we're all lucky in our family to have real nice eyes, so I blink and show her mine, and it works. Lisette walks with me to our next class, telling me about how her older brothers got that shirt at an actual concert at the Superdome in New Orleans. I've never met anyone like her.

When Willow Rose is late to meet me at the bike stand at the end of the day, I'm so restless thinking about Lisette that I'm about to leave by myself, but I know what my mother will say if I show up at home without my sister, so I wait. When she appears, Willow Rose is with another girl her age and two boys. She's wearing the stupid halter-top she put on in the morning. Daddy bought it for her, and it's grey with a glittery red heart in the middle of it. Willow Rose waves off her friends, who slink away except for one boy who looks at me and smirks like he knows something, but I don't care because I have something good to think about too.

Willow Rose perches herself on the back of the bike where there is an old rack, and I stand up on the pedals as we turn down the road away from the school while Willow Rose sticks her arms out wide to feel the air rush past, then she dumps a package of pop rocks that one of her new friends gave her into her mouth and presses her mouth into my ear with the sound of all the little candy explosions. We made it through the first day, and we're both relieved. At home, Mama is sitting out back smoking. When she takes in Willow Rose's shirt, she stubs out her smoke and turns to me.

"She wore that to school?" she asks, as if it's my fault. I shrug and lean the bike against the back of the house. "That's not a school shirt." Mama follows us into the house where my father is sitting at the kitchen table. In front of him are stacks of bills — likely all the money he has — and he is counting it into piles, bundling them with elastics.

"You bought this shirt for her?" Mama demands, one hand on her hip.

"She liked it." Daddy barely looks up. He pauses his counting and slams a pile of bills on the table. "Fuck," he says. "I lost count." Mama looks at Willow Rose dead serious.

"Don't wear that to school again," she says.

"I'll wear what I want," Willow Rose says and puts a hand on her hip, imitating Mama.

"Oh no you won't. And someone needs to buy you a bra."

"Mama!" Willow Rose shrieks and stomps to our room, where she slams the door behind her. Mama rubs her forearm across her brow and watches Daddy counting.

"Goddammit," she says and goes back outside, and I can smell Mama's smoke coming in the open kitchen window.

"You see this?" Daddy says to me. I nod. "It's all we got. You got that?"

I don't know what I'm supposed to say, so I keep nodding.

"You got nothing to say about that?" my father asks.

I take a breath. "Have you gone back to work yet? At Antoine's?" I know it's the wrong thing to say, but I feel sore just seeing my father's mean face.

He slaps down his hand. "You think you're too smart to help out?" my father says, voice almost hoarse with anger.

"I'm supposed to be in school," I say.

"I always worked when I was in school," he says.

"And look where you are," I say and gesture around the room.

"You little bitch. Even your sister's more of a man than you," he says.

I pause for just a second before I open my smart mouth. "I bet I can make more money than you while staying in school," I say.

"I'd like to see you try," he says.

Suddenly, I am filled with rage at him for introducing us to Antoine and leaving us here alone with so little money. I want it to be his fault. "Do you think everyone who was on the rig acts like you? Or are you the only one turned crazy?"

"You shut your mouth," he says.

"Big hero, tried to save a man but you couldn't, so now you've gone out of your mind," I say.

My father's eyes get real big and then narrow. I keep on. "Scared of a little fire? Huh? Bang!" I clap my hands to make an exploding noise and as soon as I do it, I know I've gone too far.

I wait for my father's rage, holding my breath, bracing for a punch or a slap, but instead he shakes his head and looks down.

"You don't know half of it," he murmurs, and his eyes turn red and watery like I've hit him.

I slink out of the kitchen thinking if I stay any longer, I'll see my father cry and I'd rather see anything but that. When I burst into our bedroom, Willow Rose is trying on one of Mama's floppy beige bras.

"Get out!" Willow Rose screams.

"Jesus Christ," I say and fly back out of the room, out the front door, and grab my bicycle and bolt down the highway.

SEVENTEEN

RUN TO YOU

ANTOINE IS UNDER A jacked-up black Mustang when I find him. He's dressed in coveralls covered in old grease, and his hands are up inside the car, whose underside is lit by a lamp. I imagine punching him in his massive face.

"Damnit," he says as I slink into his shop and stand near enough that I could touch his arm. With his neck tilted back like that, he doesn't notice me. I say his name. Still nothing. This time I practically bellow, "Antoine." He swivels his head towards me, and for a second all I can see is the sickening, smug look he had on his face when I saw him with Mama. I narrow my eyes and focus on what I want.

"You break another window of mine?" he asks and wipes his hands on his coveralls then against each other.

"No sir," I say. I have decided that if Daddy doesn't know about Antoine, there's every reason to take his money. I may have lost my chance to kill him, but I can make him pay.

"Good," he says, and then he claps me on the shoulder like we're pals, and I let go my breath that I didn't even notice I was holding.

"You broke that window real good," he says looking at my hand and smiling like he thinks it's funny now.

I look at it too. It's still scratched up, but it doesn't sting so much anymore. Antoine holds open my palm for a second, looks it over and nods.

"You'll be fine," he says and whacks me on the back in a friendly way.

"Antoine, sir? I need a job," I say, acting all polite, remembering what Daddy said about him being loose with money.

"I knew it," he says. "Your Daddy gone again?" he asks.

"Naw. He's home."

"He came by here a couple of times lately, and then he just quit," Antoine says. "You know anything about cars?" I shake my head. "Your Daddy didn't teach you?" He shakes his head and tsks. "You'll have to be my apprentice then. I'll pay you cash — real money — but not as good as your Daddy. Fair?"

"Fair," I say, and we shake on it. He grins at me and I pretend-grin back feeling like I'm hiding a sneaky, mean side of myself that even I don't know very well.

Antoine brings me under the Mustang and points up and into the car. He's changing a muffler, he tells me, and step by step he shows me what he's working on. He lowers the car so that I can reach it, and my hands get black with grease. He points me to the rags he keeps behind the desk he calls his office. I duck down to pick out a soft grey rag that I can tell used to be a T-shirt, and piled high on the floor he's got more than a dozen books — some novels and then books about different American wars and presidents. Buried in the pile, he has one by Ernest Hemingway called *A Farewell to Arms*. I've never read it, and I consider swiping it, but then I catch sight of the stack of girlie magazines — *Playboy*, *Juggs*, one called *High Society* — behind the books. I wipe my hands and rifle through one real quick before I return to the car.

"You find my reading material?" Antoine asks. I nod, too embarrassed to say much.

"Philosopher or man?" he asks with a smirk and a laugh. When I don't answer he shakes his head and keeps talking. "A man can be a philosopher, but a philosopher can't always be a man. You see what I'm saying?"

I have no idea what he's saying. I nod anyway.

"You like those magazines, don't you?" he asks.

"I guess," I mumble.

"You guess? Everybody likes that," he says. I wish I were older so I would know what say. Instead, I keep on wiping my hands on the rag, trying to take the grease out from the creases in my knuckles while Antoine watches me and shakes his head.

After he finishes with the car, he brings me back to his desk, and I feel my cheeks burn. "I'll give you twenty for today," he says, and pulls out cash from a messy drawer filled with bills and other papers. We stare at each other for a second, and remembering why I came here, seeing the thing in his face that I hate, I keep holding my hand out. He peels off another twenty and I pocket it. There is much more in his drawer. He nods, and as if he feels nervous, he chuckles and looks down at his pile of magazines. "You take one of those too," he says.

"Really?" I ask.

"Anyone you like," he says.

I want to go through all of them, to choose the best one, but I snatch the one on top and roll it up.

"You sure that's the one?" he asks.

"Yes sir," I say, again pretending my politeness.

"Sometimes it's good to be fussy. Or maybe it don't matter," he says.

I look at the magazine I've got in my hands, flip through it in a hurry, heat creeping up my neck as Antoine watches me. I tell him this one's real good.

Antoine shakes his head and tells me that if I had dug a bit deeper, I would have found the one with the famous pictures of the Miss America — she was the first-ever Black Miss America and real pretty too — who had to give up her crown because of those pictures. I look back at the pile of magazines, now regretting my choice. He grins and says, "Damn shame she had to give that up. She's a beauty, and smart too. Naw, I wouldn't have given that magazine to you, anyway."

I pull my hand back from rifling through the stack.

"Now you don't show no one you got that, all right?" he says.

"No sir," I say. Holding my magazine, an image of him and my Mama flashes in my mind. I suck in a deep breath. "I want a book. And more money," I say.

He looks real surprised and tries to laugh it off like I'm joking. "Don't get too excited. There's plenty of time for that. Take whatever book you want, though," he says rubbing his hands on his pants.

"You should give me more money," I say. The serious sound of my voice surprises even me.

He pauses and looks at me like he has a question but doesn't know the words.

"My father," I start to say.

"You come here on a shakedown?" he asks.

"Naw," I say. "I'm just trying to help out my family. Like you said — not much in our icebox." I put my hand out and kick my toe into the floor as if I'm all humble and shy.

"I see how it is," he says, and he passes me another twenty.

"I don't want to tell no one," I begin again.

He pulls out two more twenties and hands them over. It's the most money I've ever held. Then I snatch a book — *Zen and the Art of Motorcycle Maintenance*. Antoine shrugs at my choice and says, "So this is how we do."

"I'll come back another time," I say, and he nods, claps me on the back, pretending we're buddies, but I shrug him off and stare into his eyes. I imagine I've just knocked him out. I imagine his head hitting the floor of his shop. I imagine blood.

I tear away from his shop and bike just far enough that I am alone before I stop and look at the magazine in the dusky light. I speed past the pages of half-shown tits and asses, feeling myself grow hard and my breath heavy before I flatten the magazine up inside my shirt and tuck it into my jeans so that no one will know it's there.

Willow Rose lies on my bed when I return home so that instead of sneaking a look at my magazine in peace, I stand there, all sweaty, pages plastered to my belly, bothering her about why she's in my bed and so early.

"Mama says we're too old to share a room, so you're going to have to use the couch," she announces, her legs kicked up against the wall, bare heels against my map.

"It's my bed," I say, holding my hand against my shirt.

"You've had it all this time. Now it's my turn. Ask Mama," my sister says.

I clomp back down the hall and find my mother sitting in the kitchen, smoking her cigarette down to a stub. Her face is hard against my complaints.

"You both need privacy," she says.

"So, stick Willow Rose on the couch," I say.

"She's a girl. She's younger." Mama stubs out her cigarette.

"It's not fair," I say.

"You're right," Mama says. "A lot of things aren't fair these days. You should get used to it." She reaches to me to wrap her arm around my shoulder, and as she leans into me my magazine crunches into her side. My mama lifts up my shirt, and her face grows dark. She yanks the magazine from me, but I cling to it.

"Jesse, where did you get that?"

I let go of the magazine. "A kid at school."

"Get rid of it." She holds out the trash bin to me. I hesitate, but Mama taps her foot and orders me to dump it. I let out an angry huff, let it fall from my hands and watch the pages flick open, trying for a last glimpse.

"I'm sorry," I say and keep looking at the magazine now splayed open in the trash.

"Is that how you think of girls?" Mama asks.

I mumble that I don't.

"That's not how I raised you," she says.

"I'm sorry," I say again, but I'm only sorry Mama caught me.

"Stop looking at that and move your things to the couch," Mama says, and she shakes her head at me as I leave the room to do as she says.

Long after I drag my sheets and pillow down to the sofa, and hours after Mama and Willow Rose have gone to bed, I tiptoe to the kitchen and look for my magazine, but Mama's no fool — she's gotten rid of it. Back on the couch, I sulk and then conjure up some images in my head, telling myself there are plenty more magazines at Antoine's and plenty of reasons to go back there. Thinking of all the pictures in the big pile on his floor, I find my release and then I turn to my new book, and from the first page I wish the author — Robert Pirsig — was my father. The way he describes the swamps and the redwing blackbirds and seeing all of this on a motorcycle, I would give anything for that kind of adventure. A few pages in, he describes places that sound like Grande Isle, or even like where we live now and how much better he thinks they are than cities, and I think he's obviously never lived in the middle of nowhere, but I read on into the night, wishing I had a father who read aloud to me the way he describes with his son.

I don't know what time it is when my father comes in the front door. I hold my breath and watch his dark shadow creep down the hall to Mama. The door of their bedroom clicks shut behind him. In minutes his and Mama's voices rise and fall and then Mama's erupts, and Daddy comes back to the front room. My father's weight sinks down next to me, and I sit up, smell the drink on his breath, the smoke on his clothes and in his hair.

"You been kicked out?" he asks me.

"Yes sir," I say.

"So that's how it is. All the women are mad at all the men, and all the men have to sleep on couches." He throws an arm around me and sinks in.

"Mama kicked you out?" I ask.

"Said I'm too drunk. Didn't want me near her," he says.

"You smell drunk," I say.

My father sniffs his shirt with a big snort. "I stink," he announces. "I stink real good."

"Real good," I say sniffing his shirt like he did, feeling his warmth press into my rib cage.

"You only wish you could stink like me," he says, and he laughs real hard. I can't think of the last time my father laughed like that, so hard he throws himself against the back of the sofa, holding onto my arm. He groans and tells me that he's definitely going to pay for this tomorrow. "I should drink less," he says, and I mumble that I agree. Then he notices the book I'm reading, and he picks it up. "I read this once," he says.

"You did?" I have not seen my father read a book in a long time, though he used to, before the explosion.

"You are a romantic and I am a classicist," he says.

"I don't know what you mean," I say.

"Keep reading. The book says they're both good, but I know which I'd rather be," he says and then he puts his hand to his head.

I go to get him a glass of water and then another, making him drink it all. He thanks me and comes back to his senses a bit. "Damn it's hot," he says and waves his hand in front of his face. He takes off his clothes down to his underpants, which are saggy and white like mine.

"Where're you going to sleep?" I ask my father.

"Right here," he says and points at the couch. "Two can fit." He takes my pillow, then points at the other end of the sofa. "You take that side," he says, and he presses himself into the cushions, stretching himself long and patting the space beside him. "Bedtime," he says.

I arrange myself on the opposite side, legs glued together, arms rigid by my sides. I have never slept so close to my father. I can feel the weight of his legs next to mine, smell his feet near my armpit, as his breath grows heavy.

I'm too aware of my father to sleep. I prop myself up and watch the twitch of his eyelids that are so thin I can see the twisting vessels in the pale moonlight that comes into the room. Beneath his grizzled jaw and the hollows of his slackened cheeks is something soft and small in his face, almost like he's a child. When I see him like that, I think about what he must have seen on the rig that night. I suppose I'm afraid of dying, but I have never looked at death in the eye like my father must have. His face is relaxed as he sleeps, a look I haven't seen on him ever since he came home the day of the blast. In my memory from the time before, my father is brave, much braver than me. I always figured he wasn't afraid of anything. I snake an arm around his ankles and hold on so that I won't topple off the couch. I lie there holding tight, listening to the rhythm of my father's breathing.

Daddy rustles and mutters and then moans like a ghost. The noise comes from deep in his throat, a hollow sound that grows into a wail, like he's trying to say something, but nothing he utters is words. He starts to howl louder, then whimpers. He writhes from side to side, hitting out against the air. I lie there, paralyzed, while his wail swells and becomes a full-body screech. He jolts upright, grasping the side of the sofa and screams words that I can't make out. His eyes are wide and shining, but blank.

I put my hand on his arm, but he doesn't notice. His breath is shallow and fast. On his forehead a thick vein stands out and pulses. His skin feels clammy.

"Emmett." Mama comes into the front room. She sits down beside him. "Shh," she says. "I'm here." She wraps an arm around him and touches his shoulder, then his face. My father pants like a dog as he turns to her. His body releases into a slouch.

"Fuck," he says.

"I know," Mama says.

He puts his head in his hands, covering his face. He rubs his ear, stands up and leans into Mama, letting her walk with him back to their room.

I lay awake for the rest of the night thinking of the look on my father's face, like he could see clear to the other side.

EIGHTEEN

YOU SPIN ME 'ROUND

AT SCHOOL I LUST over Lisette and scheme ways to get close to her during classes. She's part of a group of kids from Golden Meadow who've gone to school together all their lives, played sports together and dated, even had sex with each other like sex was a thing you shared like a bag of chips. Her older brothers — three of them — are only half-brothers, and I've heard the rumours about parties and drugs. But Lisette gets good grades and wears T-shirts that are just the right amount of tight. Nobody bothers her.

On the day she wears an I Love New York T-shirt to school, I am practically dizzy with envy — I don't know anyone who's been to New York — and I can't stop staring at the big red heart that lands right on her left tit, making me want to squeeze it all day long. In science class, we're standing over our lab stations, trying to light rickety Bunsen burners when Cole — a kid who plays basketball and has a smart mouth — taps me on the shoulder.

"Stop looking at her," he says.

I pretend I don't know what he's talking about by fiddling with the lab instruments in front of me, but he snickers and fake whispers, "I've seen what's under that shirt."

The flame of my Bunsen burner rips to life, and my cheeks flush with the heat. Cole laughs. Lisette is at the far end of the room, and I pray she can't hear us.

"Fuck," I say messing with the flame to bring it down.

"Real nice. But definitely not for you," Cole presses on, watching me fumble.

"Piss off," I whisper to the flame. Lisette crosses back to the banks of lab stations.

"You're still looking," Cole taunts.

My flame is now small and blue like it's supposed to be, and I can't hide my face in playing with it anymore. "It's okay, you can look, but don't touch. Catch you later," Cole says. He shakes his head, tsks and walks towards Lisette, tearing away the paper towels she has in her hands. She grabs them back.

"Get your own," she says and saunters to her station where she joins her friend Gina, who glances at me and nudges Lisette. I force myself to look down at my own work. Cole has had sex with her. I know it. My heart pounds when I think of that. A burst of laughter rings out and suddenly Lisette is beside me, her warmth real close. The hairs on my arms stand on end.

"Could I borrow your lab instructions?" she asks.

I'm working alone, still I hand the two typed pages to her. She looks at me instead of them.

"Thanks," she says and puts them back down.

"You can take them," I say, even though I'm not done my experiment.

"I don't need them," she says. "I just wanted to know if I could see them."

"Okay," I say. I feel like I'm caught in a rainstorm without an umbrella.

"Thanks again. You better finish up," she says and shakes a mocking finger at me before returning to her own station.

Wiping my sweaty palms on my shirt, I realize the period's almost over. Lisette brushes by me and says, "See you." Then Gina passes me and hands me a note that says *Someone likes you* and beneath it is a phone number that says *Lisette* beside it. I run my hands through my hair and am too wound up to say anything back before the two of them stroll out of class, all long limbs and long hair. I shove the note in my pocket. It doesn't matter if we don't have a phone, I have something that belongs to Lisette. I memorize the number then and there.

At the end of the day, I wait for Willow Rose beside my bike, half in a daze, half ready to explode with excitement when she approaches from one direction, but from the other Cole is coming my way bellowing something about me being a piece of shit.

"Hurry up," I hiss to Willow Rose, who's loping towards me like she's on a lazy holiday. When she finally jumps on the bike, I tear away just in time to hear Cole calling after me that he'll beat my ass, and I pedal away with practised speed, sweat plastering my back as we rip down the highway for home.

NINETEEN

AGAINST ALL ODDS

MAMA'S HAIR IS A wild mess, tangled and frizzy, and she sits in the kitchen next to Daddy, who has a lit cigarette hanging from his lips and an open can of Miller that he clenches and unclenches, making a crunching noise. Mama lights one up and breathes in all tight. Her eyes are bloodshot.

"Mama?" I ask.

"I'm pregnant," she announces to me and Willow Rose. We stand there paralyzed, still holding our school bags.

"She's pregnant!" Daddy repeats and blows smoke into the kitchen.

"Holy shit!" Willow Rose yells.

"Willow Rose!" I say.

"She's right," Daddy says. "Holy shit balls." Now he sucks back the last of his Miller and crumples the can down to a flat disc that he throws my way. "Holy fuckin' shit balls."

"When?" I say.

"Spring," Mama mutters, watching the orange glow beneath the ash of her smoke, but not inhaling.

"Somebody around here better be making money by then," my father announces, standing up from his chair, banging his knee on the table as he does and rubbing it with his hand. "Fuck," he says. "Goddamn fuck. Fuck." His voice rises now to a bellow.

"Stop it!" Mama says.

"Can everyone just shut up?" my father says.

Willow Rose backs towards the kitchen door. "Spring," she says, soft like she's calling someone's name.

"Motherfucking spring," my father says.

"Enough," Mama says.

"Wow," I say, and then look down, embarrassed at the childishness of my own voice.

"Wow," my father mimics.

"Fuck off," I mutter.

"Fuck all y'all," my father says. "Fuck the spring."

"I'm leaving," Mama says, and stands up. "Make your own damn dinner," she tells us. She brushes by Willow Rose and closes her bedroom door behind her.

Daddy looks at me and asks, "Well? What are you cooking?" He opens the icebox to pull out another beer and the shelves gape, near empty.

"Motherfucking spring," my father murmurs and slams the icebox shut.

Willow Rose scurries to her room, and with nowhere private to go anymore, I follow her, leaving Daddy to his mood. With the mattress now shoved into the shed, Willow Rose has spread all of her clothes on the floor of the room, turning it into a colourful carpet of crumpled T-shirts and tired jeans. Her school notebooks — two of them — are also open on the floor, along with a dirty plate, an empty pack of pink bubblegum and a clump her own dirty blonde hair that she must have pulled from her hairbrush. I sit down on the floor on top of a red shirt and she clears her throat.

"Watch my stuff," she says.

I pull the shirt out from under me and pretend to smooth it out.

"Better," she nods.

Willow Rose has kept my habit of hiding the radio in the bedroom, and we turn it on to break the silence. Willow Rose hums the lines about wearing sunglasses at night while she yanks at the ragged edge of an old orange blanket, pulling threads, winding one around her finger until her finger turns white. I remember that blanket from when we were kids. I remember when we lived in our first trailer, and Mama would tuck both me and Willow Rose under that blanket and put us to sleep together on a narrow bed, like we were her dolls. I try to remember Willow Rose when she was a baby, but I was only little when she was born, so in my earliest memory of her, she's already running after me outside on the beach, wearing just a diaper and a white shirt that lifted up to show her outy of a bellybutton. I'm running towards the water, and she's coming after me, sand in both hands, until Mama calls to me to not let her in the water, and I stop running and pick her up under her arms, and she shrieks and tries to hit me until I drop her back in Mama's lap. I must have only been four or so, but I remember the look on her face when I picked her up — eyebrows coming together in a V and lips pouting in frustration like she was so much older and madder than a kid with a sandy diaper should be. That day I complained to Mama that I couldn't do anything anymore without Willow Rose bothering me, and Mama told me that I should feel proud she wanted to chase me, because she wanted to be big and strong like me.

Willow Rose is chewing her fingernail when I finally speak.

"Do you think —" I start. But I can't finish the sentence.

"Do you know you can't get pregnant if you do it standing up?" Willow Rose says.

"Who said?"

Willow Rose shrugs. "I just know."

"I don't believe you," I say.

"Ask anyone." She rips her nail off between her teeth and spits it onto the floor. "Everyone knows that."

"Shut your mouth," I say.

Willow Rose starts in on another fingernail and says, "Don't have a cow."

"Well at least, then it's not..." I begin to say, but Willow Rose interrupts me.

"You should have killed him."

The way my sister looks at me now, I know she means what she says. She's right. In my mind, I imagine it: I go outside and find Antoine hurting Mama. She calls my name. I pull the gun, only this time it's loaded and as Antoine opens his huge mouth to say something, I pull the trigger and get him right in the heart. When his massive body collapses, Mama tells me that I saved her, and I go to hug her, stepping over the blood that seeps from Antoine. Mama and Willow Rose and I hold each other real tight and everything is okay.

"Do you think Daddy knows what happened?" I ask my sister.

She shakes her head and looks down. "Mama would never tell. He'd be too mad."

Daddy's footsteps are in the hall now, and he goes into Mama's and his bedroom, clicking the door shut. Ever since I last saw Antoine, I have kept his money tucked in the pocket of an unwashed pair of jeans like a hidden jewel. Back in the front room, I pull the soft bills from my jeans pocket. I finger them and think of what I could buy with a hundred dollars, but I know what I have to do. This is why I took Antoine's money. I take a deep breath and knock on my parents' bedroom door before bursting in on them. They are standing on opposite sides of the bed. Both of them have blazing eyes.

"Here," I say. I drop the five twenties on the side of the bed where Daddy stands, nearest to the door.

"What's that?" Daddy's voice is mocking, like I have dropped a piece of trash on his bed.

"Money," I say.

Mama rubs her forehead with the fingers of her right hand.

"That real?" My father asks.

"A hundred dollars," I say.

"Well that's something," he says and picks up the bills, holding each up to the light one at a time, like he might be pleased.

"It's for you," I say.

He smooths the bills between his fingers. "Damn well better be," he says.

"Jesus," Mama says.

"You got a problem?" my father asks her.

"It's his money," Mama says, though she must wonder why I have it.

"Where does this one-hundred dollars come from?" my father asks.

"I been saving," I lie. Even if Daddy doesn't know what Antoine did, he doesn't have to know where I got the money.

"Saving all that Christmas money?" Daddy says.

I nod.

"Liar. You ain't got no Christmas money." He comes closer to me, crunches the bills in his hand.

"Where does this come from?"

"I told you."

"And I said you were lying."

"Leave him alone," Mama says.

"He got that money from your coonass cousin, didn't he?"

At least he got that wrong.

Mama slaps her hand on the table beside their bed. "Leave him be. He hasn't been to see PJ in weeks, and if he had, what do you care? You told him to get a job."

"Stop lying to me. All of you." Daddy throws the bills down on the bed, but they flutter like feathers and land too soft for his anger.

"Fine," I grunt, and I reach my arm to get my bills back.

As I do, Daddy fakes me out, making a fist like he's going for me and then pulling it back. "Boo! Scared you, didn't I?" he says.

"Emmett!" Mama gives him a real dirty look.

"He can fend for himself," my father says and makes a pair of fists, stands in a boxing pose. "Come on," he says, taunting me.

I stare at my father until he puts down his fists, and as he does, I think about how stale the room smells, how faded my father looks. He waits for me to do something.

"C'mon," he says and raises a fist again, lightly hitting me on the arm. I brush him off. My mother draws a breath in.

"I'm not afraid of you," I say. My father lowers his eyes and mutters "Goddamit"as he slumps out of the room. I let out my breath real hard. The truth is, I have no idea if his anger is because Mama is pregnant or because he figured out all on his own what happened. If he suspects what happened while he was he away, he must hate me. An image flashes in my mind of me holding the unloaded Colt like a useless fool. Mama rubs her belly and shakes her head at me, and when she turns away, I can't help myself. I snatch my bills away and scurry back to the sofa where I turn my back to the world, money safely stuffed in my pockets, heart crashing around with so many questions.

TWENTY

LET'S GO CRAZY

SOME DAYS IT'S BETTER to be invisible. The day after I learn that Mama is pregnant, I make sure me and Willow Rose get off to school before Mama and Daddy even come out of their room, and I make Willow Rose stay real quiet until we shut the door behind us. For weeks, everyone at home stays near silent, like we've forgotten all our words, but it's the kind of hush that feels like a storm coming. You can sense it from miles away.

One morning I wake up early and turn the TV on real soft so I can watch the Space Shuttle *Challenger* take off. It's the closest I can get to the real thing. As it disappears into the blue sky, I wonder how you know where to steer when the only thing around you is space. If there are no roads to follow edged by murky waterways, I guess you could go anywhere. That morning on my bike, I imagine myself free like that, weightless.

When me and my sister come home from school, Daddy's truck is gone and Mama sits in the kitchen, knees curled into her chest, bare feet on the creaky wooden chair. Though it is fall, she wears cutoff shorts and Daddy's old, faded jean shirt with the snaps. The shadows under her eyes make her look tired. Not just tired like she hasn't slept enough, but tired of everything. For once she isn't smoking, just staring, and when I tiptoe into the room to greet her, she doesn't even look at me, as if the effort is too much. I never thought of Mama as old — not like the old people sitting on porches in Grand Isle all toothless with strands of grey hair slicked back — but I think about how long she's already been our mama, and now, she has to start all over again.

In the blue house on Grand Isle, Mama always kept the kitchen clean. It was the first time she ever had a real kitchen like that, and she got real fussy about making sure the dishes were washed and put away as soon as we were done eating. And though me and Willow Rose complained about it all the time, it felt good that the kitchen was all tidy like that for once. Eventually even Willow Rose got bossy about the dishes, snarking at me every time I'd lay a plate in the sink to wash later. It was like she and Mama became the kitchen cops. Now I look past Mama to the sink full of dishes and the ripped window screen and, in front of her, the full ashtray. This is not what she wanted for us. She pulls a cigarette from the package but doesn't even light it, just rolls it between her fingers. I slink into the front room and find the soft bills in my jeans pocket again. I hold them in two hands and stare at them for a long time, crouching on the floor, surrounded by my clothes and schoolbooks. If I give them to Mama, she'll feel better for at least the next week. I have to do it. It'll make her proud of me.

When I peer back around the kitchen door, Willow Rose is already there. She has brought Mama a glass of water and is rubbing her shoulders. I stand in the doorway watching. Mama puts her hand on Willow Rose's smaller hands, and she says, "Thank you," and Willow Rose nods like she knows something, their eyes locked. Mama leans on Willow Rose's arm. "Come on," Willow Rose says, and Mama nods like she is the child. Willow Rose looks at me and mouths at me to get lost as she and Mama move like sisters real slow, down the hall and into Willow Rose's room. While I tiptoe behind them, Willow Rose wraps Mama in the orange blanket and eases her into the narrow bed. Willow Rose pats Mama's arm and says, "I'm here." Mama focuses on Willow Rose's face.

"I know," she says.

I watch, fist clenched around my bills, as Mama's lids close and my sister rubs her back in circles. I have never seen my mama hurt so much. She must feel more alone than any of us.

It's dark out when my father comes home. The truck pulls up in front of the house and the motor cuts off, but that's it. There's no sound of Daddy getting down and coming into the house. I open my book and read about motorcycle maintenance and how the author feels like he is in church when he fixes his bike. I'm not sure if I understand everything he says, but it makes me wonder if Daddy feels that way with cars or if he felt that way on the rig, like maybe when he's fixing something that makes sense, he can keep away all the things that make no sense. When my father doesn't come into the house, I close my book and I peer out the open window, only peeking so that Daddy won't see me. I can hear the faint sound of music. The truck sits there, lights off, with my father a shadow inside. I go out.

The radio is blasting, and through the closed windows, I hear Dolly Parton beg Jolene not to take her man. When I try to get in, the passenger door is locked. I knock on the window until Daddy rolls it down and says, "Men's room only." He cranks up the music, sucks back on a bottle of Jack Daniels.

"Mama needs you," I yell at him.

My father clears his throat. "I'm busy," he says.

"Let me in. I want to talk to you," I say.

"You want to talk? To me?" He sounds surprised, like talking to his son never occurred to him.

"About Mama. Just let me in," I say. He unlocks the door and I climb up into his truck.

"Well," he says.

"Hi," I say like an idiot.

"What's with you?"

"Mama — she needs you. She seems real scared and sad."

"I know it," he says. His voice is raw as a fresh wound. He flicks open a lighter so that in the dark of the truck his face shines as he lights a cigarette. When he says that, my lips and tongue go dry, like I am resisting the words that come out next. Mama told me not to tell, but every day I feel like the heaviness of knowing is going to kill me, and seeing her so sad like that is more than I can take.

"Daddy, when you went away, Antoine came over." My father sits up straight and clears his throat some more. He takes a big swallow from his bottle, finishes his drink and then tosses it to the floor. I keep on, though I can hardly get the words out. "He brought us Cheetos and Cokes. He was real drunk," I say, my voice creaking out of me. My father wraps his hands around the steering wheel real tight.

"He made Mama give him dinner. He talked so much," I say.

My father breathes in what feels like all the air in the truck.

"He kept drinking," I say. I feel breathless as my father turns to me real slow and grabs my shirt in his fist. His voice is quiet, calm.

"And what did you do when all this happened?" he asks. Even in the dark his eyes pierce my chest.

My breath is heavy, almost heaving. "What did you do?" my father repeats.

"I got the Colt. I made him go away, but he took it and he left with it."

My father thrusts me against the door and sucks hard on his smoke.

"That son of a bitch," my father says.

"I'm real sorry," I whisper.

"That gun was my father's."

"I know." My voice is almost a squeak.

"You better get that back," he says.

"I will. I promise," I say, and I mean it.

"Is that all?" he asks. I nod, willing myself to breathe. My father sits back in his seat and closes his eyes. When he opens them he flicks open the flame on his lighter and lets it linger. I swear I can smell the flesh on his thumb getting singed, and the light beneath his face makes his eyes look wild. I see a look in them close to what I saw the night he slept on the couch and woke up screaming. It makes me think of how it hurts to know something bad and to feel like you can't do anything about it.

On the radio Stevie Nicks comes on singing about a white-winged dove, and Daddy turns the volume up loud. We sit there and listen, both of us silent.

"God, I love her voice," Daddy says.

"Me too," I say, though I've never really thought about it before. Her voice sounds like she knows how I feel right now.

"I saw her in concert once. She was real good." My father leans back into his seat, lights another smoke and inhales hard.

I take a deep breathe. "Daddy?" I ask. He doesn't look at me. I keep talking, staring straight ahead. "When you jumped with your friend. Did anyone see you try to save him?"

At first my father doesn't answer. He sucks back on his smoke, exhales and inhales again so fast he even coughs a bit before he blows smoke in my direction.

"What the hell kind of question is that?" Now he's gone fiery.

"I just wanted to know," I start.

"You got something you think you know?" he asks.

"Never mind," I mutter.

"Everyone else was either dead or gone ahead in the lifeboat. Is that good enough for you?" he says.

"I'm sorry," I say. For a flicker of a second I meet his eye, and even with only the light from the ember of his smoke I can see that look again. He turns away from me.

"Is this meeting over?" he asks.

"Yeah," I mumble.

"Go help your mama," he says.

"She needs *you*. Please." I can't shake the image of Mama looking so weak as Willow Rose put her to bed.

"I have a gun to retrieve," he says and revs the engine.

"Daddy, no. I'll get it. I swear," I say.

"You better. Now get out of here," he says.

I nearly tumble down from the truck, and as I go inside the prickles on my skin feel like a thousand tiny knives.

TWENTY-ONE

LET'S HEAR IT FOR THE BOY

BEFORE LUNCH THE NEXT day, I flunk a math test and realize I forgot to finish a history assignment. I shove my work in my bag, papers crumpling, and pull out the dry ramen noodles I have for lunch. I hide in a bathroom stall and shove the broken noodles into my mouth in a hurry, feet pulled up on the toilet so no one will recognize my tattered tennis shoes.

When I go outside, I let myself get drawn into a soccer game on the no-shirts side. I strip my T-shirt and shove it down the waist of my jeans, check for chest hair, compare myself to my teammates, grit my teeth. When I get the ball, I charge with it down the field and find a guy open for the pass. It's Cole who blocks me, but I keep the ball away from him, angling it just right so that the other no-shirt tips it into the net real fast. I pump my fist in a cheer and Cole shoves me to the ground. My ribs, already bruised, make a crunching noise, but I don't care about the ache. I leap up and smack a fist against Cole's cheekbone before I think. He lands one in my gut, and I take him down with another crack to his head. Someone grabs my shirt from my waist, but I keep on kicking Cole until I am tackled by another shirt and we three wrestle on the field. Everything stings: my fists, my ribs, but a mass of people has swarmed around us, and all I want is to make Cole's face bleed. Grabbing him from behind, I wrap an arm around his neck and hold him down. The other shirt stands up and kicks my back, but I hold on while Cole claws at my arms, kicks at the dusty field.

"Say uncle," I say.

"Fuck you," Cole says.

"Say it." I wrap my arm tighter around his throat.

"Get off me," he gasps.

"Last chance," I tell him.

"Motherfucking get off me."

Cole kicks out at my thigh, but it barely lands and we both scrabble up from the ground. He lunges at me, but I shove him away and punch his face hard and then again. I don't want to stop. It feels like winning, like screaming out everything that has happened. I barely notice the blood on my hand until two or maybe three other boys drag me away from him and throw me to the ground.

"Eat shit, assholes," I yell and stand up, wipe my hands on my stomach and feel the crunch of my ribs. Blood stains his cheek, Cole cusses at me after I walk away, but I know he won't follow me. It's over. The kid with my shirt whips out his dick and pisses on it. I don't care, I tell myself. I smear my bloody fist on my jeans. I'm sweating, and I think it smells like victory. There's nothing left but to head for my bike.

"Fighting's stupid," Lisette says, coming up from behind me.

I'm standing over my bike, not sure what to do with myself — I can't go back to classes without a shirt, and I know I'll get in big trouble. Speechless, I stand there and rub my sore ribcage.

"Your face is all red," she says.

I cross my arms across my chest, suddenly self-conscious. She laughs like my half-nakedness makes her nervous.

"I guess I need another shirt," I say.

"Don't you have a gym shirt in your locker?" she asks.

I shake my head. She nods like she gets it, even though I know she doesn't. She moves a little closer.

"I'm going home," I say.

She puts her finger on my stomach where there is a long scratch.

"Wow," she says.

A feeling comes over me like a crushing wave. I put my hand on the small of her back and bend down. I press my mouth onto hers, shove my tongue into her mouth. She doesn't pull away. She tastes sweet and I can smell her heat. I put my hand behind her head and my mouth to her neck. I grow hard. She backs away, right hand pushing at my shoulder. I am panting, my chest warm, moist with sweat. We stare at each other.

"See you tomorrow," I say to break the silence.

She runs her hands over her hair. "Cool. See you," she says and turns away. She walks towards the school but looks back real quick and then away again. I can't catch my breath. Sweat creeps down my back as I notice how swingy her hair is when she walks, and then she disappears inside.

The house is dense with quiet when I tumble inside, holding onto my ribs. Mama's fallen asleep in front of the TV. My father is flopped on his and Mama's bed, mouth open, eyes closed. I nudge him and he swats my hand away. I grab his shoulder and shake it. Without opening his eyes, he shoves me away. I shove back. He looks at me.

"What's the matter with you?" he asks, looking at my naked chest.

I show him my still-bloody hands.

"I got in a fight."

My father sits up.

"Did you win?" he asks.

"Yep."

He punches me in my shoulder.

"Atta boy!" He punches me again. "Where's your shirt?"

"I dunno," I say.

"We've got to celebrate," he says.

Suddenly Daddy is up and about. He rustles in a kitchen drawer until he pulls out a few bills. "Let's go," he says, and he's out the door and in his truck before I even have a shirt on. He wants to know all about my fight, and as he listens he grins real big. In Golden Meadow, where we stop at the dingy liquor store, Daddy picks out a six-pack of Bud and a box of Twinkies. "It's a party," he says as he pays, and the clerk — a young woman with blue hair —

doesn't even look up, as if she's seen him before and knows better. "A real party," he says again and tosses me a can before we're even out of the store.

He cracks into a beer and presses it between his thighs as he drives back towards the highway, one hand on the wheel, one on his drink. I don't know what time it is, but it finally dawns on me that I left my sister with no way to get home.

I tell my father that we need to stop to get Willow Rose and I expect him to turn on me, but he's still happy about my fight and veers the truck towards school, stopping across the street, blocking a no-parking sign. Kids are starting to come out of school.

"Drink up," Daddy says and clinks my can with his as I push back the tab. It tastes real good. I dig into a Twinkie and keep watch for Willow Rose. We drink until we're both done our beer but still no Willow Rose. When there are no more kids in the yard, Daddy opens another beer and sucks on it.

Now I really expect him to let me have it. Instead, he takes a long sip and revs the engine.

"She'll be fine," he says.

I think he's lost his mind even more than usual, and I can't stop looking over my shoulder for my sister, as my father careens down the highway for home.

When we get there, Mama is glued to the TV watching that new game show where they give the answers and you have to ask the questions. Mama always knows the right question for the answers about anything to do with geography, like if she hadn't been born in this swamp she'd be travelling all over the world. There's no sign of Willow Rose. Daddy and I sit together in the kitchen. He tells me about fights he got in when he was my age, while I eat the entire box of Twinkies. He tells me about how he and his brother were wrestlers on the school team, so they knew how to fight, and one time they ganged up on a kid at school who was real rich and also a terrible snitch, always tattling about kids who skipped school or who hot-wired their own father's car, so he had it coming. Daddy tells me he and his brother got in big trouble — at school, at home — but it was all worth it because that kid never opened his mouth about him or his brother again. When my father talks like this and laughs so easy, it reminds me of how — when things were good — it always felt like I was lucky to have him as my father because he was funny and brave and handsome, and everyone knew it. Daddy tells me he's proud of me. I don't know what gets into me, but I start talking like an idiot. "We fought because of a girl," I say. My father grins real big, wraps an arm around my shoulders and rubs my head with his knuckles.

"That's what I like to hear," he says and bangs me on the back so hard I nearly fall out of my chair. "What girl?" he asks.

"Just a girl," I mutter, wishing I'd kept my mouth shut.

"Well at least it's a girl," he says and punches me in the arm.

I feel heat come up inside me like an angry wave, and I'm about to cuss at him when Mama walks into the room and turns on the stove to boil water. Daddy tells Mama about my fight and sounds all happy when he tells her it was over a girl. Then he wraps his arm around her waist and reminds her that he was once a wrestler, saying maybe I have his genes after all. Mama mutters, "Fantastic," and tells him that next time, if I get brain injured, Daddy'll have to look after me because she already has her hands full. Daddy rumples my hair and smiles before he goes back to their room.

From the TV, the host announces a question that I could never crack: "Chief Justice appointed by Eisenhower, he served until the Nixon Era."

"Earl Warren," Mama calls out.

"How do you know that?" I ask.

"I've been alive longer than you. Where's your sister at?" Mama asks.

I don't look at her. "With a friend."

Not wanting to talk more, I go to Willow Rose's room, where my last clean clothes still are and pull out a shirt. Willow Rose's room smells different now. I can't name the smell, but it makes me think of old Pop-Tarts, and I steal back to the front room to get away from it.

Mama is in the kitchen, standing over the stove, slurping ramen noodles from a bowl. She offers me some, but I'm full of Twinkies and shake my head. I go to the couch and wait for my sister.

I'm on Willow Rose right away when she breezes through the door.

"How'd you get home?" I ask.

"No thanks to you," she sings her answer, acting cool.

"We came for you," I say.

"I didn't see you." I can tell that she can't decide whether to believe me.

"Me and Daddy. In his truck. I got in a fight."

"Yeah. I heard," Willow Rose says, her back to me as she fusses with her school bag. "Good job. That guy's a real jerk," she says, and I think she means it.

"Where you been?" I ask her and pat the seat of the couch beside me. Mama comes into the room then and asks the same question. Willow Rose mutters that everyone's so nosy around here. Feeling big, I pipe up.

"She had to work on a school project with a friend. I'll wait for her next time."

"Good. No reason for her to come home alone," Mama says.

Willow Rose and I sit on the couch together and grin, and when Mama leaves, Willow Rose mouths her thanks to me and I nod, like I know.

TWENTY-TWO

SAY SAY SAY

I WAIT AND WAIT to be punished the next day at school, but nothing happens. Finally, I figure Cole is too proud to tell, and I'm strangely grateful to him and also happy when I think of how it felt to hit him. At the end of the day, Willow Rose doesn't show up at the bike rack. I wait, but finally I turn for home, thinking of excuses to fend off Mama's anger. Lucky for me, at almost the same time I arrive on my bike, a black truck shows up outside our house all thunder and no muffler. Willow Rose is in the passenger seat with some boy behind the wheel leaning into her neck. I can't see where his hands are. I flush all hot and watch her tumble out of the truck, hair messy, cheeks pink. She greets me like nothing has happened.

"Who was that?" I ask.

"Nobody. You just get home?"

I nod, but for a reason I can't name, I feel like I've been kicked in the gut.

Inside, Willow Rose dumps her school bag on the kitchen floor. She leans against the kitchen counter. "We got anything to eat?" she asks, raking her fingers through her knotted hair.

I open up the pantry door and toss her some crackers. She mumbles that she's hungrier than that but takes a handful anyway.

"Who dropped you off?" I ask.

"Your girlfriend's brother," she says, mouth full of crackers.

"She's not my girlfriend," I say, but hearing her say it makes me feel excited.

"Well, yesterday she was looking for you after school at the bike rack, and then her brother showed up to pick her up and said he'd take both of us home. Then today he came just for me. It's way better than your bike. He invited me to a big Halloween party at their house."

I nod, pretending I know all about it. "Could you at least chew with your mouth closed?" I snap at my sister.

Willow Rose shakes her head and tells me she's still hungry. She gets up and grabs a bag of ramen noodles from the cupboard. With the bag still closed, she breaks up the noodles, crushing them between her elbow and the counter.

"You should come too," she says, tossing chunks of dry noodles into her mouth.

"Maybe," I say, even though I already know I'll go.

"Please, Jesse — you have to go, or I'll never be able to go," she says and grabs my arm, petting it like I'm a dog.

"Maybe I will and maybe I won't," I say.

"Please, please, please," she says.

"Why's it so important to you, anyway?" I ask.

"I just really like — carving pumpkins," she says.

"Nice try," I say.

"Please don't tell Mama," she says.

She pats my arm some more until I tell her to stop acting like I'm a dog, which makes her bark at me until I agree to go with her to the party, as if I'm the one doing her the favour. We shake on it like it's a bet or a dare.

TWENTY-THREE

SMOOTH OPERATOR

LISETTE SMILES AT ME a lot in science class and then finds me unlocking my bike, waiting for Willow Rose. She's wearing a jean jacket and her hair is pulled into a side braid. "Did your sister tell you about our party?" she asks.

"Yeah."

"You should come. Your sister'll be there."

"Cool. I guess she met your brother," I say. I hold my breath waiting for her answer.

"Yeah. He came to pick me up and took her home instead." She shrugs like it's no big deal. "Anyway, it'll be a fun party," she says.

All I can think of is how sweet she smelled that time I kissed her. Like candy or flowers. Halloween is a week away.

Last Halloween, Willow Rose and her best friend dressed as Stacy and Linda from that movie, *Fast Times at Ridgemont High,* we all snuck into the theatre to watch. Willow Rose was Stacy, and she found a pair of real tight red shorts to wear with a white T-shirt tied at the side so that it showed off her flat stomach. She wore her long hair up in a side ponytail, snitched Mama's big sunglasses and wore lipstick that turned her mouth bright red, like a flower. She and her friend both wore red bowties around their necks. Everyone noticed Willow Rose that day, and I noticed everyone noticing her. My own friends looked at her different, and when one of them told me she looked hot, I told him to shut up his mouth. Willow Rose knew it though. Everyone wanted to talk to her at school that day, and after that there was always some boy who would pay her attention. I don't even think there was a boy in particular that she liked. She just liked being liked. It used to be that everyone knew her as my little sister, but after that I began to feel invisible beside her.

Willow Rose puts on a tight T-shirt and covers it up with a sweatshirt and an oversized jean jacket before nudging me to hurry up. I tell Mama we're going to a dance at the school, and she waves at us from the front room, where she watches TV. When we leave the house, Willow Rose bursts into nervous laughter and produces a can of beer from inside her sweatshirt. I wish I'd thought of the same.

I didn't know there were any nice houses in Golden Meadow. All I've ever noticed from my bike ride are small, dirty clapboard houses on stilts, but Lisette's house is real nice. It's all lit up and when you walk through the thick wooden front door, there's a fancy rug with a paisley design and a huge glass chandelier overhead. From another room, there's loud music and voices, and I take a breath before I follow Willow Rose out back where everyone's gathered around a pool that is surrounded by jack-o-lanterns, one on each corner. Willow Rose's eyes are sharp and searching.

Lisette and Gina dance with each other at the edge of the pool. They both hold cans of Coors and bounce around to Madonna's song "Lucky Star" and then sway to Cyndi Lauper singing "She Bop." Their hips swivel, and their thin arms trace shapes in the air. Lisette's lips are very red. She wears a short yellow skirt and a Joan Jett shirt with open sides that show her blue bra underneath. I grab a beer from an open cooler near the pool and try not to stare. Willow Rose stays by my side: this crowd is older than her, but she acts cool, sipping on her beer, while I do the same. We edge into each other, quiet, looking around. I talk to a kid from my history class, and Willow Rose huddles beside me.

The cool air settles on our skin, and me and Willow Rose shuffle inside, looking around for something to drink, someone to talk to. When Lisette and Gina tumble into the kitchen, I lift an empty beer can to my mouth and act like I'm deep in some conversation with Willow Rose, who wrinkles her brow and mouths "Talk to her!"

before slouching against the counter, turning away from me. She looks around the kitchen like she's bored, but I catch the shine of hope in her eyes and the disappointment in her hunched shoulders.

Lisette yanks open the fridge and pulls out a six-pack, flips back the tab of her can and drinks. She says hi to Willow Rose and comes right up to me. She is shorter than me, but not by much, and I can smell the heat on her. Her cheeks are flushed.

"I told Cole not to come," she says.

I have no idea what to say, so I just tell her that's cool and keep on pretend-drinking from the empty can. Willow Rose looks my way and raises her eyebrows. I'm too shy to ask for another beer, so I stand there and force myself to say something.

"Good party," I say.

"My parents are in Baton Rouge. They left my brothers in charge." She gives me the thumbs up.

"You got family in Baton Rouge?" I ask.

"Naw — my dad's work. He works for Shell. Big convention this weekend."

My father says all the oil companies are filled with sons-of-bitches in offices who know nothing about life on the rig. He hates those men, but looking around this house I think it must be better to be one of them. I nod and pretend-finish the beer, putting it down hard on the counter. Willow Rose elbows me.

"Where're your brothers at?" I ask. My sister rolls her eyes for my benefit.

"They'll be here. They're probably out at some other party."

"Cool," I say again. And then I get up my nerve to ask for a beer. Lisette pops it open for me and touches my hand when she passes it over. She smooths her skirt.

"Come see my house," she says and gestures for me to follow. My skin prickles all over, and I leave Willow Rose standing in the kitchen with my beer. Lisette takes my hand and leads me from the kitchen to a quiet hall with family pictures hanging in big black frames on the walls and thick carpet beneath my feet.

She points at the hanging pictures. This one is her when she's five, and when she's eight or maybe nine. In one she's in her grandmother's arms. She tells me her brothers came from her father's first marriage, that she sometimes wishes they weren't part of her family, but they're in all the photos, an imposing gang. She wants to know about my family.

When I lean in to kiss her, I brush her hair away from her mouth and wrap my arm around her back. I hold the back of her head and push myself into her. I snake a hand up the back of her shirt, feel the warmth of the small of her back and then let my hand run over her ass, press her to me. She braces her hands at my hips and in the darkness of the hallway, I run my hand to the heat between her thighs and feel her arch her back. Under her skirt, I put my hand inside her panties, and with one finger, I find my way inside her wetness. I shove her against the wall and say her name, thrusting into her, grabbing her tit with my hand, moving my tongue into her mouth.

"Let's go to your room," I whisper.

She kisses me harder but doesn't make a move.

I moan her name again and ask which door in the hallway of closed doors is hers, but this time she pushes me away and tells me she needs to get back to the party. She straightens her hair, pushes down her skirt and rubs her lips together. She smiles at me and makes her way back down the hall, sidling into the bathroom, closing the door behind her.

I linger in the hallway, breathless, the feeling of sweat and electricity covering my skin, and I look at pictures in faded colour. Beach scenes. Christmas. A big family. I stay there until after Lisette slinks out of the bathroom and back towards the party without me. When I finally saunter back to the noise and the smell of beer in the kitchen, I look around for Willow Rose. I peer into the living room, where I find her with a trio of boys — older, taller — but Willow Rose stands among them, beer in hand, in charge like she's the ringleader. They're laughing at something she's said. All three of them are close in height, but the youngest — I guess it's Sterling — is shorter, stockier than the other two, who are skinnier and have darker hair. I know from school that the oldest, Jed, dropped out of high school but then finished his GED and rents his own house in Galliano. He works construction. The middle brother is nicknamed Trigger. He looks and talks like Jed, though he's supposed to be smart, and the youngest, Sterling, is a junior and a good athlete who doesn't go to school very often and is now putting his arm around my sister's waist, urging her to let him take her for a ride. Willow Rose acts like we barely know each other. She waves at me, all casual, and then looks away.

"Hey," I say to the room. The brothers barely notice I'm there. They look up for a second and then back to my sister. I tell Willow Rose it's time to go home, but she shakes her head and mutters that she's not ready yet.

"The night is young," Trigger says and slaps Sterling on the back.

"I'll take you home after we go for a ride. Promise," Sterling says to Willow Rose. She tells me I should go without her and gives me a look that makes me think she'd like to strangle me. I tell my sister she should come with me, that we've got to get home. She pauses and takes a step towards me, and I mouth the words *Mama will kill you* and run a finger across my throat. Sterling sniggers and drapes his arm across her shoulders, sloppy, as if she's a piece of furniture, and he runs his tongue along her ear. Willow Rose backs into him. He gropes her and says, "That's my girl."

Willow Rose pushes him away slightly and says, "Watch what you do in front of my brother."

Trigger punches Sterling in the arm and gives him a look like he's got a live one, and he and my sister slip out the front door leaning into each other, hands everywhere.

I stand there, left alone with the two remaining brothers, and shove my hands in my pockets. Trigger and Jed swig at the bottle of Southern Comfort they pass between them. Trigger looks up at me and says, "Hey, you're the guy who beat up Cole, aren't you?"

"Yeah," I say.

"He had it coming," Trigger says. I grin and they offer me the Southern Comfort. I take a swig.

"Who's going to get laid first, you or my little brother?" Trigger asks.

"Don't talk about my sister like that," I say.

"Guess I could tell you to back off my sister," Trigger says.

"That cherry ain't going to pop itself," Jed says.

"My sister's a kid," I say.

"Some kid," Trigger says and tips booze down his throat.

"Game on!" Jed taunts and throws an arm around Trigger's shoulders. "So far our team's winning."

"Fuck you," I say. Part of me wants a fight, but there are two of them, so instead I say "I'm out of here" and skitter off to the restroom down the hall, their guffaws behind me. While I piss, I try to think of what to say. I want to get close to Lisette again so bad, but when I peer out back again, she and Gina share a chair and they're passing a cigarette back and forth, whispering to each other. When the song "Thriller" comes on they jump up and start dancing with one another. They know all the words and the dance that goes with them. I stay in the shadows and eventually give up and find my way back to the front door alone. Outside, I walk down the block and look for the black truck and try not to think about what my sister is doing or what Mama will say if I go home without her.

They haven't gone far: the truck is parked only a block away in front of a quiet park, and I knock on the passenger window. It's dark inside, but I know what's going on. When Sterling blasts the horn, I back off, embarrassed, and in the darkness I can just make out Willow Rose scrambling, and then rolling down the window, head turned away, she pleads with me to cover for her.

"What am I supposed to tell Mama when she hollers at me?"

"Just tell her I'm with a friend."

"It's not a lie," Sterling chimes in.

"Ha ha. And I suppose your friend will take you home?"

"Naw, tell her my friend's mother will. That's better," Willow Rose says.

"Better," Sterling says.

"She's going to be pissed," I say.

"Not if you tell her what I said — come on, Jess."

"You owe me," I say.

"I know," she says and waves at me.

"Bro!" Sterling calls out and honks his horn like it's a friendly greeting before he revs the engine and peels off down the street, leaving me alone.

Back in front of Lisette's house, the music from the party still blasts. The feeling of touching Lisette crashes over me until I am at once shivering cold and feverishly hot. The whole way home, I kick myself for leaving too early and agreeing to help Willow Rose.

When I show up without Willow Rose, Mama cusses and looks real mad when I tell her that she's with a friend, and anyway, she makes her own choices. Mama guesses I'm lying and says driving around with some boy isn't a good choice, and I should know better than to let her. Then she turns on the TV and tells me she'll wait right there for my sister.

In the kitchen I steal one of Mama's Pall Malls and take it out back, where I light up and inhale real hard, forcing the smoke deep into my lungs where it burns. My head gets light and all the heaviness spins away from me. *I should smoke more*, I think, and go inside to grab the whole pack. I'm outside, arms wrapped around myself against the chill, when Willow Rose appears. She is trying to sneak in the back door and whispers a cuss when she sees me. I pull the smoke into my lungs and exhale hard in her direction. She plunks herself down in the chair beside mine.

"Is Mama up?" she asks.

I nod. She cusses again.

"Can I have a drag?" She reaches over and I pass her the smoke. She sucks it in.

"That's real nice," she says. I agree and we pass the cigarette back and forth until it's a stub, and still I smoke it down to the very end wanting to get all the good feelings I can from it before I put it out under my foot.

"What should I do?" Willow Rose asks.

I consider telling her to piss off, but her voice is small as she shivers under her jacket. She pulls the elastic from her hair, letting a mess of knots tumble onto her shoulders. She picks at one of them, combing through her mane with long, skinny fingers. We have never really talked to each other about that night and what we saw out here. I light up another cigarette with Mama's blue plastic lighter. Willow Rose takes one too and holds her smoke out for me to light with the end of mine. She flicks the orange embers to the ground and asks if I know how to blow smoke rings. I don't. She does, she says. She watched Mama do it and figured it out for herself, and then she shows me and looks almost glamorous except that she curls her legs up onto the chair like she's still a kid, a kid with a cigarette and a knowing look.

"What was Mama doing?" she asks.

"Nothing. Just waiting," I say.

Willow Rose nods. "She doesn't do much anymore," she says.

"At least she talks to you," I say.

"Barely," she says.

"It's like she hardly knows we're here," I say.

Willow Rose nods. Her teeth chatter.

"Fuck, it's cold," she says. I offer her my jacket and she takes it. The cool air raises bumps on my skin and I rub my arms to keep them warm. Willow Rose unfolds her legs, bumps her knee against the table, and it collapses between us. Willow Rose startles back and nearly falls from her chair. She cries out before she pulls herself back up, wipes her legs and sits back down.

"God, I hate this place," she says.

"Did you see how nice that pool was?" I ask.

"So nice," she says.

I try to set the table back up, and Willow Rose tells me not to make so much noise. I rearrange myself in my chair.

"Did you and Sterling —" I start to ask, but she cuts me off.

"Seriously?" she asks.

"C'mon," I say — the dark makes me bold.

"You stay out of my business, and I'll stay out of yours," she says.

"Fine," I say.

"Good," she says, and chews on her nails, smirking. "Did you and Lisette?" she asks.

"Hey! Mind your business," I say.

"Just checking. At least Sterling has a truck," she says.

"That's what you're excited about? A truck?"

Willow Rose stops chewing on her nails and says, "At least it's something. I don't want to ride on the back of your bike forever."

"You wait and see — someday I'll have a real nice car, maybe a Mustang or a Corvette, and then you'll wish you could get a ride with me," I say.

"I can't wait," she says and puts out the last of her smoke and then sneaks another into her pocket for later.

When I go inside to check, Mama's gone to bed, and there's no sign of Daddy, so I tell Willow Rose that she should come in now. My sister flicks her hair over her shoulders. It's barely visible in the dark, but on her neck, just over her collarbone, is a deep red mark. "Nice hickey," I say.

Willow Rose slaps her hand to the small mark, but before she leaves me in the kitchen she says, "You only wish." Even as she says it, I grow breathless thinking of getting that close to Lisette, close enough that I could dig into her flesh that way.

Lying alone on the sofa, I grab myself and release a soft groan thinking of Lisette's wetness. I float in that perfect thought until I fall asleep.

TWENTY-FOUR

LOVE IS A BATTLEFIELD

MY FATHER CUSSES ABOUT Ronald Reagan being elected president again. He calls him a lying bastard who's never worked a day in his life, which is, apparently, the thing that bugs him the most when Mama watches his victory speech. Daddy screams at Mama to turn that crap off, yelling "Trickle-down economics, my ass. We got millions of barrels of oil trickling into the Gulf. That's the only trickling we got."

I'm too distracted to pay any attention — I'm like a dog with an itch I can't scratch. I skulk the halls at school, linger outside classrooms waiting for Lisette, who always smiles at me, even talks to me about homework, but never gets near enough for me to smell her hair, her neck. I notice the light brown fuzz on her arms and the way her eyes sometimes look light brown and sometimes shine almost golden. All I can think about is wanting to touch her. I notice everything about her.

At home I look in the mirror in the bathroom, hanging in front of it like a girl examining myself. Hairs — some soft, some wiry — sprout above my top lip and on my chin, so I swipe Daddy's ancient, gummed-up razor and shave them off hoping I'll get some stubble that'll make me look real tough, but instead I get nicked by the dull blade and walk around for two days constantly aware of the red cuts that sit on my face and sting like the devil. Willow Rose calls me hopeless and flicks back her hair to reveal a red mark just beneath her ear and a shiny new stud with a pink sparkly stone in her left earlobe. Sterling gave it to her, she tells me, and she used a safety pin to make the new hole herself. It glitters like an announcement.

It is a grey Thursday, almost a month after the Halloween party, and I am in science class, tinkering with an experiment whose instructions I didn't read last night. Cole leaves me alone now, but Lisette chatters with me like nothing ever happened, like I give a crap about homework or her colour-coded periodic table. Today I notice her hair is short, cut to fall to her chin, and she looks like a supermodel in her jeans with the cuffs rolled up to show her skinny ankles. I say hi and she smiles, but I can't figure out if she's just being friendly or if she thinks of me the way I think of her.

I try to concentrate on the steps I'm supposed to take with the acid and the base and the litmus strip. Back in school in Grand Isle I always finished labs early. I knew what to do, but today I stare out the window and wonder when exactly I changed. Lisette's voice says my name, and then she is next to me, showing me what to do, saving me from fumbling my experiment. With the glass eyedropper she squeezes water into the solution in my beaker and the litmus paper turns pink. She reminds me to take notes, invites me to her house after school to write up my lab report. I suck in my breath and try to get closer to her, but she moves aside just a little and tells me she'll meet me at the bike rack after school. I can't think straight for the rest of the afternoon.

I offer to double Lisette to her place on my bike, but she shakes her head no, so instead, we walk together through Golden Meadow to her quiet street. When the sun strains through the clouds, I notice how her hair shines almost golden. Walking so close, I can feel her brush against me. She asks about Grand Isle, and I tell her about how the sunset looks over the Gulf and about the coloured houses on stilts. She's never been there, she says, never crossed the long bridge. They take holidays in Georgia and Florida. Next year they're going to Mexico, she tells me. Real holidays with beaches and clear water. I nod like I know, even though the places she describes are nothing but names on my map that I could dream about. Every time I am with Lisette, I make a mental list of all the things I will do someday. Maybe if I can get a job like Daddy's job on the rig, I can work my way up so that I'm the one in the office ordering around the men on the platform. I figure if I start young, I can catch up, even live in a house like Lisette's and go on real holidays.

Her house is quiet when we get there. She tells me that her mother's a nurse at the hospital in Cut Off and is sleeping so she can leave for her all-night shift in a couple of hours. Her father, she says, is always at work late, and her brothers are never around. The light brown carpet in her bedroom feels plush under my feet, and her bed is made with a white bedspread and piles of pillows that she tosses aside along with a bear who wears an LSU T-shirt. She presses play on her stereo and Prince comes on. I have no time to say anything at all before she kisses me real hard and reaches under my shirt, tugging it over my head. My shirt is torn at the hem, but she says nothing about it as she looks at my chest and arms. I yank her T-shirt and lift it off in a flurry. I unbutton her jeans and she pulls me into her bed as we fall under the sheets, all elbows and knees and the smell of her. Her tits are firm like tiny fists and her nipples are buttons. When I put my mouth to one, I bite down, suddenly animal. At the last second, she pulls a package of three purple condoms from inside a thick notebook inside the drawer of her white night table and tears one off, pressing it against my chest. The packaging makes me think of fizz candies, and the writing on it says Ribbed for her pleasure. I fumble, burning to get inside her.

"Shit," I say, and then I clap my hand to my mouth.

"Never used one before?" The sun from her bedroom window lights her from behind, making her look like a beauty queen, and she tells me she wants to be a doctor, not a teen mom. With delicate fingers she unrolls the rubber thing, touching me so I think I might die, before she climbs on top and opens herself to me. At first, I can't find my way in. Breathless and pulsing with need, I try to roll on top of her, but I pin her hip, and she cries out. When I ask if she's okay, she nods and pulls me to her. Finally, I tremble into her, and I swear an electrical current bolts from my groin to my chest. Muscles I never felt before contract and throb as my torso presses into hers. I groan, she does too. I think of a thunderstorm and rain that makes everything slick.

When she peels away from me, she pats me on my back, like I am a pet. The purple rubber sags as I grow soft, and I flush with embarrassment.

"Have you ever done that before — I mean, with a girl?" she asks.

Startled, I mutter that I have, but I can tell she doesn't believe me. I wonder how many other boys she's done it with, maybe in the very spot I'm in now.

While Lisette plucks her bra from the pile of clothes like discarded candy wrappers on the floor, I look down. The skin of my stomach looks raw and red, strange, like it's not even mine. I reach for Lisette as she dresses, put my hand on the inside of her thigh, wanting more, but she shakes her head and jumps into her jeans without even putting on underwear. Her mother will be up soon, she says; she pats my hair down, throws me my clothes, tells me to hurry up. Even after I'm dressed, I can smell her on me, I can feel her in the heat of my skin, and I am swollen with want. She murmurs about our lab report and cracks open her bedroom door before the drunken feeling clears from my head.

In the living room with the soft grey sofas and the tall lamps, we go through each step of the report. Her writing is messy; she's practising to be a doctor, she says. She tells me about doctors who travel around the world; she wants to deliver babies in faraway countries. I tell her about my map, and she drags a dusty atlas from a tall bookcase mostly covered with expensive-looking knick-knacks: pottery vases, a wooden mask. We turn the slick pages of the book and draw our fingers around the edges of places like Brazil, India, and Egypt. These are places Lisette plans to see. She has the page open to South America — her mother's from Venezuela, she says. She met her father while he was there on a business trip, and that was that. She points to other countries: Saudi Arabia, Iraq. Her father's been there and there, she tells me. Oil. They have all the oil and all the money. I want to tell her about my father and the explosion and what it did to him, to the beach back home and about all the terrible-looking fish that washed ashore. I'm so close to telling, I can feel the story bubble in my throat, but her eyes light up when she talks about her father and the faraway countries, the way people on Sunday morning TV look when they talk about Jesus, so I keep my mouth shut and listen hard.

When Daddy first got the job on the rig, he looked like that too. He took us out for dinner — just burgers because he hadn't been paid yet — but he kept cracking jokes, teasing my mama about how she'd have to get used to nice things. She'd put her hair up in some fancy way with a big clip at the back of her head, and the light in the restaurant made the makeup on her eyelids sparkle silvery blue. The thing I remember most is the feeling I think we all had that night, like we could breathe, like maybe a door we'd been groping for all along finally opened up and let in the air.

Roasted chicken dripping with juice and fat. That's what Lisette's mother — she tells me to call her Mrs. Salazar-Dulac — serves us for dinner. I haven't eaten meat like this in so long, and I swear I could eat the blue and white china plate too. Mrs. Salazar-Dulac speaks to Lisette in Spanish and Lisette speaks back to her in English, telling her mother it's not polite to speak Spanish in front of guests.

"Such a rich country, but they can't teach their children a second language," Mrs. Salazar-Dulac tsks, but there is laughter in her eyes. "So, Jesse — if you're going to come around, you better learn. First lesson: *Quieres más de pollo?*" she asks.

I look at her blankly and she sighs. "Chicken. Do you want more? You seem hungry."

I am embarrassed as if maybe I've been eating too quickly, but Mrs. Salazar-Dulac doesn't seem to mind. She says, "Teenage boys should eat."

I fill up my plate again and mumble, "*Gracias.*"

Lisette's mother nods and with a grin she says, "*De nada.*"

I don't know what it is about Mrs. Salazar-Dulac. She doesn't look much older than my mama, but she's smooth, like a TV mother, like someone who's used to getting what she wants.

Mrs. Salazar-Dulac hugs me before she leaves and says, "I'll see you again, *mijo*," and I feel like I've been chosen. Once the house is ours, I try putting my hand back up Lisette's shirt. She lets me, but only for a second before she tells me she wants to do her homework in peace, which, she tells me, means being alone and putting a Prince tape in her Walkman and blasting it while she works. In a lightly mocking voice, she tells me to keep my hands to myself. I am so worked up I think I might pop when she says that, but I act polite, because Lisette's voice is firm, not like she wants me to keep bothering her. I tell myself it means she has real feelings for me and not just sex feelings. Before I leave, Lisette kisses me nice and soft and then tiptoes into the living room and snatches the atlas from its shelves. She tucks it into my bag, tells me no one looks at it at her house anyway. No one has ever given me something so good.

On the bike ride home, I am a glowing hot ember against the cool night. I finally know what love is. It's Lisette's eyelashes against her cheeks when I kiss her. I've liked other girls before, but none of them made me want to be better the way I want to be better, smarter, now that I know Lisette. That atlas. Her plans. Everything she wants, I want now too. I imagine her thin arms, her pinkish-brown nipples. I remember noticing the softness of her lips, and I want to be the only one to know all the parts of her.

The night that Daddy took us out for burgers, we ran to the beach to watch the dolphins at dusk. I swear I will tell Lisette about that, about how Grand Isle — even though it's not Mexico — has something beautiful. I tell myself that next time I'll tell her everything.

In the streaked grey light of the next morning, I take pity on Willow Rose's sulky mood and on the fact that she is scraping at a crust — the last of the grits that Mama's made — in a pot on the stove. The stud in her earlobe glitters, but I can tell she's never felt how I feel.

Back at school the next morning, Lisette pushes through the wave of students slamming locker doors, checking for books. She moves slow. Her neck is thin and beautiful. I imagine kissing her right there, touching her collarbone with the tips of my fingers, but when I look her way, her own eyes are moving across the crowd like a searchlight over water. First, she smiles at me and then looks down, almost like she's nervous. The sight of her dark hair spread across the white of her pillowcase flashes through my head, and I move to greet her in front of her locker.

I want to feel her lips again, so I wrap my arms around her waist, pull her towards me, press my hips against hers and put my lips on her mouth. I murmur her name. In my arms, her body is rigid and when I face her, her eyebrows are raised in a question as she slides away from me.

"What are you doing?" she asks like I'm someone she's never met.

"I thought —"

Her face is a car driving down a highway, getting farther and farther away.

"Yesterday —" I choke out.

She shakes her head and keeps saying "Not here," as if I am a dog that won't stop licking its privates in public. I back away from her, aching for an escape even as she reaches out her hand and then lets it drop.

"I have to get to class," she says, her voice soft, but I feel like I've just run straight into razor wire.

I have to stop myself from doubling over in pain as she turns away from me and walks towards class, books clutched in her arms. I slouch towards the front door, where, on my way out, I pass Gina and Cole pressed up against his locker. His hand cups the small of her back, fingers tucked into the waist of her jeans, and I know.

TWENTY-FIVE

UNION OF THE SNAKE

I DON'T GO TO school the next day because there's no point.

Before my father worked on the rig, he always said that someday he'd move up in the world. Everything good would happen someday. One time when he was at home, we sat around the new kitchen table eating crab — but not that we'd got ourselves. Mama had actually bought it in the store with money from Daddy's paycheque. He pretended to say grace before we ate, but really he thanked the oil company, and we laughed so hard. "Crab!" Mama exclaimed, digging into the meat. It was real good, and we all knew it.

Only two days ago I thought I'd join Lisette on some adventure, somewhere. I'd be an oilman, she'd be a doctor, and we'd get the hell out of here, but today I know better. Dreams like that aren't for people who live in broken-down houses. I swerve my bike south and head to Leeville, where there is money for fuck-ups like me to make.

That night we ate crab, I said I guessed someday good had finally come, and my father put down the knife he was using to pick his teeth and said, "From now on, we're going to have lots of good somedays."

He picked his knife back up and scraped every bit of meat from the shell. Then he took the shell from Mama's plate and scraped it raw too before he piled the last bite into his mouth, whacked my back and told me that I was lucky to have a Daddy with a rig job and that I better get smart and do like him some day. He grinned so big that night and didn't even care about the crab meat stuck between his teeth.

It's early when I show up at Antoine's, the sky still tinged with pink, and I push my way into the darkness of his shop, inhaling the comforting smell of oil and gas, thinking of the two things Antoine has that I want: money and Daddy's gun. When I find him, Antoine's got his feet kicked up on his desk as he reads a newspaper and slurps back a mug of coffee. He raises his eyebrows when he sees me and says, "You tempting me to call the truancy officers?"

"I want to work today. And I want my gun back," I say before I lose the guts to spit it out.

"I don't hire extortionists," he says, lowering his coffee mug with a heavy thunk.

"I came to work. For real," I say, feeling the meanness rise inside of me even as I soften my voice.

He flips through the paper, ignoring me, leaning over his desk like he's studying the news real hard.

"Please. I need that gun back," I say.

He looks up at me and asks, "Why should I help you?"

Looking at my toes I say, "Because I need a job. To help my mama." I know that'll land.

"You going to help me take care of things around here? Make a commitment?"

"Yes sir," I say.

He nods like he's thinking it over and then he agrees. "Fine. I'll pay you, but a regular wage. No more shaking me down."

"And the gun?"

"We'll see about that," he says.

That day Antoine begins to teach me things for real. He shows me the underside of a car and the heavy tools he uses to fix them. He shows me how to change oil and a flat tire. By the end of the day, I feel strangely happy as I sweep his floor and then go to wash my hands with heavy-duty soap that dries out my skin and makes it smell like bad perfume. Antoine even tells me I did good today, and then he says, "I ain't paying, though — you owe me with everything I gave you last time."

A fiery rage surges in my chest and head and I think to really hit Antoine right in his stomach. Instead I breathe in and out heavy and slow, thinking things over, remembering why I'm here. Finally, I squeak out, "I want my gun."

"I forgot to tell you — I sold that," he says.

"You lie," I say, and the anger rages back.

"No lie. I sold it to a pawnshop in Galliano," he says.

"That was my father's. I need it," I say. My heart pounds real loud.

"You saying I should go get it back?" he asks.

"Please," I say. He knows he's got me.

"If I do, I'm going to take money off your pay for my time," he says.

"Please get it back," I say, and I hate myself for begging like that.

"I'll think about it," he says and sits himself down behind his desk.

My fists clenched up, I can't stop myself. I whisper, "You're a real sick son of a bitch."

He shrugs his shoulders and flicks a page of his newspaper.

As I clatter out the door, Antoine calls after me, "Next time I'll give you something for your mama."

My hands shake with rage.

On the way home, I spot PJ's ginger tom by the side of the road, and to calm myself I follow him to an abandoned skeleton of a house where, I realize, there are at least a dozen other cats. One has a stump for a tail, another walks with a rhythmic limp. I have a bit of cash in my pocket from the last time I visited Antoine. I can help the cats. I stop at the store in Leeville and buy a bag of cat food, which I haul back to the house, and sprinkle around my ankles so that the cats surround me as they feast. The ginger tom bumps up against my legs, and I promise myself I'll come back whenever I can, so the cats won't have to be hungry anymore. At least I can get that right.

In Grand Isle I never skipped class except once when Fin and I left before the end of the day, following a girl he liked — she was tall and a grade ahead of us — out the front door of school. Fin said he was going to ask her out, so we trailed after her, always a half a block behind. I shoved him ahead, but he hung back as she strode away from us, hair swinging down her back against her jean jacket. She was listening to her Walkman, so Fin kept saying he couldn't call her because she wouldn't hear him, but we both knew that was a lie, so when she turned a corner down a quiet street, I hollered her name — *Debbie!* — and then pushed Fin ahead of me. She spun around in her red tennis shoes, smiled for one second and then squinted at us like we were space aliens. "Hi," Fin said. And that was all. I stuck my elbow in his side, but he just said hi again, as if he was out being neighbourly. Debbie said hi back, but the way she said it I knew what she was really saying and it wasn't friendly, so I tugged Fin by the arm and we sped away back to where we came from, me reassuring Fin, arm thrown around his shoulders, telling him he's wasn't a total loser, even though I'm pretty sure we both looked like it as we slumped our way to Landry's Quickstop and comforted ourselves with Cokes and chips.

No one notices when I miss a week and then two weeks of school, so I just keep going to Antoine's, and he starts giving me money. Sometimes he gives it to me when I'm done working, and sometimes I just take it for myself. When he doesn't bring me the Colt, I start to take other things too. A magazine that I hide from Mama, cigarettes, small tools. It doesn't take much until I've nabbed the keys to a car Antoine has just fixed — a red Pontiac Fiero — and I sneak back at night, after everyone at home is asleep, to take it for a ride. It's easy. Antoine keeps the cars he's done with out front. I slip into it, turn the key and it purrs to life. I have never driven alone before. I gun it up the highway, whip past our house and blast the radio. I drive all the way to Golden Meadow and turn the music down in front of Lisette's dark house. I lean into the horn with all my weight, and the noise tears into the quiet night. I press on it again and again until a light goes on in Lisette's house — her parents' bedroom. "Fuck all y'all," I holler out the window as I floor the gas pedal and plunge myself back down the pitch-black road to nowhere.

At home, I silently add to Daddy's stash, but I keep plenty for myself. Like Daddy, I find real crazy places to keep my growing piles of money, counting the dollars worn soft with use each evening when no one's looking. At night I read from *Zen and the Art of Motorcycle Maintenance* or memorize pages of the atlas. The atlas has facts about the earth written in tiny print on each of the pages: the highest mountain is Mount Everest. The lowest point on earth is the Dead Sea. The largest sea is the South China Sea, and the largest hot desert is the Sahara. I memorize these facts like they are the combination of a lock. I tell myself that someday I'll take all my money and buy a motorcycle and learn to fix it — maybe I can learn to be a classicist like Daddy, and I'll get out of here and never come back.

TWENTY-SIX

LET THE MUSIC PLAY

DARK COMES EARLY NOW, so it's strange when Mama is in the kitchen one night instead of lying in her bed. We're the only ones at home and she's chain-smoking, then wiping the counter with a wet rag over and over. Her face is all tight like someone sucked it part-way into a straw. I try to ignore her, leaving the kitchen for the safety of the sofa in the living room, where I keep wading through Pirsig's Chautauquas. By now I know for sure I don't understand everything he says, but still, I hold my focus. Anything so that Mama will leave me alone. She's eagle-eyed tonight, though, and she ignores my ignoring her.

"Homework?" she asks.

"Uh huh, English class," I say like I'm thinking real hard.

Mama sinks back into the brown armchair she and Daddy both like and she taps her fingers on the wooden arm. She looks out the window.

"It's late," she says. I keep my face in the book and nod. She breathes out all heavy.

"Did you bring Willow Rose home from school today?" she finally asks. Real slow, I put down the book, but thinking fast.

"She went off with a friend," I mumble. Mama nods and winds a lock of hair around her finger.

"You take her to school this morning?"

"Yes ma'am," I say, and look her in the eye. I'm lying. Most days I take my sister to school on my bike, but this morning, she never came out of her room, and I didn't bother her because it's easier if I don't have to go in two different directions. If she wants to skip school, I figure, who am I to tell her otherwise? I know she's been with Sterling until late most nights, and I also know because I can smell it on her that she's drinking and smoking with him, but I keep my mouth shut because no one likes a hypocrite, and anyway — I'm not her father.

Mama stops tapping on the armchair.

"I don't think she came home last night," she says. I draw in my lips and offer to go check Willow Rose's room, as though I will find a clue there.

I toss aside clothes, pull back Willow Rose's thin blanket to find her beat-up stuffed dog, but of course there's nothing there to tell me when my sister was last home. I assumed she came in after I fell asleep, but what did I really know about what she was up to? Her room smells faintly like dirty laundry, or stale Cheetos. I stay up there as long as I can, opening drawers full of old markers and notes passed in class, pretending I'm some kind of detective and not a lousy brother who lost track of his sister. I lift up her mattress, straining my arm as I peer at what it reveals. A tiny plastic bag. Weed. Mama comes in just as I pick it up. In a flash I drop the bag and let the mattress fall in a heavy crash back on the creaky metal frame. I feel the red crawl over my cheeks as Mama asks what I'm doing. I shake my head and try to act normal. I know that with her belly so big, Mama won't try to lift the mattress up herself.

"What's under there?" she demands.

"Nothing," I say.

"You better tell me what you saw and where she is."

"I told you, she was with a friend. I swear," I say.

"And now? Where is your sister right now?" Mama demands.

I say nothing.

"You need to go find her or I will," Mama says.

"I'll go. I'll go," I say.

"You better before I whack you." Mama looks at me like I am something she spat from her mouth.

I scurry away from her angry gaze and run out to the shed where

I grab my bicycle. The highway is dark and has no lights. I push all my weight into the pedals as I pound my way north to Golden Meadow. All around me I can smell the swampy stench of bayou and it fills my lungs as I breathe it in hard. The air is chilly and the sky is hazy black without any stars. I hope the truck will be in front of Lisette's house, but it isn't, so I steel myself, like I'm preparing for a fight. Standing in front of Lisette's door, sweat pours down my sides, and I pat down my hair, try to brush the dirt off my jeans, but they are stains. A light comes on in the front hall, and the door opens. Mr. Dulac. He wears jeans and an untucked, blue button-down shirt and fancy tennis shoes. He has eyes like Lisette's.

"Hello sir." I take a deep breath and ask for Lisette, and tell him I'm from her class. He looks at me in a strange way but calls for her, and stays by the door when she shows up. Her face rearranges itself in quick surprise when she sees me. I mumble that I need to talk to her, and her cheeks grow pink. Her father leaves the door open, and we huddle just outside, under the yellow light of the porch lamp.

Lisette tries to hug me. I back away as she asks, "Where've you been?" I'm surprised she's noticed I've been away. Inside my chest a commotion of something like anger beats at the same time that I want to grab her and kiss her all over.

"I've been away. I'm looking for my sister." I don't know what I expected her to do, but I don't expect it when she puts her hand on my hand and says, "I missed you, Jesse." I'm still mad, so in spite of the heat I feel telling me to reach out to her, I pretend I didn't hear her.

"Do you know if she's with your brother?" I ask.

"If she is, they'll be at Jed's," she says, and she darts inside to write down his address and directions to his place. She passes me the note and I notice she's drawn a heart at the bottom of the page. It's not far, she tells me, and she looks down then up in a slow way that goes right to my groin.

"Have you been okay?" she asks.

"I'm fine," I tell her.

"I'm glad," she says and smiles and I begin to smile back.

"Your sister — she's," Lisette starts to say.

I take a step back. "She's what?" I ask.

"Never mind," Lisette says and crosses her arms across her chest. She has goosebumps on her arms. She backs towards the light inside the doorway.

"You don't know anything about my sister. You don't know anything about me," I hiss at her. Her father is visible through the living room window, or I'd say more. Stupid rich people. What would she understand anyway? I take the address and pedal fast all the way there. I don't even have to ring the bell of the small house because the black truck sits out front; even from the curb, I can hear their music. Bruce Springsteen's song "I'm on Fire" plays real loud. I hesitate. I feel like I'm some kind of asshole cop out to stop Willow Rose from having fun just because I'm not. I almost turn around and go home, but then Mama would really let me have it. When I knock on the passenger door, I catch a glimpse of Willow Rose, who ducks down and pulls a sweatshirt over her head before she rolls down the window and gives me a real stink eye.

"You again?" she says.

"It's not like I want to be here. You've got to come home. Mama's ready to kill you. Or me." Willow Rose's face twists into fear.

"Does she know where I am?" Willow Rose asks.

"Not now she doesn't," I say trying to act tough.

Sterling leans over my way and acts friendly like we're just out having an evening chat. "Hey bro, how about I'll race you to your place?" He looks at my bike.

"Yeah right," I say. He starts his motor. "I'll bike you home," I say to Willow Rose. She shakes her head and says she doesn't want to get cold.

"You heard her," Sterling says and revs the engine. I pick up my bike and think how I'd like to throw it at Sterling. I mutter at him to fuck off, but he calls out the window "Why don't you ride with us? It'll be fun. You know, like a three-way?" This time I do tell him to fuck off, but he honks the horn and tells me to throw the bike in the bed of the truck. It's late and I'm trembling with cold. I heave the bike into the bed of the truck and jump in. Sterling sticks his head out the driver's side and yells at me to hang on. Even though I'm shivering, the cool air feels good on my cheeks, and I wish I had a truck instead of a bike. When Sterling stops the truck near our house, he lets it rumble while I wrestle my bike from the bed and then wait there, watching Willow Rose press herself into Sterling. Willow Rose jumps down from the truck. Sterling gives me the thumbs up and calls out the window "Go team!" and then lurches his truck in a U-turn, leaving us in the cold and dark.

"You happy now?" Willow Rose asks, and I tell her not really. Glaring at each other, we go for the door. Mama's waiting in the living room where the TV is on, but she's not watching, which is obvious because her arm is tossed over her brow and her head rolls back against the armchair, neck stretched like a chicken about to be axed. She bolts up when we tiptoe in and watches us for angry seconds before she heaves herself up, feet wide like she is steadying herself for a fight. I realize for the first time that I'm as tall as Mama, even taller. Willow Rose greets Mama while scurrying through the living room towards the hall, eyes on her nails that she chews up, but Mama's having none of it. She moves fast, especially for being pregnant like she is, and she grabs Willow Rose by the wrist, stops her going to her room. Willow Rose's whole face turns scared or shocked, and I catch my breath as Mama drags Willow Rose up to her and smacks her across the face. Willow Rose squeals as she tries to tear her arm from Mama's grasp, but Mama's fingers are tight around her like talons, turning the flesh on my sister's skinny arm blotchy and red as her cheeks. Mama backs Willow Rose into the wall. "Where you been?" Mama's voice is gruffer than ever, and she pulls Willow Rose to her, taking her other arm, shaking her.

My sister mumbles, "Hi to you, too." She lowers her head, trying to hide her face in her hair. My mother, whose arms have grown fleshy, grasps Willow Rose's arms and jerks them as if she's trying to yank them off.

"You stay out all night? Sleeping with some boy?" Willow Rose flails her arms, still trying to wrestle Mama off her as she raises her voice to a shriek.

"I stayed at a friend's. Jesse stopped taking me home from school."

Mama drops my sister's arms and backs away, now keeping me fixed in her glare. Willow Rose won't look at me. She rubs her arms and keeps her face down.

"Not true," I say.

"He ain't been in school in weeks," Willow Rose says.

I yell that she's a liar. I call her a little bitch, and in a blur, I pound into her room, pull back the mattress from Willow Rose's bed and dangle the bag of weed in front of Mama like it is a dead rat. The look on Willow Rose's face is white hot. She denies ever having seen that before. She tells Mama it must be mine because she wouldn't even know what to do with that. My sister, face pinched up, but voice calm, tells my mother that this must be the reason I stopped going to school — to get high — and it has nothing to do with her. Mama grabs my wrist now, but I twist away from her easy.

"Is it true you haven't been in school?" I don't answer. I want my mother to stop looking at me like that. I want to hide from her, but our house is too small, and that look she has on her face — I could feel it from miles away. If it were my father, I would lie, I would say anything to keep him from hitting me, but this is my mother. I run to the front room, trying to think fast what to say next. She batters me with questions.

"Where you been if you haven't been in school? Doing drugs?"

"I don't do drugs," I say.

"Then what in hell have you been doing?" Mama yells.

I make my voice real quiet as if I can keep from hurting her.

"You haven't even noticed the money I've been putting in the drawer?"

"What are you talking about? What money?"

Mama stands over me, arms folded over her belly. I keep my voice real soft.

"Mama, I've been working."

She lets her arms fall to her sides. "Working?" she asks.

"Someone had to," I say. I lean under the couch and dig into the pocket of my work jeans. I pull out bills. Lots of bills. My mother reaches for the money, and I pass it to her. Her breath is heavy.

"Who gave you this?"

"I told you, I got a job."

"You selling drugs?" She blinks fast.

All along, working with Antoine seemed like a game to me, but now I see it — hurting Mama is no game. I make my voice even lower than before and look down as I speak.

"Mama, I took Daddy's job. I'm working at the garage."

My mama has never hit me in all my life, but now she reaches out her hand. I could have pulled away, I could have shoved her arm back, but I let her, and her hand crosses my face with force that makes my neck twist. My cheek burns and my eyes water as my mother backs away from me. She speaks to me in the tightest, angriest voice she's ever had.

"You work for that man?"

"Yes ma'am," I whisper and hang my head, hold my hand to my cheek.

"Get out of here. I don't want to see your face again," she says and drops the cash onto the sofa.

Inside of me, everything is on fire as I take my money, run out the front door and grab my bike. Even though it is late now, way past time for anyone to be riding down the highway, I flee the house and make for Leeville.

TWENTY-SEVEN

RUNNING WITH THE NIGHT

PJ'S AWAKE, ALL WOUND up, listening to the Rolling Stones sing something about starfucker when I show up. He says they're the best rock 'n' roll band ever, and he jumps around singing into a fork while I follow him around his trailer and tell him that Mama wants me out of the house for good. Over the music he hollers at me that I can stay a while until things cool down whenever that is. His eyes are red and he's more hyper than I've ever seen any adult. PJ thinks it'll blow over, but I tell him I don't know if I should ever go back. Things don't always work out so good in families, he tells me, after all, it's not like you choose them, and even when you do it ain't no picnic, he says. He offers me a can of Old Milwaukee, which I gladly take. We drink together and he cackles something about falling off the wagon and then he points to a set-up on his kitchen counter where he's got white powder in a bag plus a box of baking soda, a glass pipe and a pad of Chore Boy. The next thing I know, PJ's cooking his powder into rock and he's talking real fast and loud about how much his goddamn oysters are worth now, and how everyone in New Orleans is doing the same shit he is, and how it's too bad there's no drug you can do that makes you feel happy enough to stop doing drugs. He lies back on his bed and announces that he's the best fucking oysterman in Leeville and maybe the world. For a second, he offers me his glass pipe, then pulls it away and tells me I should never, ever, try the big C because, he says, it's like the worst kind of girlfriend — giving you a good time then making you pay and pay with everything you got.

I keep trying to tell PJ what happened at home and how much Mama hates me, but he can't stop talking. His ideas jump around and make me think of how it sounds when someone keeps changing the TV channel. He takes me out back to show me something real good, he says, an art project he's working on. PJ has spread out a big blue tarp, and it's covered with oyster shells. He's drying them out, he explains, and collecting them by the hundreds because putting oyster shells back in the bayou can make a barrier against the encroaching water, he says. He's sure the next real big hurricane is bound to come sooner than later, and it'll make the water rise so high we'll all be gone, so he's getting ready. Flood insurance he calls it, and he sits down next to a bucket of fresh oysters that he starts to pry apart with a knife and suck out into his mouth. Then he tosses the shells onto the tarp. When I ask him if he thinks oysters'll really help if there's a big storm, he scratches his head and repeats my question over and over and keeps calling himself a fucking oyster insurance salesman, and he says that since all he's got is oysters and no insurance, it better work. A man with oysters isn't nothing, he yells and tells me to yell it with him. We start to laugh together. We laugh so hard, PJ rolls on the ground and pulls me down with him. Even without being high, I start to feel lighter lying there, howling like that.

For five days, PJ smokes his happy rocks — that's what he calls them. He barely sleeps. He drinks Dixie, plays the same Stones tape on his tinny tape deck and fidgets with his oyster shells, arranging them in patterns that he says the Russians will understand if they come to bomb us, and they'll know we're the good guys. When he tells me that, he laughs and then he gets serious and says that everyone's so worried about the Russians, but the only thing to really worry about down here is the goddamn rising water taking us all with it, but ain't no one in Washington who cares or even knows about life down here.

Every time PJ goes outside to mess with his oysters, I think he'll fall into the bayou and drown, but he doesn't. One day he pulls a baseball out from under his bed and piles up his Dixie cans so he can knock them over with the ball, and he manages to dent his wood-panelled walls in three places. After that he pulls out his AR-15 to play the same game, and I thank God or whoever's paying attention that he has no ammo because I swear, he'd go shooting up his own trailer if he could. Then he talks to me about how maybe nuclear war would be better than dying by hurricane because it might be faster, unless you got radiation poisoning and died real slow. But he says he'd rather do himself in than choose between a hurricane or death by nukes. I start to realize that even if I wanted to leave, I'd be scared that PJ would die, so I stay and cook boxes of Kraft Dinner that PJ eats by the bowlful, and I take out the cans when they're covered with ants, clear the spoiling oysters from behind his trailer so he won't eat them, but when he catches me doing that he screams at me that I'm ruining his flood insurance, and I hide outside his trailer until he forgets.

PJ doesn't have a need to sleep, but I'm exhausted and only manage to sleep in fits on his couch. One morning I wake up and PJ's gone. I find him in his boat, standing up and rocking like he wants to topple over. He hollers at me to join him, and fearful he'll kill himself if he goes out alone, I jump in. "I got something to show you," he tells me. "A piece of family history." Somehow PJ steers the boat through the water, not far from his launch, and he pulls us up to the edge where the water meets crumbling earth and right there, inches from where the boat idles, the corners of a wooden casket jut out at us as if preparing to set sail. "I call it the floating cemetery. It used to be a regular cemetery, above ground like they do, but with the water rising up and the land falling away — even the dead can't rest here," PJ says. It's impossible to read the name on the tombstone PJ points out. It sits at an angle, sinking into the muck. He gets right up close and touches the casket. "This is where my *memere* was laid to rest, and I ain't sure this is her, but all these fuckers — they didn't plan on a burial at sea," he says. "I hope all these coonasses like the water 'cause it keeps rising," PJ says. I say that even the dead need to buy his flood insurance, and PJ stands up to salute the cemetery, hollering about selling insurance to ghosts while the boat lurches from side to side. "You better be careful not to die down here. If you do, you'll drown in the afterlife, some kind of special hell for coonasses," PJ says, and then he sits down and talks real quiet, but fast. He tells me that down here the only way to make money is oil, but those oil fuckers are killing everyone. Humans, animals — they're even killing the dead. "So, which do you choose?" he asks. "Do you keep yourself fed, or do you go hungry while watching other men get fat off of all that black gold? No wonder people down here turn crazy," I agree, but then he says, "At least crazy can be fun, right?" When I say I'm not so sure, he carries on. "C'mon Jesse, we're having fun. Have fun!" he orders until I admit he's fun.

After that day, PJ runs out of coke to cook. Between that and Christmas coming on, he grows dark, lying around all the time, sleeping or complaining of headaches and pain all over his body and telling me to turn off all the lights because if he uses electricity, they'll find him. At night he sleeps with his AR-15 by his side. One night he wakes me from a thin sleep panicking about a migraine trying to kill him. I sit beside him on his bed, smooth out the blankets and hold him like he's a baby and I'm his nurse. He's so skinny, I can feel his bones as he curls into me. Suddenly he's crying and he tells me how of all his kids, only two ever wanted to know him, but after a while, their mama — Wanda, he calls her — said enough bad things about him that even they quit trying to see him. Even still, he tells me, his daughter sometimes calls and he's real proud of her, even if he don't see her so often, even if she's got a problem with the bottle. He tells me to go get a picture of her that he keeps in a drawer in the kitchen. It's been damaged by water and the colours have run. She looks young, not much older than me. PJ holds the photo up to the light and tells me, "There's something you should know. Love is about letting people fuck up and still loving them even when they're too fucked up to know you do."

The next morning, PJ lights a cigarette and plops himself down next to me on the couch. He looks more like himself than he has in days. When I ask him if I can make him some Kraft Dinner for breakfast, he tells me he's had enough Kraft Dinner for this life and the next one. I offer to make something else, but he interrupts me and asks if I have any smokes on me. When I tell him I don't smoke — which he knows — he tells me never to start because once you do, the smokes own you, but right now, he really needs to smoke.

It takes me no time to run from PJ's trailer to the nearby store and buy two packs of Marlboros, which cost me way too much, and bring them back to PJ, who wants to smoke and talk real talk. He lights up, inhales hard, hand on his head. Then he sits up straight.

"It's near Christmas. You have a family. You should go to them," he says.

"They don't want me," I say.

"You only think that because you're chicken," PJ says. I tell him there's no way Mama wants me back, and he says that no matter what I've done, my mama wants me home at Christmas.

"I really hurt her," I say.

"You won't understand this because you're not a parent, but even if your mama is madder than all hell broke loose, she loves you. Your father — I'm not so sure about him, but your mama will always want you." PJ laughs a bit when he says that about my father and I think he might be right. Then he pats me on the shoulder as if to make me feel better. Right then, I come real close to telling PJ about Antoine and what he did, and how I saw it but still went to work for him just so I could prove something to my father and bring home money, but it sounds too awful, and I can't bring myself to say it even though it hurts not to. Instead, I tell him I quit going to school, and so Mama was real disappointed in me.

"Go home. Make that shit right," PJ says.

"You ever going to make shit right with Wanda?" I ask him.

"Hey now, that ain't none of your business. And anyway, she's not my blood like you are to your mama."

"Are you going to be okay?" I ask. He looks small now and I don't want to leave him alone.

"Don't make me your reason for not going home. I'm fine. Just fell of the wagon again is all," he says. "It ain't the first time I got to start over."

I gather up my few things, feeling real bad about an adult looking lost like PJ does.

"Tell your mama, Merry Christmas," he says and he lights up another smoke.

"I will," I tell him.

"I'm okay," he says, and I nod.

PJ claps me into a hug and I hug him back hard as if I could comfort him for the kind of troubles he has.

As I leave, I can picture him there, on his couch like that, in a hundred years, his whole trailer drowning in the rising water and him not having anywhere else to call home.

TWENTY-EIGHT

TIME AFTER TIME

LAST CHRISTMAS WE WERE happy. I mean real happy like some family in a Christmas TV special. Mama cleaned the blue house and made seafood gumbo while Daddy put on a clean shirt and cooked sausages on the barbecue. Even our neighbours came over for Christmas dinner, and for once I felt like we were a regular family.

I get home on the twenty-fourth. The house is cold and dark, and inside everyone is ignoring everyone else. Mama's in her room with the door closed and there's no sign of Willow Rose. My father has spread himself out to nap in the front room, taking up the whole of the brown sofa with his sprawling legs and his snores. There's no sign of Christmas anywhere: not much food in the icebox, no tree, nothing.

In the shed there is a box of Christmas ornaments — Mama used to collect them — and I pull it out from under the piles of other dusty boxes. Back in the kitchen, I rummage through them. After we ate Christmas dinner last year, all of us — Mama, Daddy, Willow Rose, me and the older neighbour couple from next door along with their daughter and her husband and their baby girl left our house and traipsed over to our neighbours' place because they had a piano, and we must have sat around it for an hour or more singing all the Christmas songs we knew. We'd never done that before, and I was near shocked that even my father knew all the words and had a nice voice. We sang and ate two kinds of cake, and Mrs. Hebert told me and Willow Rose that if we wanted, we could come over anytime to learn piano from her. She was old and must have been lonely. At school I'd learned to play enough clarinet to pass band class without ever even caring about the clarinet, but piano — that was for making real music.

I pull out the ornaments from Mama's box. Some of them are real old, but not all of them are very nice like the one in the shape of an alligator with reindeer antlers, and the one that looks like a crawfish wearing a Santa cap. Mama's favourite is a gold ball with the words "Joyeux Noel" written on it in glitter. She says her mama gave it to her, and even though it's nothing fancy, she loves it best. Last year, for the first time in a long time, we had a proper tree, and even presents, but there's nowhere to get a tree anywhere near here, so I take the shiny balls from the box and put them in a bowl like they're apples, and then I sit at the kitchen table and put my head down, wishing for sleep, for something to erase the memory of how PJ looked when I left.

After Christmas last year, there was one day when I thought I'd drop in on Mr. and Mrs. Hebert to ask about getting my hands on that piano. I had to work up the nerve to go over there and kept thinking about what I would say. I combed my hair and put on clean clothes. When I went to leave, my father stopped me in my tracks, asking me if I was going out to visit some girl all cleaned up like that, and when I mumbled about the piano, he nearly peed himself laughing and told me I'd be better off chasing girls, or at least a football, and then he sent me to buy him smokes instead.

My father rustles into the kitchen and looks at the Christmas balls. I can smell the booze on him. He plucks a Christmas ornament from the bowl — an old green one — and he examines it up close.

"Christmas, huh?" he asks.

I nod, watching the green ball that he turns over and over in his hands.

"Your mama loves these," he says, digging around in the bowl, pulling out a delicate silver ball.

"That one's real old," I say and reach for the ball he's holding, but he hangs onto it.

"No one's in the mood for Christmas this year," he says.

I nod.

"You nearly killed your mother with that job you went and got." My father says the word *job* like it is a filthy cuss. The kitchen is silent and still. The single light bulb casts a harsh shadow on my father's face, and I can imagine how he might look when he is old.

"I just wanted to help," I say.

"You ever go back to that man's place, and I will beat you within an inch of your life, and then I will beat you again. You hear me?"

"Yes, sir."

My father puts down the silver ball and picks the green one up again. He tosses it between his hands. He is not finished with me.

"Did you at least get money from him?" he asks.

"Plenty," I say.

"I should still whack you." My father's breath is shallow and fast. I can smell it from across the table.

"You said I needed to look after us, and I did," I say.

"You got some nerve going to that man for help," my father says.

"Why? What's so special about Antoine?" I ask, waiting for him to tell me what he knows, silently pleading.

His chest rises and falls fast. He goes to touch his ear. "Nothing," he mutters.

I exhale. "I told you I could make more money than you," I say.

My father lets the green ball fall from his hand. It makes a light crashing noise on the floor.

"Those are Mama's!" I say.

"You little son of a bitch," he says and picks up the silver ball.

"Don't!" I say.

"You take money from that man instead of finding your own way to help out around here, and then you run away. All you are is a crybaby, not fit to do things right," my father says.

My mother comes into the room. Her belly looks bigger, and her cheeks are pink and puffy, her long hair swept into a messy ponytail. She spies the Christmas ball on the floor, just as Daddy lets the silver one fall from his hand.

"Emmett!" she says, real angry. She clutches her belly and bends down to pick up some pieces, but then she moans and stands back up, face redder than ever.

"Angeline — I didn't mean to," my father says.

"It's Christmas and those were my mother's," she says.

"I'm sorry," my father mutters.

Mama closes her eyes and says, "You always are." She holds her swollen belly and my father tries to touch her, but she pushes his hand away.

My father lowers his face and slinks to the door, but before he leaves he turns to me and says, "It's time for you to grow up." He slams the door behind him as he leaves the house.

Mama and I listen to the engine of his truck sputter to life and the sound of his tires squealing down the road. "Mama," I say. I want to make things right with her, but when I put my hand on her arm, she brushes it off and squats down to the floor to pick up glimmering pieces of her ornaments. I kneel down, picking up tiny coloured glass pieces like a broken rainbow until Mama sighs and says, "I don't know what you said to him, but you should have kept your mouth shut." The look on her face is the same one she showed to Daddy. I let go of all the glittering shards and get on my bike to follow my father.

TWENTY-NINE

MIDDLE OF THE ROAD

OF COURSE, I KNOW where my father goes. I follow him because I have nowhere else to go and because thinking about the look on Mama's face makes me want to draw blood from my father. When I get to Lafitte Lodge my father sits at a barstool two beers in, and even though it's Christmas Eve there are enough other men there — mostly alone or in pairs — to make up a pathetic crowd. All the broken faces lowered over cheap bottles of beer make me want to puke. I edge into the smoky room and plunk down beside my father, hot with rage, ears stinging from the cold air outside. A Cajun band with two fat men and one skinny one bangs out that twangy music on an accordion and a fiddle that everyone around here plays, and it's loud enough that no one has to talk to each other. No one notices or cares that I'm too young to be there and when I join him, my father raises two fingers to the bartender, who cracks open a single bottle of Bud and hands it over, nodding at me. My father raises his finger again. "I'll take one more for my son," he says.

"He don't look old enough," says the bartender.

"It's Christmas," my father says.

The bartender is old, and his eyes have that watery half-blind look in them. He looks like he should be off being someone's grandfather and not here in this shitty bar serving beer to this crowd of misfits. "Christmas," he mutters. His bottom jaw has no teeth, and he has a cigarette hanging out of his mouth that looks like it's been there his whole life. He shrugs and cracks open another bottle, sliding it across the counter to me and my father. My father actually thanks the old man and passes the bottle to me.

"Drink up," my father says and bangs his beer bottle against mine. "To Christmas." He tosses back the liquid and belches real loud. He finishes his third while I sip on my first, and he asks the bartender — Felix is his name — for two more. Five beers in and my father teeters on the edge of his barstool and tries to sound like he's talking sense, going on about how Jimmy Carter became president even though he was only a peanut farmer, which should mean America is great, but it usually don't work like that; six and he's barely talking anymore. He keeps up his pace for one more round then swivels around on his stool, and when the waitress passes by, he grabs her arm and asks her to bring him a whisky. Like all the waitresses, she wears a tight skirt and so much makeup you can see its thickness seeping into the cracks of her skin even in the dark lighting. Up close I can see she must be at least Mama's age, maybe older. When Daddy grabs her, she barely bothers to turn his way.

"Ask the bartender. He's right there, baby," she says, and takes her arm from my father's grasp, a teacher's look on her face.

"I want you to bring it," my father says.

She gives him a dirty look, but Daddy doesn't notice, cajoling her to serve him, so she slams her tray on the bar and then bangs down a bottle in front of Daddy, telling him he better tip her good. Daddy says he'll tip her real good and before I know what he's doing, he takes my hand under his and grabs her thigh, shoving my hand up under her skirt where I can feel the heat and the edge of her panties. I draw my hand away even as the electricity runs through my arm. I pull away so fast I whack my father in the chest and he bends over gasping with laughter. The waitress cusses a stream of words at Daddy, and then she smacks him on the head with her tray so that his laughter turns to moans as she yells at him to get the fuck out.

Felix calls out from behind the bar that he can't leave until he pays up, so while my father holds his head, I grab his wallet from his back pocket and drop everything he's got on the bar and then dig into my own pocket and add another twenty. Felix cusses at both of us, so as fast as I can, I yank Daddy from the barstool, get him to lean into me and walk with him outside, where the cold air hits us both like a slap in the face. Daddy is laughing and carrying on, asking me if that felt real good or what, telling me it's never too late to make a child into a man.

My father starts to get up into his truck, but he's so wasted I tell him if he drives, we'll both end up drowned in the bayou. He looks real serious for a second and says, "Is it better to burn up or to drown? Or to live?" I tell him to fuck off and let me drive. He laughs and calls me chickenshit, but he's so fucked up that it's easy for me to snatch his keys as he fumbles them, and I tell him no one's going anywhere unless I drive.

When I was a little kid, Daddy used to sit me on his lap and let me hold the wheel while he pressed the pedals of his truck. He'd always have a beer in one hand and his other hand on the wheel while we drove up and down the road through Grand Isle. We haven't done that in years, and he doesn't know I've driven by myself. No one knows. And Daddy's truck is way bigger than that Pontiac I took. I jump in the passenger side and shove Daddy, practically lifting him out of the driver's seat and dumping him outside. He's too drunk to fight me off. I slip over to the driver's side and rev the engine and threaten to leave without him. He takes his time getting in the passenger side, pisses outside the truck, tells me he'll call the police on me for stealing his truck, but I start to drive away anyway and watch him chase after me for just a few seconds before I stop the truck and tell him to get the fuck in and he does.

I drive real smooth up the straight highway, nothing like the last time when I slammed on the gas the whole way. Daddy tells me to pull over and when I do, he stumbles down from the truck and pukes. When he gets back up, he stinks like the vomit that is all over his shirt. "Don't tell nobody about this," he says. I put the car back into gear and take us home as my father fusses over his filthy shirt, making the stench rise to fill the cab of the truck. As we get home he grabs me by the shoulder and says, "Remember what I said about taking money from Antoine. I meant it."

THIRTY

DANCING IN THE DARK

DADDY COLLAPSES INTO HIS bed like he's near dead, but I glide into the house real proud that I got to drive my father's truck. Even Daddy pats my shoulder and mutters that I did good. The next day, even though it's Christmas and our lives have turned to shit, I still feel like I have a secret power.

Christmas morning used to mean presents, even just small ones, but I know better than to expect anything this morning, so I lie on the sofa in the front room, refusing to get up. Willow Rose gets up first. I know it's her because she hums that "Last Christmas" song that was on PJ's radio all the time last week. She rustles around the kitchen before she comes into the front room and plunks herself down in front of the TV with a box of Ritz crackers in her hand.

"Ho ho ho," I say from my spot on the sofa.

"Shit! I didn't see you," Willow Rose says.

She asks where I've been and I tell her PJ's, but I skip over the details about him being ripped the whole time. Willow Rose offers me the box of crackers she's eating out of and tells me she's glad I'm home because Mama's been watching her like a hawk on a squirrel, and between Mama and Daddy it's either screaming or silence.

"You think Mama ever thinks about leaving him?" I ask.

"Not since she's pregnant," Willow Rose says. I look away.

I tell her about driving Daddy's truck last night. "No fair," she says. I shrug and tell her she'll get to someday. When she asks me to teach her right then, I shake my head and tease her about the trouble she causes me when I show her new things. That shuts her up for a minute while the Jesus lovers on TV — that's the only thing that's on — prattle on. The glassy-eyed couple tells us that if we send them money and pray real hard we'll be blessed sevenfold, which makes us snicker together on the sofa.

Imitating the woman on the television with the huge, blonde hair and all that makeup, Willow Rose uses her thumb as a microphone and turns on a loud voice. "If you accept the will of the Lord Jesus Christ and send us ten or twenty or even one hundred dollars, you will receive back the gift of eternal prosperity."

"But all I got is this crappy house and no money," I tell her, turning on a fake southern accent.

"Then you must take that as a sign that the Lord in Heaven wants you to have more, which you will have as soon as you send us all your money." Willow Rose lifts her hand and closes her eyes as if in prayer. Then she digs into her cracker box and says, "From crumbs you will have great riches in Jesus's name." She tosses me the last of the crackers, which I shove into my mouth as Willow Rose begins to sing a pretend song about Jesus and I call out Amen a half-dozen times.

When Mama comes into the room, I swallow in embarrassment like I don't have the right to eat or even be in her presence, but she taps me on the head and tells us Merry Christmas. It's not real friendly, but it's not nothing, either. From behind her back, she pulls out two small gifts for my sister. The first is a small, dusty blue bottle in the shape of a swan that's made to spritz perfume. It's supposed to look like glass, but I can tell it's plastic and that Mama probably got it at Dollar General. Still, Willow Rose acts like it's real special and hugs Mama around the neck for it, but it's the next present that really gets her going. From inside the newspaper that Mama has wrapped it in, it falls onto the floor and Willow Rose picks up a silver-coloured chain with a pendant made from a .22 bullet dangling from it. My sister clasps that necklace around her neck in no time. Now she has her own secret power too.

Mama doesn't say anything about a gift for me, but I act like I don't care and offer to make her coffee, and she lets me join her in the kitchen. Four unbroken Christmas ornaments sit on the counter: gold, silver, green and blue. Mama places them in my hands and says, "You find a safe place for these. Someday we'll have them out again." When she lets go my hands, she rubs her belly like the baby inside is her someday, her something better still to come.

"Mama?" I ask. Now she keeps her back to me, watching the coffee drip. "I'm real sorry for everything," I tell her.

"I know. You ought to be. But I know," she says. And that's it. I can tell from her voice that she doesn't want any more talk, but her face is softer than it looked yesterday, and she pats me lightly on my shoulder.

I cradle the ornaments, clutching them to my chest, and I hide them back where they came from. When I do, I have the feeling that I'm putting them to sleep until the light comes back to us someday.

There is less than nothing to do on Christmas day in the middle of nowhere, so Willow Rose and Mama and I turn back to the TV, and the three of us sit in the front room, dozing, not talking, but at least no one's screaming at anyone else. When I look at Mama's face and her pregnant belly, I wonder if we had known last year at Christmas what was going to happen to Daddy months later, and if we had known everything that would happen after that, would we have still had fun then? Maybe it's better not to know the bad things that are ahead of you. If you don't have a life raft ready, it's not worth knowing what storms are going to come.

I tense up when my father joins us, but he just nods at Willow Rose's necklace, makes room for himself on the sofa, pushing aside Mama's feet, then letting her rest them on his lap. He wishes us Merry Christmas and whistles "We Wish You a Merry Christmas." The rest of us hum, then sing along. In my mind I take a picture. I tell myself to remember Daddy stroking Mama's feet, and the way Willow Rose touches the chain around her neck, and the feeling I have when I think about how good it felt to be behind the wheel of Daddy's truck, driving down the highway, just us two.

In the afternoon, Daddy forces me to come outside with him. We walk for five or more minutes down the bayou and I'm sure he's taken me out to whack me one, but instead he points high up in a cypress tree to a huge nest. He tells me there are a couple of bald eagles nesting, likely waiting for their babies to hatch. I tell him I wish I could see the look on their faces and my daddy surprises me. "It's a good thing I brought these," he says and pulls out a small pair of binoculars. When I use them, I can see everything. The bird I guess is the mama eagle sits unmoving, while the male spreads his wings as if to threaten anyone who might come near. As he scans the horizon, I imagine him waiting for a fight. "Merry Christmas," my father says and hands me the binoculars.

"For real?" I ask. I have no idea where he got them, but I don't care.

"For real," he says.

When we go back inside, he tells me to keep the binoculars hidden from Willow Rose, even Mama, and I agree, doing my best to keep my grin to myself.

THIRTY-ONE

CARELESS WHISPER

AFTER CHRISTMAS, I SLINK back to school and act like I never left. No one asks anything about where I've been, and I don't say anything, like a chunk of time can be erased if you just act like that's how it is. On my last science test, I got an A, and my teacher gave me the thumbs up when she returned it, but it made me wonder if she'd even notice if I disappeared again.

In civics class, our teacher takes us to the library, a windowless room with long, tall rows of shelves and dusty books that look like no one's ever taken them out, and she shows us the local and even faraway newspapers that go back at least five years, maybe more. The library keeps them all bound together in huge black books, year by year. When I see that, the question that Daddy never answered comes back to me, and I get the idea to rifle through old newspapers after school when I'm by myself. I know exactly what date I want and when I find it, everything I'm looking for is all over the front page. The blowout. Eleven men. The huge blaze that burned the sky black. I read everything. On that first day after the explosion, it says eleven men are missing, but it doesn't name them. By three days later, it says they are presumed to be dead. After a week, the paper reports that no bodies have been recovered, and since the rig has sunk, they will probably never be found.

I'm still reading when Lisette shows up alone. I nod at her, pretending we hardly know each other even though all I can think about is her hair and the way she smells, and that feeling like drunken heat comes over me again. She pulls out a math textbook, flattens it open on the table along with a notebook, and she starts writing down a series of equations. If she feels anything, she hides it under a stone face. She writes and the sound of the squeak of her pencil on paper makes me shiver. The lead breaks. She sighs and flips her hair, now grown almost to her shoulders.

"Do you need a pencil?" I ask.

"Thanks," she says and reaches for the stubby one I offer. Her fingers touch mine. My stomach and groin go taut. I close the newspaper I'm reading and fold it up so she won't see.

"Jesse?" she says, and I look up, trying to be all casual. "I missed you before Christmas," she says.

"Okay," I say.

When that's all I have to say, she fidgets with the pencil until it goes flying across the table and onto the floor. I pick it up. "I shouldn't have," she starts to say, but I cut her off.

"It doesn't matter," I say.

"I'm sorry," she says. I don't want to look in her eyes because if I do, I'll know whether she's sorry for what we did or sorry for what she said after, and I don't want to know.

"It's okay," I say, face down, fingernails digging into my palms.

"Jesse," she says and then she says it again like she's singing a song. I'm trying not to look at her, but she comes around to my side of the table and takes my face in her hands, pats my hair, puts a finger over my lips, and without thinking I half bite half suck on it and she smiles. "What are you reading?" she asks.

"Nothing. Just something for class." I don't want her to know. She lets it go without another word, but I think she must know. I crease the page I'm looking at and slam the book shut.

"Want to come over to study?" she asks, wedging her way onto my lap.

At first, I shake my head. I'm not that dumb, so I say no, but then I grab her hands and kiss and bite each of her fingers, making her laugh, feeling myself grow hard even as I tell her no again and again, even as I pull her to me and put a hand on her tit. She pushes my hand away and asks me again. "Come study with me," she says, and this time I say yes. I can't take out the book with all the newspapers, so with Lisette following me, I tuck it away on its shelf deep in the back of the library. I know I'm the only one who ever looks at the old newspapers. I can tell by how stiff the binding of the book is. In the darkness between the shelves, Lisette kisses me long and slow and then she takes my hand and leads me out of the library. I double her to her place on my bike, her hands wrapped around me going everywhere.

I tell myself not to have any feelings — it's just sex, and I treat it rough, like all I want is her body. I want the curve of her back and the soft wetness between her thighs. I want all of her, but I won't let myself feel anything. I just concentrate on her body and mine and what we're doing. When we finish, I pull away from her and I scoff at myself for everything I imagined last time. This time, I'm the one who gets up and tosses my clothes back on, and I smile at her, lying there, all soft and warm, and tell her I should get home. She smiles like she gets it, or maybe like she's happy that I get it. Whatever it is, I drown out the voice that says *maybe, maybe*, and even when I kiss her goodbye — deep and hard — I stay focused on ending it, cutting it off so she'll know who I am, but just as I'm about to feel the relief of pulling away, she presses herself into me and tells me we should study again soon. It takes the whole bike ride home to shake the fuzzy feeling as I tell myself *she's not for you, it's only sex*, but even without feelings, I am lost.

Each day after that, I go back to the library to read and to hope Lisette will show up. I skim through weeks and weeks of newspapers. At first, the blast was in the news every day, all over the first section, and then it got less and less space until about ten days later there was nothing left to say except how many barrels of oil had gushed into the Gulf. By two weeks, there were pictures of filthy sea turtles and pelicans, but nothing about the men.

And then I find the treasure I'm looking for. On the one-month anniversary there's a huge spread: it's all over the front page and takes up two more pages inside. It details everything they know about what went wrong. I read every word from a long article whose title — The Men Who Were Heroes — is splashed on the page in bold, black writing. It describes the gas that was under pressure deep beneath the sea floor and the mud that came up first before the explosion, and how much time it took to try to close off the well. I read about the men who were believed to be in the driller's shack and in the engine control room, and about who pressed which button, and who made the first mayday call and then the second, their words: "We've got a problem on board," and then "Fire on the derrick — copy?" apparently spoken in calm voices, the last anyone outside the rig heard from them. I read about men — my father must have known them all — who tried to keep the explosion from happening and who must have known it was already too late. And I read what Andy told me. That everyone at the company assumed that all the men who were never seen again died on or near the rig floor. There is only a single mention of a nameless man — just one — who was believed to have jumped, but this, the newspaper says, is unconfirmed.

I slam the paper closed and push it from me. I want to tear it up, but I also want to bring it home and ask Daddy a hundred questions about why he turned so crazy if he never had a friend who died after all, but I won't. I know now that it's better to keep my mouth shut around him. Still, I come back the next day to read the same piece. I memorize words I never knew about how the rig worked, and I learn the professions of the men who are no longer alive. My father's story about a man who drowned is nowhere in these pages.

That day, Lisette comes to find me in the library. She sits on my lap and kisses me on my eyelids. She lets me unbutton her jeans and put a finger inside of her and I nearly explode when I feel her there. Again, I slam shut the book with the newspapers, but this time, I leave it on the table and I lead her out of the library and to the bike rack and take her to her place in a hurry. Lucky for us, no one's home, and this time I can't stop. I have my hands all over her, and I kiss her everywhere, saying her name again and again until finally, we lie beside each other, bathed in sweat, breathless.

"Why did you move from Grand Isle?" she asks, tracing the line of my jaw with her finger.

Lisette's bed is so comfortable, with such soft sheets, and I'm sleepy and buzzed, but her question pierces me awake, even as it leaves me without any words. I graze her nipple with my fingertips, but she presses on.

"Was it the rig? I heard your father was in that."

I pull my hand away. My skin grows cold and my heart speeds up. What if she knows how crazy my father's been since the rig or that he lied about everything that happened to him? Then I begin to think it all might be a trap. What if he did try to help a man and now her father's going to get mine in big trouble because that man drowned? Maybe everyone knows something about what happened except for me.

"You can tell me," she says.

The first time I was with Lisette, I wanted to tell her every secret I had, but now that I know my father's worst secret, all I want is to bury everything. I swing an arm across my brow and blurt the first thing I think of. "Yeah. He was in that. It made him real crazy and broke, so we had to move. Now it's here." I reach for her warmth, mad that I can't find the words to tell her the truth about the oil and the beaches and how the explosion wrecked so many people's lives.

"That's tough," she says and keeps her gaze on the ceiling.

"Yeah," I say and curse myself silently. *Crazy and broke. She didn't need to know that.* But now I know it's even worse — my father is a liar.

Lisette kisses my head and like a chill's got her, she wraps herself in a blanket, so I won't see her pull on her panties. I leave her house just as her mother comes home and greets me with a smile that is too knowing to be comfortable, and I guess she must be relieved when I leave. I imagine Mrs. Salazar-Dulac meeting my mama or my father, and it's like a cold shower or a slap in the face. *Crazy and broke. Crazy and broke.* The whole way home, I repeat it to myself like a reminder — *she's not for you.*

"I am having this baby soon and you better be ready." That's what my mama is screaming at my father when I get home. They're in the kitchen and for some reason the lights are out as they holler at each other. My mother's belly is huge and her eyes wide. Next to her my father looks skinnier than ever and scared. Mama yells that he needs to get back to work, get some money so this baby doesn't die of hunger. Daddy tells her no one has died of hunger so far, to which Mama sweeps a counter-full of empty beer cans onto the floor and he ducks his head as he watches.

When my mother sees me standing in the doorway of the kitchen, she turns on me.

"Where's your sister?" she asks. I shake my head. Mama turns back to my father. "Your daughter is out there chasing around some boy because she has no good role model for a father." She rubs her belly.

"Your daughter is out there chasing around some boy because her mama never finished school," my father says. My mama takes a step back, stunned.

"You saying I got pregnant all by myself?" she says.

"I ain't saying nothing," my father says. I suck in my breath as Mama goes to hit my father. She hits him with everything she's got. She slaps his face and then, shocked at herself, she backs away. My father tries to grab her hands, so she kicks him until I jump between them, but my father pushes me out of the way, and my mother starts battering him again. She's shrieking that she should kill him for saying that, that she's so sick of babying him, and I am yelling at both of them to stop, leaping between them again. My mother kicks my father's leg and he tumbles to the floor pulling her down with him, rolling into her as they land. My father pulls my mama's hair and my mama goes for his throat like she wants to strangle my father. He holds her back and then my mother moans and her moans keep getting louder. My father looks the most scared I've ever seen him as my mama keeps saying "the baby," as she clutches onto herself and heaves from side to side on the floor. My father cusses and then leans into my mother's belly to check on her, but she shoves him away and groans at him to go get help fast. In my father's frozen face, there is nothing but terror.

THIRTY-TWO

EMMETT – BANG YOUR HEAD

I MISSED THE BIRTH of Fortune. No one wanted me around after what I did to Angeline. I used to think I was a drunk, but not a bad man, but after everything I did – it's different now.

It doesn't take long to drive from New Albany back to where we live, but I drew it out, stopping in small towns — every one of them looked the same — and drinking until I blacked out and woke in my truck, sometimes in the morning, sometimes in the afternoon with the full sun blaring through my windshield. You'd think someone would stop you sleeping in a parking lot, dead drunk night after night, but I bet there are parking lots all over this goddamn country filled with drunks escaping their wives, or their lives, or something too sorry to name. I don't remember most of it. I wish I remembered less.

I don't know what town I was in. I don't know her name. That's how bad I was. It was night and I drove off the highway looking to forget. After I met Frank's wife, I felt everything, I mean I felt every motherfucking thing sitting there right on my skin, pressing down on me all day long. Everyone else — all the men sitting in bars eating burgers, drinking beer — looked like they were gliding through life, while I wanted to die every minute of the day. It happened at some beat-up bar in a nothing of a town, just like every other place I'd stopped in.

Couldn't she see it on my face? Or maybe she could and that's why she liked me. I bought her cheap beer. She told me she was getting married. I told her it didn't bother me if it didn't bother her. Then I told her about the explosion, and she looked all sad, her face the way every woman's face looks when they think they can rescue you. I brought her to my truck, and she said it was a big adventure to do it in a truck, like everything was funny to her. Of course, I couldn't do it. All I could think of was Angeline and then Frank, and I couldn't even get started. I don't remember her face or her voice, I just remember the feeling of shame and wanting to go to sleep and never wake up again.

I spent two days in my truck after that. I didn't eat, just slept huddled against the door of the driver's side. When I finally had to eat, I staggered back into the bar and ate foul eggs that made me feel good because of how bad they made my stomach feel. On the TV over the skinny bartender's head, a news report flashed an update about those brothers who had escaped from death row in a Virginia prison and were recaptured last summer. One of them was slated to die by electric chair in October and all I could think about was that even those men — stuck on death row — had more will to live, more fight in them than I had in me. It wasn't just the explosion or Frank that made me want to die. It was knowing that none of it had to happen. The thought of the electric chair made me feel sick, but feeling like you're dead while you're still living might be even worse. Like me, those brothers grew up in a shit place, but at least they had courage. I put my head in my hands and nearly cried with how pathetic I felt. When the bartender asked me if I was okay, I nodded and left the last of my pale eggs behind.

No one had to know where I'd been. I got behind the wheel and told myself *get your shit together. No one cares if you live or die, but if you're going to live, at least get your ass home and act like a man.* I drove the rest of the way without stopping.

I didn't mean to hit Angeline. I would never hit Angeline. Christ — when I first met her, the only thing I wanted was for her to like me, to stay with me. Now she'd never ever want to look at my face again. After it happened, she moaned and panted like a dog. When Jesse saw her like that, I could hardly look at his face. He screamed at me that we had to take her to the hospital, and like a fool, all I could think of was the money. Jesse screamed and screamed while I stood there until he went and took my keys and ran out the door, gunning the engine and charging off alone. I went after him in Angeline's car, and I stayed on his tail, gunning it the whole time. When I pulled up beside him at the first red light in Golden Meadow, I gestured at him to roll down his window.

"Where are you going?" I hollered.

"I'm getting help."

"Like hell you are," I said I had no idea where he thought he was going to get help without paying for a doctor.

Jesse leaned out the window, real calm and he told me, "Back off. I'm taking care of this." He rolled up his window and shot away from the intersection, bearing down streets I didn't know, stopping in front of a real nice house. Jesse rang the doorbell until a man answered. Minutes later, a woman emerged and jumped in my truck with my son. I rolled down the window again, looking for an explanation.

"She's a nurse," Jesse yelled.

"I'll follow you," I said.

"Do what you want," he said and tore off.

I missed the birth of Fortune. I stayed away, shivering inside the truck, parked on the side of the road, too afraid to go into my own house because I'd already done enough things wrong. I didn't need more proof of that.

THIRTY-THREE

JESSE – UPTOWN GIRL

MY BABY BROTHER IS born on the kitchen floor, into the arms of Mrs. Salazar-Dulac, and surrounded by old towels and bloody sheets. He's got the bluest eyes, raw red skin, and a cleft in his chin that's all I can look at for days. Every time Mama sits in the kitchen and feeds him, I stare at his chin until it starts to look like a third eyeball. No one says a word about it, including me, as if truth is something you can pretend away.

Lisette's all excited about how I helped her mother deliver Fortune. She keeps talking about it after school, calling me Dr. Jesse so that I let myself feel like some kind of a movie hero when she looks up at me, eyes all shiny and proud. She tells me that her Mama said I was gentle and smart, and I tell her stories about how cute my baby brother is, even though all he does so far is sleep, cry and nurse. But it works because Lisette invites me to the Golden Meadow Mardi Gras parade with her. It's on Friday before Mardi Gras — a night parade like some of the ones in New Orleans — and it's all I can think of until the end of the week.

Classes finish and I sprint to meet Lisette. I can hardly breathe. She shows up with Gina — they must have picked each other over Cole — and I want to collapse in disappointment, but I keep the sting to myself and walk beside them, always just outside of their conversation, back to Lisette's house, where Mrs. Salazar-Dulac prepares a crawfish boil in the kitchen, while Mr. Dulac barbecues corn and burgers on the front lawn. Their house is on the parade route, and it looks like all their neighbours and friends and maybe some people they work with have gathered outside their house, drinking bottles of beer from the tub of ice that everyone digs into. There are gold and purple and green streamers on the outside of their house, and men and women wearing beads. The air smells heavy with meat and smoke and speakers blast the Rajun' Cajun radio station's mix of Cajun music and swamp pop real loud. I follow Lisette to get a plate full of crawfish, but then Lisette and Gina take the only two chairs in the kitchen, so I wander outside to wait for the parade.

In the early evening, the street is lined with pick-ups parked so the beds face where the floats will be, waiting to catch beads and all the other trinkets. Tough guys wearing leather with patches stand in front of their bikes, and couples float down the street, girls with tight jeans and lots of makeup, boys with baggy pants and ballcaps, they all swagger past. By the time the first brass band marches by, Lisette has come outside. She's eating a cob of corn with her hands and keeps brushing fallen kernels from her hair. She's put on a hooded Saints sweatshirt. When I ask about Gina, she tells me she went to find her parents. I stand close to Lisette and wrap my arm around her waist when the first float, lit up with gold fleur-de-lis, comes past. We yell for them to throw us beads and I pass mine — tiny silver disco balls — to Lisette so that she can add them to the few she already has around her neck. The music from the bands blasts past us and the floats whir with dancers and lights. Lisette cries for more necklaces so that they grow into a heavy pile of shiny beads around her neck. She competes with all the other girls, and I swear everyone wants to throw something at her: necklaces, stuffed animals, a purple foam football that we toss back and forth and then turn over to a boy who throws it to his father with a gleeful shriek. I pull Lisette close to me. She lets my hand trail over her ass before she jumps back in front of me calling out to the float in front of us to throw her something and they do.

When the parade is done, kids from our school drift down the street. Trucks pull away, some of them with bags filled with necklaces in every size and colour, and the bikers rev their engines. Me and Lisette wade into the thinning crowd. The road is dotted with beer cans and glittering beads. We take turns kicking a can down the road, pass by some girls Lisette waves to, and I snake my arm around her hips, inch my hand up her sweatshirt to feel her warm skin.

"Let's go to your house," I say and kiss her hard.

She kisses me back, but then she says, "We can't go to my house. Everyone's there. My parents' friends. People they work with."

"No one will notice," I say, hands all over her.

"They will." She pulls away just a bit. My heart races. I can't stand not to be with her tonight.

"Lisette." I kiss her ear and then pause, prickles covering my skin. "Do you want me?"

For an instant she says nothing, and in that time, I feel like I've jumped off a cliff with no parachute, but she catches me.

She wraps her arms around my neck and brushes her lips across my face. "Yes. I've always wanted you."

I think I might cry as I pull her to me.

"I felt so scared. I thought I was a joke to you," I say.

"Why would you think that?"

"My sister. My father," I tell her.

"I only care about you. And you're different."

"Different how?"

"Good different. Like you have things on your mind besides getting in my pants," she says and rests her hand on my face.

I grab her to me, pressing her to my chest hard. I grab her ass and slip my hand between her legs. "You're right. I want a lot of things. I want to go places with you. I want to watch you become a doctor. I want to go to college and learn Spanish. I want everything you want."

She kisses me light as a feather and then harder.

"*And* I want to get in your pants," I say.

She laughs. "Are you asking?"

"Lisette Dulac, please can I get in your pants? And then spend every afternoon studying with you in the library?" I bat my eyelashes at her. "Pleeeease?"

"I know where we can go," she says and grabs my hand. Laughing and shivering in the cool air, we tear down streets that are not yet empty. I nearly twist my ankle when I slip on a purple beaded necklace and Lisette laughs and pulls me up. I place the beads around her neck and call her my Mardi Gras princess. She corrects me and tells me to call her Queen.

"Queen bee," I say. "My queen bee. Let's go find a hive."

"Cheesy," she says, but laces her fingers back through mine and we dash all the way to her place, where she tells me to stay outside.

Plenty of cars and trucks are still parked outside her house, and through the front window, all her parents' friends are there, lingering, drinking, laughing. Someday I'll be like them, I tell myself.

When Lisette reappears, she jangles a set of car keys that she tells me she snitched from her dad's dresser. She tells me his car is real nice.

I'm so ready, I don't care where we do it. Her daddy's car *is* real nice. It has smooth leather seats, and Lisette, who has jumped in the driver's seat, leans it all the way back. I bang my hip on the stick between us as I try to get over to her side.

"Lean your seat back and let me climb on top," she says.

"God, I love Mardi Gras," I say.

"So do I," she whispers.

That night, I undress Lisette, taking time to kiss every part of her that I uncover. I tell her I want to kiss her in places she's never been kissed, and she tells me she wants me to. I unclasp her bra and put my hands on her. She puts her hands on mine, purrs my name from deep in her throat. We roll around, tugging at clothes and banging elbows and knees into the car door and dash. She wraps her hand around me, stroking me slow and then faster. I tilt my neck back and feel like I'm going to die.

"*Mijo,*" I say.

Lisette laughs. "That means my son."

I feel my cheeks flush, but I don't care. "Can I get inside you?" I whisper. "Please."

"I don't have a condom. Can you pull out on time?"

"I've never done that," I say.

"Can you?"

"Yes," I say.

"It's important."

"I will."

I push aside her panties and she parts her legs to let me in. I rock my way deep into her wetness, pushing and groaning so that she giggles and puts a hand over my mouth, afraid of us being heard. I bite at her fingers and feel unstoppable as I grab at her breasts. She goes first, a quiet moan, but it takes no time — not even a minute and I feel the release coming over me. I don't know if I can do it, I want to stay inside her so bad I would almost die for it, but I think of what she said before and just as I tilt my head back to let it all go, I do it. I pull myself from her and in the darkness of the car, her belly looks like it is covered in glistening honey.

"You did it," she murmurs and pulls me to her, wrapping herself around me, holding me in our wetness, in our heat, cocooned inside the quiet bubble of her father's fancy car.

"I really love Mardi Gras," I say.

"So do I," she says and rests her hand on her belly, her head on my chest.

THIRTY-FOUR

OBSESSION

ANTOINE. WHEN I GET home, his red truck is parked, bed up against the tree nearest our house, and he's standing at the base of the tree throwing a steel cable over a branch. Even from where I stand on the roadside, he looks half-mad, white T-shirt pulled up over his belly, cigarette hanging from his mouth. Mama must be inside. I want to kill him. "What the fuck!" I yell, throw down my bike and run towards him. An alligator. In the bed of his truck, there's an alligator with a chain wrapped around its body and under its front legs, and the giant animal must be ten feet or more. A monster. Cable strung over the branch, Antoine lumbers into the back of his truck, and attaches the hook of the cable to the chain around the alligator's body and calls out, "Wait'll you see this."

I scream at him to get the hell away from here, but he pays me no mind and jumps out of his truck, squats down at the base of the tree so I can see the crack in his ass, and he starts working the lever of the winch that he's fixed there. He tugs it back and forth, stopping to take a drag of his smoke as the alligator begins to move up and out of his truck and towards the tree as I stand there and watch, amazed.

When he winches it as far as the cable will go, Antoine looks up at it and gives me the thumbs up, like I am in on his madness. Then he gets in the cab of his truck. He sticks his head out the window and says, "I'm about to drive out from under the tree and this motherfucker'll fly." He lurches forward and the alligator jolts, whacks against the side of Antoine's truck and then swings out, bangs against the tree and dangles there, tail just brushing the ground. I wait for the crack, for the branch to come down, but it holds. The alligator turns one way, showing its white belly, and then turns again just enough to show its gleaming teeth.

Antoine leaps from his truck. I try to block him. I get in his way and shove him back. I can feel the heat of exertion on him. I smell the stink of whisky, but I can't stop him pounding on the front door. Mama answers. She's holding my baby brother in her arms, and she gasps and covers his tiny head. I scream at her not to let Antoine in, but the screen door is flimsy, and Antoine blows past it like it's not even there. Mama tells Antoine to get out. She says it over and over as if she's possessed. Antoine takes up all the space in the front room. In the low light, his shadow covers the far wall, and he stands there solid as a bull.

"I heard that baby was born, and I figured at least I should get a look at him since I've been helping out your family all this time. I came with a gift," he says. He wipes his face with his hands and tells Mama she should go look outside. Mama clutches my little brother to her, so tense she almost vibrates.

"You've been no help to us. We don't need your gift," my mama says, voice real low.

"All I've done is help you — didn't your boy tell you how much money I gave him? He came to me, and I helped him. Damn near bankrupted me, but I gave him money. That was for you, for the baby, for your family. And now I want to see that baby." Antoine reaches his arms out. Mama backs away from him.

"Get out," my Mama says.

I lunge towards him, fuelled with guilt and hate, but he blocks me with his arms and moves to the other side of the room. I go for him again, scratching at his arms, but he shoves me aside. The last time Antoine was in this kitchen, I start to think, and as if he's thinking the same, he says to Mama, "You sure made a nice dinner that night. And I set the table. And you liked that. And then your boy came to me. He came to *me*. Just let me hold that baby for a minute."

Mama looks like an animal backed into a corner, and her voice is a bellow when she says, "Get the hell out of here right now."

"Aw, come on now, Angel baby. Don't you want to know what I brought for you?" Antoine is a huge man, but I jump on him. I jump on top of him, and I try to grab him around the throat, but he grabs my wrists and slams me to the floor. I lie there for a second, stunned by his strength. He stands up, looming over me like a bear. "Angel," he says. "Come on and show me the baby. Then I'll show you what I brought for you." Fortune whimpers into Mama's neck. She keeps moving away from him, but he gets up and goes for her again. I try to trip him, but he doesn't fall. He follows Mama deeper into the house, into the kitchen. I sprint ahead and pull a knife from a drawer, and I grasp it in my fist while Antoine reaches for Fortune and Mama.

The back door slams open. Willow Rose holds the .410. She holds it right against her shoulder like I taught her, her finger at the ready, eyes huge. Everything gets real slow. I hear Mama say "Willow Rose — don't," but I don't think she hears Mama. For some reason I notice that my sister still wears that bullet around her neck. She pulls the trigger. I hear the crack like it's far away and Antoine falls to the kitchen floor, slumping over himself in slow motion. Mama whispers my sister's name. Antoine howls and grabs onto his thigh, curling into himself, fetal, bleeding. I drop my knife to the floor beside Antoine. Willow Rose kicks it away from him, reloads the .410 and says, "Don't move." We're frozen in our places, each of us panting, the room electric.

When my father walks through the door, we all gasp. Willow Rose cries out, "Daddy!" and falls into his arms.

THIRTY-FIVE

EMMETT – WE DON'T NEED ANOTHER HERO

I KNEW IT WAS Her as soon as I came home and saw the whole goddamn scene. It was like a fucking movie happening in my own kitchen. Antoine — that monster — he was lying on the floor bleeding while everyone else — Angeline clutching Fortune, Jesse, and Willow Rose stood over him all wide-eyed like they'd just slayed a lamb. I knew it was Willow Rose. That look on her face — I would know that look anywhere. Willow Rose is like me — all raw and restless — a gun is a dangerous thing, but a girl with a gun? I knew it was her.

I thought Willow Rose would put the gun down, but she didn't. She kept holding it even as I held her.

"What the fuck is going on here?" I must have screamed a dozen times.

"He came for Mama," Jesse answered. "It's my fault."

"No, I did it. I shot him," Willow Rose said.

"He was going to hurt Mama and Fortune," Jesse said.

Angeline had backed away from Antoine and was holding Fortune's head to her chest. Fortune didn't even cry. Angeline's hand covered his entire head as if he was her doll. Willow Rose held the .410 upright, ready to snap it into use. Antoine groaned from the floor that he was dying, and when I looked at his leg, blood oozed from a gash and made a dark lake on the floor.

"Shit. Christ," I said and then ordered Jesse to get a towel or something — anything, but Jesse wouldn't move and Willow Rose wouldn't either, so Angeline tiptoed around the bloody mess and came back with three thin, ratty towels and put them in my hands.

"You move, and I'll kill you," I told Antoine.

He grunted and then, eyes closed, he told me, "I'll kill you after. All of you." Willow Rose kept the gun on him, and I motioned for her to point it away. I wasn't going to get shot by my own daughter. I could have let Antoine bleed. I could have let him die right there, right there on our kitchen floor on Mardi Gras, real slow, and I don't know why I didn't. Maybe I felt guilty about every other terrible thing I'd done, or maybe I knew what that would do to Willow Rose, to Angeline, but for some reason, I couldn't let that son of a bitch snuff out in front of me, so I wrapped his bloody leg, even checked his pulse like I was a nurse, but he wouldn't stop bleeding. I've never seen so much blood come from any human or animal.

"He needs a hospital. He needs a hospital or he's going to fucking die," I said.

I made a lousy tourniquet with a shirt. Then we rocked Antoine onto a sheet and pulled him outside that way, heaving the big man out the door. His eyes rolled into his head, and his giant head lolled onto his chest, and I thought how pathetic we are when we first see death.

"I'll drive," Jesse said.

"Like hell you will," I said.

"I'll drive — not either of you," Angeline snapped, and she handed Fortune to Willow Rose. "You clean this place up," she said to Willow Rose, who nodded mutely.

"We need to tighten this thing," Jesse said, re-doing the tourniquet.

He was right. We needed to keep it pulled tight, so we tugged on the shirt sleeves and held on, praying he'd stay alive. Jesse didn't know it, but that night I thanked God he was there. As we raced up the highway, Angeline gunned it. Blood still seeped from Antoine's leg, but at least it had slowed. My fingers turned wet and then sticky. In the darkness of the car, his blood looked black like oil.

At the hospital in Cut Off, we screeched up to the entrance, called over the first person who looked like she knew something, and as soon as they had him on a stretcher, I said we should flee before they started asking us questions. Angeline said we should stay, make sure he lives, but I said I didn't give one crap if that man croaked as long as he didn't croak on my kitchen floor. Of course, I didn't want anyone to die, but more than that, I didn't want my name attached to Antoine's problems. I needed to disappear. With more force than I knew she had, Angeline smacked me across the cheek, a real hard smack, and she cussed at me that I should have stayed the hell away from Antoine from the start.

I knew Fortune was Antoine's. I knew it even before I saw that cleft like a goddamn canyon on Fortune's chin. I knew it because when I came back from New Albany, Angeline couldn't stand the smell of me, wouldn't come near me, and that was fine by me because of everything I'd done. I knew her silence was rage, but we both pretended otherwise. When Fortune was born, I wanted to kill Antoine, but instead I kept my mouth shut real tight and tried to keep myself drunk enough to forget I'd played every move wrong.

I talked Angeline into leaving, or maybe I yanked her by the arm back to the car. We tore back down the highway. This time Jesse drove while Angeline sat silent in the passenger seat, and I sat in the back and hung my head. My heart raged in my chest while Jesse sped through the nighttime fog. He didn't stop at our turnoff. He blew past it all the way to Leeville, stopping in front of Antoine's place. He told me and Angeline to wait in the car while he slipped into Antoine's house. I sweat and thought I might burst into a thousand pieces while I waited for him to come back. Angeline stared ahead the whole time. Time passes real slow when it's night and all you can think about is men who've died on your watch. When Jesse came back, he clutched my Colt, a pile of cash, and of all things — a book. He refused to answer anything about anything, so we raced back for home, and I swear to God, I half-expected Antoine to have come back by then and finished off Willow Rose, and even Fortune, or for our house — our shitty little shack on the edge of the marsh — to be swarmed by cops looking for me. Game over.

PART THREE

THIRTY-SIX

JESSE – EVERYBODY WANTS TO RULE THE WORLD

DADDY SAYS WE HAVE to leave. He says if we don't leave now, we could get in real trouble. When I say that me and Willow Rose have to go to school, he says "Fuck school," and like some demon's got him he tosses things — clothes, blankets, some old flashlight, and all the money he's got — into Mama's car and he tells us to hurry our asses. While we scurry around like each of us is our own human tornado, Daddy dumps water on the kitchen floor, scrubs it and then bundles all the bloody towels into the trunk of the car. Mama tells him he's gone crazy, that she doesn't want to go anywhere, but he says that staying here in this goddamn swamp all this time was what was crazy, and now it's time to go. He says he ain't leaving without us. He yells at Mama to set the chickens free from their coop. He tells her it's better this way. Her face twists in sadness and anger, but he is fiery, and she gives in. I follow Mama outside into the darkness and watch her spread food out on the ground for the hens. She pats them, gentle, scared, and whispers goodbye to them, holding each one to her in turn. They are confused and go right back into their coop, so Mama leaves them there, the coop open, and she turns her back on them with her hand on her heart.

Finally, we all settle into the Chevy, me in the front, Willow Rose and Mama sit in the back. When no one is looking, I tuck *A Farewell to Arms* and *Zen and the Art of Motorcycle Maintenance* under the front passenger seat. I keep the binoculars with me. Mama clutches Fortune tight against her body. The last thing I see as we drive away is Antoine's truck and the alligator, a dark shape dangling in the night. When we reach the highway, Daddy stops on the side of the bayou, wraps the bloody towels around stones and lets them sink into the water.

For the first time in my life, we are going somewhere. At first, the highway unwinds with familiar names: Raceland, Houma and all the way to Lafayette. We leave behind the bayou and its smell, and I wonder if I'll ever see pelicans dive-bomb into the water again, if I'll ever see our crumbling house and the big trees that surround it again. Maybe together we'll find our next real good thing. Daddy stops at a gas station and buys a great big map. He says we'll keep going until there's nowhere left to go. I trace my finger over lines and more lines that lead to places I never thought I'd see. Texas. Arizona. California, and then nothing but ocean. Maybe if we travel far enough, I'll forget about Mardi Gras and Lisette, Antoine's face and the smell of the bayou. Maybe we'll end up somewhere good.

Hours later dawn cracks the sky open. We cross a muddy river, and a roadside sign welcomes us to Texas. We are somewhere, and it's like nowhere I have ever been. From the backseat Willow Rose stifles sobs. Mama tries to quiet her, but finally she lets out a real cry. "What are you crying about?" Mama asks. Willow Rose keeps sobbing. "You crying about that man?" She looks at her in the rearview mirror, eyebrows raised. Willow Rose nods, her legs folded up to her chest.

"What if he dies?" she asks.

"He's not dying," Mama answers.

"But what if he does?" Willow Rose asks.

"You think he was worried about us when he came into our house?"

Willow Rose sucks in a big breath, making herself hiccup. "Will we ever be able to go home?" she asks.

"We are home. We're together," my father says and even Mama looks at him, surprised as he reaches back and touches Willow Rose's knee. I don't know if anyone else thinks it, but I know it's my fault and not Willow Rose's that Antoine came over, that we had to leave. I stay silent and look out the window of the car.

Before we reach Houston, I trade places with Willow Rose and offer to hold Fortune. Mama hands him to me and curls up for a rest. Since he's been born, I've hardly spent time with Fortune. Mama's always got him in her arms, and he's always suckling at her breast. They are a unit with no need for anyone else, but now that I'm holding him in our warm car, I notice his eyelashes have grown in and his hands have gotten chubby along with his cheeks. I tickle his arm and he smiles at me, puts his hand on my mouth. I nuzzle him with my nose and say, "We're going on a road trip, little brother." He smiles and makes a little squealing noise, drooling on me. I grow sleepy with his warm skin stuck to mine.

We enter Houston, a web of highways. Daddy cusses at all the other drivers, leans into his horn and cuts into lanes. Me and Willow Rose peer through the binoculars and call out licence plates from other states. I spy one from New York, Willow Rose says she sees one from Washington. Daddy tells us to shut up and let him drive. Outside of Houston, the sky is bigger than any I've ever seen. It's so clear and blue, it makes me think of truth, of bad feelings dissolving in the air that's thin and crisp, not heavy like the swamp air I know. We blow through San Antonio, hungry and hot, and the desert is all around us. Billboards on the side of the road advertise guns and Jesus, and when we pass a giant sign with cowboys on it advertising a real Texan steakhouse. Daddy announces, "We'll go there."

The restaurant is off the highway, and it's huge, like everything in Texas, and it has a giant statue of a steer outside. I think my father's lost his mind: we've never sat at a fancy restaurant like this with checkered tablecloths and real waiters wearing cowboy hats, but my father has a plan. When the waiter comes, my father orders the 72-ounce steak challenge. Our waiter, who is not much older than me and has a thin moustache, rubs his hands together. He tells my father that he will have one hour to eat the steak plus the shrimp cocktail, baked potato and a dinner roll, and if he doesn't manage to eat it all without vomiting, he'll have to pay seventy-two dollars for his dinner. Daddy chuckles and talks like he's a Texan, "Bring it on, pardner," he says. Mama tells him he shouldn't, that we don't have that kind of money, but my father says, "Don't worry, darlin'" and elbows me and Willow Rose like we're in on the joke.

"Well giddy-up," Mama mutters.

When our food comes, along with a bucket in case my father needs it, the rest of us ignore our burgers so we can watch Daddy. The waiter asks him to cut one piece of meat and eat it to make sure it's cooked right, so my father cuts a piece so big it fills his whole mouth. He chews and chews, and his Adam's apple bobs as he finally swallows the whole thing down with a swig of Coke and gives the thumbs up. A giant digital clock on the wall is set.

My father cuts and chews like he is a dying man trying to get it all in before he keels over. At first, the steak won't shrink. It looks like a whole cow laid itself down on his plate, but my father stays focused. He saws through it and devours the meat, not slowing until he's more than halfway done. He chokes a little. "Emmet, stop," my mama says and pushes his water glass in front of him.

"I ain't paying seventy-two dollars for dinner," he says and goes back to stuffing his face.

My own stomach starts to ache as my father eats like a beast, lips glossy with fat, not stopping to pick the pieces from his teeth. After my father downs a glass of water, he gulps like he's trying to keep his food down and, making a face, Mama picks up Fortune and goes for a walk. She says she won't watch anymore. Willow Rose begins to chant "Go Daddy, go!" I have to pee, but I don't want to miss anything, so I squirm in my seat and join Willow Rose's cheer. Each time my father opens up his mouth to shove more food into it, I think of a lion tearing into flesh. Finally, my father swallows the last bite of meat. Willow Rose cheers and my father belches. I cringe, my stomach twisting in disgust. Willow Rose picks up the bucket, but my father shakes his head as he slurps back the shrimp cocktail before demolishing the baked potato. Bits of it fall down his shirt, and my father doesn't notice. Time ticks by fast, so my father stuffs the entire roll into his mouth at once, barely chewing it, crumbs clinging to his greasy lips.

With two full minutes left before the timer goes, my father finishes. He stands, raises his arms like he has just won an Olympic medal and calls out "I win!" The waiter comes over and slaps him on the back, and all the other customers look up from their meals and applaud. My father's face is so alive. He smiles and jokes with the waiter. He acts like he's real famous and when Mama comes back, he gives her and Fortune each a big kiss in front of everybody like he just became president of the United States or something. Mama squirms away and wipes the grease from her cheek. The restaurant is full of families, but none of the other fathers are acting like mine. I take Fortune from Mama and hide my face in his little neck and slip off to the restroom.

When I come back, Willow Rose is high-fiving my father and a crowd of waiters gathers around. They give him a mug in the shape of a cowboy boot, a certificate and a T-shirt that says "I Survived the 72-ounce Steak Challenge." They promise his name will be added to their steak challenge wall of fame. Willow Rose tells me that someday she's going to be the first girl to get her name on that wall. Daddy's face has begun to sweat, and he rubs the side of his head as he collects his loot. He tells us he needs some air.

At the far end of the parking lot, my father tells us to look away. He turns his back to us, and he pukes everything — steak and shrimp and potato — it runs down his chin and onto his shirt. He keeps on heaving long after there's nothing left until he wipes his face with the back of his hand, then rubs his hands on his jeans and leans against the car, panting.

Mama holds Fortune tight to her and says "Oh Emmett," and then, "What a waste." She rubs my father's shoulders with one hand, and he can only nod and hang his head while Willow Rose trots back inside and returns with a pile of paper towels. Daddy tries to wipe his shirt off, but I tell him it stinks real bad, so he throws it in a trash bin and puts on his new one. "At least I didn't pay for this," he says smoothing the shirt with its shiny decal over his chest.

"Yeah," I say. "At least."

In the gift store next to the restaurant, Willow Rose begs for a cowgirl keychain and Daddy buys it for her, and for some reason he gets me a wallet that says Everything's Bigger in Texas, and then we keep driving into the still desert air. Ahead of us the sunset flames violet and orange across the sky. When it's finally night, Daddy pulls us into a rest stop parking lot, and we settle into the car to sleep. Mama and Daddy both lean their seats back, and Mama holds Fortune to her chest. Willow Rose and I try to fall asleep in all different positions, but no matter what, we're in each other's way. The sound of trucks whooshing by on the nearby highway is constant. I slip out of the car and look up at the night sky. A day ago, it was Mardi Gras, and I kissed Lisette all over. I wonder if I'll ever touch her again. When Willow Rose joins me outside the car she asks if I think Antoine will live, and I put my arm around her skinny shoulders and tell her that he'll definitely live, and we'll all be okay.

After Willow Rose settles back in the car, I wander over to a payphone at the other end of the parking lot. I have two quarters in my pocket and the memory of Lisette's phone number scrawled in Gina's handwriting. I'm aching to talk to her, but I'm scared to dial. She said she didn't care about my family, but maybe now, after everything that's happened, she feels different. I dare myself to make the call.

The first quarter plinks into the phone, and I dial, humming back at the rhythmic tones of the buttons. An operator's voice comes on and says, "You have two minutes for this call," and I panic — two minutes! What if someone else picks up the phone and takes a long time to get her? I want to reach through the phone and touch her. The phone rings. Once. Twice. After the third ring, a questioning voice — a man's. Her father. I don't say who's calling, just ask for Lisette and pray that he'll get her. I hear his shuffling feet and a mumbled conversation. They are so far from here, but I can picture it all. Their house with the soft carpet and lights. The family photos. Lisette's hair. Her smell.

"Hello?"

"It's me, Jesse."

"Jesse! Where are you?"

"I'm in Texas. My family — we had to leave."

"Why didn't you tell me?"

"It was real sudden."

The line goes silent. In the distance, trucks rumble by. Underneath that, crickets sing.

"Lisette?"

The operator comes on. "Please deposit fifty cents to continue this call."

"Lisette? Are you there?"

"Are you okay?"

"We're going to get cut off."

I put in my other quarter, but the operator's voice repeats, "Please deposit fifty cents to continue this call."

"Lisette?"

"When are you coming back?"

"I don't know."

A tuck blares its horn, and two men holler greetings at each other from inside their cabs, windows down.

"You have ten seconds remaining."

I think of glittering purple, green and gold beads and Mardi Gras and her father's car.

"Come back soon, okay, Jesse? Okay? Can you hear me?"

"This call will be disconnected."

"I will," I say, and the line clicks dead.

THIRTY-SEVEN

NEW MOON ON MONDAY

THE SUN RISES OVER the desert in blazes of pink and gold, and before anyone else is awake, I lie down on the hood of the car and think — *this is how all the forevers in the world look.* Mama has slept curled up with Fortune, who cries himself awake, and everyone else stumbles out of the car, stretching to shake off the ache of sleeping all folded up. Around us the engines of semis idle and the smell of diesel fills the air. We fill our bellies with leftover burgers and fries that we took with us from the restaurant last night, and Mama goes into the store and comes back with soft white bread, peanut butter and a big bottle of water that she says we can refill along the way. We feast standing up in the parking lot while Daddy unfolds the map on the trunk of the car and shows us where we are. We're a speck on a thin yellow line that runs through Texas. In one day, we've come farther from home than I've ever been in my whole life. The yellow line runs all the way west through Texas, New Mexico, Arizona and right through California to the Pacific Ocean. My father says we're going to keep on driving until there's nowhere left to go. There's nothing keeping us from seeing the world. He squints at the place names in small writing on the map, draws his finger down the road until there's no more road, only water. He tells us that as long as we keep moving, everything will be fine.

It's true. There's something about driving down the two lanes of highway, staying in motion with scrubby brown hills ahead of us that makes all of us real calm. Daddy lets me take a turn driving, and after, I hold Fortune snug against my chest while Mama takes a turn, and Willow Rose and I tickle our little brother to make him smile. We're all feeling tired, but also giddy, so when "We Are the World" comes on the radio, we all join in, with Willow Rose crooning out Cyndi Lauper's solo, which I tell her makes her sound like a howling cat. Daddy sings along with Bruce Springsteen, even squinching up his face like I've never seen him. Then he does an imitation of Bob Dylan, and we all burst out laughing. Mama laughs so hard she swerves the car and nearly hits a truck in the next lane, which only makes her laugh harder and makes Daddy call out "Jesus!" but he makes even that sound like Bob Dylan so that Mama shriek-laughs at him to stop.

We make it all the way to the far edge of Texas, and my father says that if we look to the left, we can see Mexico in the hot, wavy air. Then Texas becomes New Mexico with its miles of cactuses and sky and Spanish place names. Mama wants to stop at every town, but Daddy wants to get to Arizona to see the Grand Canyon, so we keep driving until no one wants to drive anymore, and we pull into another parking lot where I try to explain to Willow Rose the difference between a classical and romantic understanding of things. She tells me to stuff it, but when everyone else goes to sleep, I lie awake wondering if I can become more classical, more rational, like Daddy. If you can fix your own stuff then you don't have to ask for help, and you'll have fewer problems, like if I'd never gone to Antoine for money, maybe we'd have fewer problems now. That thought chases sleep from me for hours into the night and I swear to myself I'll change. The next day is another day on the road through the unending desert. When we finally stop for the third night, we are in the dark of a truck stop, with idling trucks around us and the sounds of cars zooming by on the highway, their headlights streaking past us. Before we try to sleep, my father turns on the light in the car and unfolds the map. He points out our route for tomorrow. "We're here," he says, pointing at what looks like nowhere. I nod like it means something. He asks me if I've seen pictures of the Grand Canyon. I nod again and say, "It's the biggest canyon in the country."

His voice hushed like he's in church, Daddy says, "It's like nothing you've ever seen. It's a crack in the ground so big it's like God himself put his fist down in anger and broke open the earth." He promises we'll get there tomorrow. He promises it'll be the best day of our lives.

My father cusses when he learns there is a fee to even get close to the canyon. He makes a screeching U-turn and drives away from the park gate before he says "Fuck it" real loud and makes another U-turn and takes us back to the gate, where he tosses bills to the woman in the booth who gives us a map and a brochure and wishes us a splendid day. Daddy revs the engine and practically rams through the gates to the park as if he's afraid they'll turn us back. Our dumpy car looks nothing like the sleek motorhomes that cruise past us with names like Pacific Adventure and Thousand Mile Maverick painted in curly writing on the backend, but out here our crappy car doesn't matter. At first the road to the canyon is nothing special: misshapen trees and more scrub. Willow Rose kicks the seat in front of her so that Mama, who is in the passenger seat with Fortune, turns around and smacks her leg. "Where's this goddamn canyon?" says Daddy, growing impatient, as he eases the car around another bend in the road, when suddenly it's there. On a roadside turnout, the canyon gapes open before us, and Daddy hits the brake so that we skid to a stop. "Holy shit," my father says.

"Holy shit!" Willow Rose yells in agreement as she jumps out of the car, and we all follow. The canyon looks as big as the sky, but brilliant red. I don't know where to look first. The pamphlet says that the oldest rocks at the bottom are 2,000 million years old and I have no idea what that means, but I know how it feels, and my skin turns to goose flesh in the light breeze. I feel smaller than I've ever felt, and maybe happier.

"Holy smokes," Mama says, standing back from the rim with Fortune at her shoulder. "This is —"

"Fucking awesome," Willow Rose finishes.

"We should have left that shithole a long time ago," my father says.

"Can we stay here? Can we live here forever?" Willow Rose asks.

"This is way better than school," I say.

"Fuck," my father says.

For a second, I remember PJ and his sinking stick, and the way he looked the last time I saw him, and Antoine, and Lisette, but I shove it all away and try to forget the smell of the bayou, the egrets that fly into the sunset and the look of the long bridge to Grand Isle. Here the air smells like pines, and it is so clear that through the binoculars, you can count all the layers of red rock that go on and on, forever. As I gaze through them, Mama turns to me and asks, "Where did you get those, anyway?"

I think real fast and say "School," while beside me Daddy stifles a strange smile.

We drive the north rim real slow, stopping along the way. None of us has any words to say when we stand, all of us together, at a viewpoint and peer over the edge. Willow Rose squeezes my hand and Daddy's. I squeeze hers back. A squirrel with long fuzzy ears skitters by and cocks his head as if to ask if we'll feed him. My father laughs. Way above our heads two bald eagles coast around each other in a wide circle, their wings open to the wind, effortless.

"If you were an animal, what would you be?" Willow Rose asks all of us.

"Gator," Daddy says.

"Eagle," I say.

"Too obvious," says Willow Rose.

"Okay, a falcon," I say.

"Don't you think you're more owl?" Willow Rose asks, and then mouths the word, *nerd*.

Willow Rose peers into Fortune's face as Mama holds him. "He'd be a baby deer," my sister says, stroking Fortune's cheek.

"Naw, if Jesse's an owl, he's an owlet — look how much they look alike," Mama says.

I'd never thought of it before — I'd been so caught up staring at Fortune's chin, but it's true. We've got the same blue eyes and dark hair. Brothers.

"Owlet." Willow Rose smiles at the sweetness of the word. "What about you?" she asks Mama.

"I'd be a seahorse," Mama says.

"Weird — why?" asks Willow Rose.

"Because male seahorses are the ones that get pregnant, and I think that would be nice for a change," Mama says.

"I'd be a crab," Willow Rose says and then runs around pinching all of us and yelling "Crabby crab, crabby crab!"

At a wooden picnic table at a rest area, we stop to make sandwiches. My father slaps peanut butter on bread and Willow Rose whispers to me that she's never seen him do that in her life, but he does, and we sit around the table eating. I hold Fortune and tell him he'll always be my owlet. If you didn't know that we hadn't changed clothes in days or that we'd barely eaten, or that we were running away, you might think we were a regular family on vacation, just taking it all in. Mama sits next to Daddy, and when she hands him Fortune, this is the first time I've watched my father hold my little brother. They hold each other, like we all belong together after all, Fortune's small hands on Daddy's stubbly beard, Daddy's big hand on his head, protecting him, watching over us all.

"Fuck that shit" is what my father says when he learns the cost of a campground later in the day, after we've toured around some more.

"It's not like we have a tent anyway," I say.

"We'll camp in a parking lot. Car camping," Daddy says. "That's how this family does it. Real roughing it." He smiles and high-fives Willow Rose.

We linger outside a small — and very expensive, Mama says — grocery store, and after it closes for the night, we park in the far corner of the lot and settle into restless sleep like we've done every night since we left home. In the dark car, Mama begins to sing a lullaby that she used to sing to me and Willow Rose. "*Dors, dors mon p'tit, dors*," she sings real quiet, nestled into Fortune's neck. I barely remember the words, but I hum along and so does Willow Rose, joining in for the chorus. Sometimes, Daddy would get mad when

Mama used to speak to us in Cajun — it made him feel left out — but this time he joins in, just a little with the few words he knows. He hasn't had a drink since we left, and his voice is clear and gentle. When Mama finishes singing, the hush of night falls over us all.

Morning in the desert makes you feel like life itself is being born. A skinny lizard rustles up a tree and overhead a bald eagle soars. Squirrels trill to each other. Daddy gets behind the wheel and we do one more drive around the rim of the canyon, stopping at all the turnouts to take in the hush. Willow Rose turns over rocks looking for scorpions, tarantulas, snakes, while I wish we would find a type of lizard our brochure tells us about that can shoot blood from its eyes. We are silent as we drive out of the park at dusk. Mama looks out the window and waves goodbye with Fortune's hand.

THIRTY-EIGHT

BORN IN THE USA

BY NIGHTFALL WE'RE LOST. Not wanting to lose the good feeling we have from seeing the canyon, my father takes a side route off the crowded highway without looking at the map. He says he has an instinct about directions, and he says — fuck all that traffic. Parroting something I read in my book, I announce that highways are the worst and the real adventure is on the side roads. My father nods at what I say and says he's sure he knows where to go, but we're on a dark road and we haven't been joined by another car for miles. Mama passes Fortune to me to nuzzle while she unfolds the map and turns on the light. She cusses then says, "I can't tell where we are. Stop the car."

"Ain't no point looking at the map if you don't know where we are." My father's voice is loose, like he doesn't get why Mama's worried. Willow Rose leans forward in her seat like she wants to help Mama read the map, while I press Fortune into my chest and hold the back of his head.

"Stop the car, Emmet," my mother says again.

My father slaps the steering wheel and brakes too fast before he cuts off the engine just long enough to yell at Mama. With the overhead light on, I catch the pleading look on my father's face. He wants to be right. He needs to be in charge of this road trip. I hold Fortune closer and bury my face in his. I make faces at him and he smiles, surprised every time.

"We're not lost," Daddy says.

"We are. And if you won't look at the map, I will," Mama says.

Daddy starts to turn the keys in the ignition. Mama pulls his hand away and tries to snatch the keys.

"Let me drive!" my father protests.

"You need to turn back. You don't know what road we're on," Mama says.

"I'll figure it out," my father says.

When he starts the car again, he doesn't turn around. Instead, he speeds ahead while Mama hollers at him to turn back, and he tells her to stop telling him what to do. The road beneath us turns from pavement to gravel and the night turns blacker as my father races on.

First there's the sound of skidding on gravel and then the feel of Daddy slamming on the brakes as he steers wildly. He screams. Metal crunches. My head smashes against the side window and when my neck snaps back, I think — *I'm going to die now.* I try to keep my arms around Fortune. I can feel him against me, I swear I can feel him when I smack up against the back of Mama's seat and we turn upside down and then back upright, and then I can't feel him anymore. I can't tell if the shriek comes from my throat or someone else's. I can't tell if I hurt so much because I'm dead or alive.

"Get out of the car!" Daddy screeches. Somehow, he clambers out from the driver's seat, and he keeps yelling at us to get out before the car falls further into the ditch beside the road. Willow Rose finds her way out and so does Mama, but I can't move.

"Fortune!" I shout his name, and I pray for him to cry, but he doesn't.

Daddy crawls into the back seat beside me and he puts a hand over my mouth, and everything around me grows real quiet. He eases me out of the car, my arms around his neck, his arms around my waist, and together we fall onto the gravel road, my weight on top of his. "You're okay," he keeps repeating over my cries.

The car is turned the wrong way with the front facing down the ditch on the side of the road. The driver's side tire is blown. The car looks like it could slip further away with a light shove. The fender hangs off, and the hood is crunched up with the front lights blown to pieces. We stand there on the road, silent. Willow Rose presses her face into my side. Mama holds her head in her hands, and we three watch Daddy pick his way back into the car. It rocks like it'll slip. Then Daddy emerges with Fortune. He cradles my brother in his arms, but Fortune's neck hangs like an unplugged electrical cord. Mama crumples to her knees and shrieks "No" a hundred times while Daddy holds Fortune to his chest and weeps. Mama's howls fill all the space between us and the night sky.

Willow Rose grabs me around the waist, and I hold her head against me, trying to keep her from seeing everything. When she pees down her leg, I feel it on my own calf. Daddy clutches Fortune to him and trips into the desert on the other side of the road and he wails, his face buried in my brother's small body. Mama follows him and takes my baby brother against her chest, rocks him to her. She tilts her head to the sky, opens her mouth in a scream that lasts forever, but makes no sound.

My father limps back to the car and sobs. He beats his own chest and grasps his hair. Screeching like a maimed animal, he pounds his fist into the side mirror of the car until the mirror breaks. Shards of shiny glass tinkle into the desert. He slumps into a squat with his hands on his face and stays like that. Mama rocks Fortune. Willow Rose hides her face in my chest.

Even though it is dark all around us, everyone's eyes shine bright. My arms and legs are freezing cold. I hold Willow Rose to me.

We stay like that forever, each of us too scared to move. Finally, Daddy looks up, his eyes wild, and he says, "I'm going to get help."

"Where'll you go?" I ask him. A thick fog has spread itself over my brain and what he says makes no sense. I ask him again.

"I don't know. There was a town way back," he says.

"I'll come," I say.

"No. I'm going alone," he says. I protest. "I don't need you," he says and then gestures to Mama and to Willow Rose. "Don't leave them," he tells me, and he's already walking. He meets my eyes for a second, and I barely recognize his face. He walks until even his white shirt disappears into the desert and there is nothing left of my father.

The desert at night is wicked cold and we all shiver against each other. I wipe blood from Willow Rose's forehead with my shirt. She says she feels no pain, and I don't either, though I can tell by the blood on my cheek that I should. We convince Mama to get back into the car, which moans and sinks further into the ditch when we get in. Her sobs are raw, but they are between her and Fortune. She won't let me or Willow Rose touch her.

We wait all night long. Not one car passes us. Pink streaks appear across the sky, and still we wait. We pee in the desert. When the sun is up, me and Willow Rose drink from our water bottle, but Mama only takes small sips, her lips dry and colourless as the desert. The sun beats down directly over our heads, and still no one comes. Before dusk, a reddish brown hawk circles above, and I think I'd rather become prey than expire, waiting like this in the desert. We spend another night huddled in the car.

At dawn Mama wraps Fortune in a blanket as though he were still alive. With him tucked in her arms she uses one hand to help Willow Rose from the car, then she shakes my shoulders as I gaze into nothingness.

"Willow Rose and I are going to get help. You stay here and wait for Daddy," she says. I nod, trying to wake myself from the trance I've fallen into. "We'll be back," Mama says. Willow Rose passes me what little remains of the bread and peanut butter, and the water bottle, which has only a small amount left. From the rearview mirror, I watch my mother, Fortune and Willow Rose disappear in the same direction as my father.

THIRTY-NINE

IN A BIG COUNTRY

I FIND A STICK in the desert and bring it to the car. Once when I was a little kid, me and my father went hunting up the bayou, and we saw a wild boar in the woods. We weren't there to shoot a boar, so we tiptoed back to Daddy's truck, and I was real scared. When we got up into the truck, Daddy taught me that if you think about the thing that scares you and pretend it's smaller than you — like if the boar was just a rabbit — and you treat it like that, calm, like you have nothing to be afraid of, then the boar will leave you alone. Daddy said you should never act scared. Out here in the desert, I am afraid of everything, but I can't name the thing that scares me most. Everything here is much bigger than me.

During the day, the heat swells inside the car, so I sit on the hood. Later I lie on the roof and stare at the sky. When the sun is still high, I remember my books inside the car and try to read *A Farewell to Arms*. My mind jumps so much I can't get past the first pages, so I open to the final section instead, and I am hit by the words: baby, dead. I slam the book shut and run with it into the desert, where I rip out pages and tear them to shreds, filling the empty air with my cries as I do it. The pages are small and white against the endless sand and brush.

I go back to the car. Still breathless, I throw *Zen and the Art of Motorcycle Maintenance* as far out the window as I can toss it. I will never have my father's classical understanding of things. To calm down, I force myself to read the brochure we got at the Grand Canyon. Ancient rocks. Lizards. Tarantulas. The best thing I've ever seen.

Pins and needles of fear prick my skin with every rustle in the trees or scuttle under the rocks. I'm bigger than a scorpion, or a spider, I tell myself, but I know I'm still not safe. We were never safe. This heat. The endless desert. This road. If my family doesn't return, my flesh will turn to bones before anyone finds me. I stick my tongue into the water bottle, desperate. My lips are dryer and rougher than all the sand that surrounds me, and they blister under the sun's glare. I cry myself into an empty sleep in the evening and wake in a sweat, plastered to the seat of the car, still alone after nightfall.

Inside the car grows cold as an icebox, and I tremble under blankets. I feel myself edge close to sleep, but a jolt of electricity rouses me. Fortune. As if I've been yanked from a dream I'm plunged into the truth: Fortune is dead because I let him go. I killed my baby brother. And worse — the only reason I even had a baby brother was because I let Antoine in and he hurt Mama, and then, like a criminal, I asked him for money. That must be why they left me here. First Daddy, then Mama and Willow Rose. They want me to die. When I realize that, I begin to cry. From somewhere far away — or maybe nearby — coyotes howl back at my sobs, and I leave the car so that the wilderness can take me. I lie down on the road, the road that took Fortune, and I wait for the same. The desert sky is crowded with more stars than I have ever imagined. I am the most alone person in the world.

Am I dreaming or am I dying? I hear the crunch of metal, I see Fortune's eyes as he looks up at me. My ears are filled with the sound of Mama's scream. And then I swear something slithers up to me. A snake: it must be a snake. It glides across my belly, heavy and fast. It sidles right up to me, curls into the crook between my shoulder and my ear. I am paralyzed, as if daggers have pegged me down. I will myself to move, to jump up, to run, but my pulsing mind can no longer control my body. The snake rattles its tail and stretches out full, its body up against mine. It will strike me now. I know it but can't move. I screech myself awake and find myself thrashing on the road alone. There's no place to hide but the car, so I pummel myself back inside and shake, sobbing until dawn comes and with it, the heat. The sun is a sniper who stalks me. I tear off my shirt and lie down on the hood of the car and offer myself to her.

The voices come to me as if they're passed through a filter, all wavy and slow. I try to answer. I have no voice. Everything I say is swallowed by blackness.

"He's alive," a man's voice says.

"Give him water," says a woman's voice — my mother, and I feel the liquid on my face, my forehead, then it trickles down my throat and I choke it up, then wretch for real. My body twists away from the voices.

I'm still on the hood of the car and my whole body feels agony as if I've been bulldozed. *Good*, I think, and keep my eyes closed. If I'm dead, Fortune can't be my fault anymore. I feel someone's hands lift me up and ease me away from here.

There is a black hole in my memory when I try to recall how I got from the desert to this clean bed. I know now that I'm not dying, but it doesn't matter: the feeling that I'm already dead is inside me, and every time I sleep, I wake screaming. I'll be finished off yet.

Mama tells me things. Mr. Alvarez is a car mechanic. He saved us. This is his house, and he's working on our car. It's busted, but still fixable. Willow Rose is with us. Fortune is in a small white urn that sits on a table in this room. When our car is fixed, we'll all go home together, except for Daddy. He's gone.

No man is kinder than Mr. Alvarez. He feeds us for all the days it takes him to repair Mama's car, and on the day Mama says we're ready to leave, he hands me a whole wad of bills and tells me we're like family now. He smells like oil and gasoline, but also like soap, and when I fall into his embrace, I weep. While my Mama arranges our few things in the car, he asks me what my father looks like. As if I'm describing a photograph, I tell him about Daddy's dirty blonde hair and blue eyes.

"It must have been him — he came by here asking for help, but when I told him the cost for a tow, he left. I didn't know," Mr. Alvarez says.

He tells me he hasn't seen him since and promises to call me if he does. He looks very sad. He doesn't know the things that are my fault. I give him Lisette's phone number, which I still remember, and he gives me his on a soft, creased business card that I shove deep in my jeans pocket. When we say goodbye, he keeps telling us to be safe and God bless, as if something as small as a prayer will help.

FORTY

ALL THROUGH THE NIGHT

MAMA DROVE US ALL the way home. We stopped twice so we could sleep, but I don't think she slept at all. She just kept on driving, face fixed on the road ahead, and all of us stayed real quiet. Now that we're back home, back in the middle of nowhere, Willow Rose and I barely look at one another, and Mama stays away from both of us. If I see what's in my mama's or in Willow Rose's eyes, I'll know what's in mine, and I don't want to know.

There are days when I wish I was dead, and some days when I want to hurt someone. One afternoon without even planning it, I find myself at the garage standing in front of Antoine, who has at least taken his truck away from the front of our house, though the alligator still hangs, festering. When I find him, Antoine sits in his shop with a real thick newspaper folded across his lap while he stares down at a crossword puzzle. His left leg is kicked out in front of him on another chair, still wrapped in bandages. I wait for his face to turn mean, but instead he is just a man with tired eyes and stubble on his chin.

"You come back to finish me off?" he asks. He puts his newspaper in his lap and tucks away his injured leg as if to hide it. He looks me up and down and he asks, "What happened to you? You don't look so good."

I want to punch him, but I find another way to hurt him. I say — real flat, "Daddy's gone. Fortune's dead." My words hit Antoine like I got a bullseye, and he drops his paper to the floor, where it rustles under the whir of a rotating fan.

"What did you say?" he asks. His cheeks grow flushed.

"Fortune … we were in a car crash. He died, and my father… he left us there." The words tumble from my mouth, wooden, unreal.

"What in hell are you talking about? How did that baby die?"

"My father was driving and I was holding him. A tire blew. Daddy crashed the car. Fortune died."

Antoine lumbers up out of his chair and he roars. For some reason his pain makes me feel real good.

"Jesus Christ." Antoine kicks his chair. "Where'd your father go?" I shrug and tell him I don't know.

"Jesus fucking Christ," Antoine says.

"My mama —" I say, and then I stop.

Antoine limps to his work counter and pulls open his cash drawer. "Here. Take it, take all of it," he says and hands over everything in his drawer, bills stuffed in his hands. I shake my head.

"I ain't taking that anymore," I say.

"Like hell. You so rich all the sudden?" His voice thunders now. "Take it. Just take it." He hobbles out from behind the counter, takes my hand in his three-fingered one and presses the pile of bills into my palm. I let my hand drop and the bills slip to the floor. Antoine bends over to gather them up, groaning with the strain. One kick, I think, and I could topple him. "I'm not asking. You take these to your mama. Don't tell her where they came from, just take them, and don't tell her you was ever here." He holds the pile out to me. I can't think of my mama without thinking of the sound she made when she saw my father come out of the car holding Fortune. I take the bills and then I toss them at his feet.

"I ain't taking nothing from you," I say.

"I see," he says.

I give the bills a little kick. Antoine watches and does nothing.

"I'll leave now," I say, but I stand there in silence.

Antoine points at his newspaper. "They finally stopped all that oil spilling. More than five million barrels, you know," Antoine says.

"Who cares? It's too late to save anyone," I say.

"I thought you'd want to know," he says.

I kick his bills one more time and take off without even a wave.

Just loud enough for me to hear, Antoine mutters "Lord help you."

The next day, the alligator and all the flies that swarmed its rotting flesh are gone from our tree.

FORTY-ONE

CUM ON FEEL THE NOIZE

MAMA GETS A JOB — the very worst job she could get — at Lafitte Lodge after weeks or more of all of us sitting around doing nothing but sleeping the days away. I tell her that place is a dump, and she tells me I can stuff it or find a decent way to make money myself. On her first night working, Mama leaves in a short skirt, her face raw like when you wake from a nightmare, and I can't even look at her to say goodbye. Willow Rose begs me to drive her to Golden Meadow, to go somewhere, anywhere but here. She says being in this house is killing her, but I know she wants to find Sterling, so I ignore her and turn on the TV real loud and refuse to look away from the characters who, even with their big houses and fancy clothes, are jealous and mean. I swear if I had that kind of money, I'd never feel bad again. When I bother to get up, Willow Rose has snuck out, and when I look in the shed, I find that my bicycle is gone too, so I get in Daddy's truck and nearly run her off the highway when I find her heading north, pedalling like mad on the too-high seat. She pleads with me to let her go, she tells me she's so lonely she thinks she's going to die, but I tell her that after everything, it'll kill Mama if she leaves, and so she shoves the bike into the truck, and we go home together. On the way back, she starts to cry and tells me that sometimes she feels like she's dying inside, that she misses Daddy and Fortune. I let her lean up against me and I tell her that I know.

The next morning, I pull out the binoculars from under the sofa where I stashed them when we got home, and I offer to take Willow

Rose to see the eagles' nest that Daddy showed me. It seems like it was a hundred years ago. Willow Rose looks through the binoculars the wrong way and even laughs. When we gaze up at the cypress tree, the giant nest is still there. At first, I see nothing, but soon a small, strange looking bird pokes its fuzzy head out of the nest and then another. There are two eaglets, one bigger than the other, and I figure the smaller one might not make it. I watch them until they both duck back down where it's safe. When I pass the binoculars to Willow Rose, she says she can't even see anything, so she sulks back inside, while I keep waiting to see the babies again, hoping for the tiniest sign of life.

A week later the two of us take Mama's car to Golden Meadow while Mama sleeps off her shift. I take some of her money and we go to make groceries. Willow Rose scans the store, hoping she'll find someone to talk to, but I don't want to. I think about Lisette all the time, but what would I say to her after everything? After I took off like that? After my brother died? I don't want to know what she thinks of me and my family. We put Top Ramen, potted meat and Cokes — Willow Rose insists on trying the new kind — in the buggy. Willow Rose adds Twinkies. I put them back on the shelf. She takes them again and I give in. When Mrs. Salazar-Dulac and Lisette appear in our aisle, I nearly faint. My shirt is dirty. Willow Rose's hair is a mess. We must look like we crawled out of the marsh.

"Jesse!" they both say, surprised. I run a hand over my hair and feel my cheeks glow like fire.

Willow Rose stands there next to me all quiet, and I feel like I've forgotten English, barely managing some stupid greeting. Lisette's eyes bore into me like nails.

"You're back," Lisette says.

"Yes ma'am," I mutter like an idiot.

"When did you get back?" Lisette asks at the same time that Mrs. Salazar-Dulac asks if we're okay. She looks from me to Willow Rose. Lisette keeps her eyes on me.

"Yes ma'am," I say again, avoiding Lisette's gaze.

Mrs. Salazar-Dulac looks at the food in our buggy. In theirs, they have apples, tomatoes, celery, ground meat wrapped up in plastic, bread, spaghetti, cans of tuna. Mrs. Salazar-Dulac waits for me to answer if we're okay, if our mama is okay. She keeps asking questions until Lisette hisses at her to stop. Maybe if Willow Rose wasn't there or if Lisette wasn't there, I'd tell her everything, but instead I mumble that we're fine, just need to get back home with the groceries is all. Lisette grabs my arm and for a second, I look into her flushed face, trying to pretend I am a stranger, trying not to show her how sorry I am.

"Why didn't you call?" she asks and grips my arm with force.

Mrs. Salazar-Dulac watches it all and shakes her head at Lisette. "If you need anything," she starts to say.

I can barely get out the words "Yes ma'am," before Lisette drops my arm with what looks like disgust on her face and I duck away from them down the frozen aisle, wishing I'd seen anyone else in the world. Two kids alone making their family's groceries. Some family. Willow Rose stands in line next to me at the check-out and ties her hair into a long, messy braid with quick, nervous fingers while I stare at the floor. "Lisette's going to tell Sterling," she whispers to me, and I know she's right.

Two nights later, the black truck appears in front of our house, and I can hear the loud thump of music as it idles. Willow Rose runs out the door, jumps up inside the truck and is gone. The tires screech as the truck turns up the road from here, and I do nothing but think how lousy I feel about Lisette. I lie on the couch and try to shove away memories of Mardi Gras and everything good I thought could happen. Mama gets home from work real late. She is skinnier than she used to be and looks almost like a kid with her stick legs hanging out of her skirt, but above the neckline of her black T-shirt, there are lines on her skin. The stink of smoke and sweat and heat follow her into the kitchen where she dumps a bag full of singles and coins onto the counter. "Good night?" I ask, meaner than I mean to sound.

Mama slaps a hand on the counter. "You got a problem?" she asks. Her hair is coming out of a loose ponytail, and she shoves the stray strands from her face. In her eyes there is no light. She slumps down in a chair.

"I'm sorry," I say and go to rub her shoulders. She lets me.

"Where's your sister at?" she asks.

I take a step back. "Willow Rose left," I say.

Now Mama makes a fist and she bangs it on the table. "Jesse!" she whisper-yells. "Why didn't you stop her?"

"She got into his truck. She wanted to. What am I supposed to do?"

"I don't know. You're her brother."

"You're her mother," I say.

"What are you saying?" she asks.

"Nothing," I mumble.

She shakes her head at me. "If you'd never taught her to use that gun, she never would have shot that man."

"So, it's my fault?"

"Your father — maybe he'd still be here."

"Some good that would do."

"And Fortune —"

"Mama," I plead. I want it to stop because I know she's right.

I go to her, but she won't stop crying. My mama, who has seemed wooden for so long, is sobbing, and it's a storm that I think will end us both. I am useless, useless because I can't rewind time, and Fortune is ashes in a small urn and that will never be different. I am useless because I am not Daddy. I can't find electricity from nothing, or catch the biggest snapper, or even fix a car right. I am worse than useless.

I stalk my sister starting the next day. It is the Fourth of July, and everyone is partying but me. I drive to Galliano and park on the far end of the street. I spot the black truck, but for hours no one moves from inside Jed's small house. This time I am too embarrassed to knock. I want to be invisible. It is past dusk when they emerge. All three brothers, grasping cans of beer, strut down the street to the truck and my sister is with them. Her light hair is loose and long, and she wears an oversized sweatshirt that must belong to Sterling. His arm hangs across her shoulders. She flicks her hair and swigs from a beer as they all jump up into the truck, slam doors behind them. I turn the key in the ignition and follow, try not to get too close, but close enough so they won't slip away from view. I trail them onto a side road that ends in a parking lot up against an open field and trees. I park at the far end of the lot, in the shadows, and watch Willow Rose lean into Sterling as they all lope over to a group of kids already gathered, drinking, blasting music from someone's truck. More kids arrive: couples, boys. A bunch of them are kids I know from school, but mostly they're not my crowd. Lisette doesn't show up. I roll down the window to let in the warm, damp air, and from the field, the sound of voices and laughter drifts my way. I roll the window back up to be invisible. I clench the steering wheel so that I don't scream, and I wait. I have no idea what time it is when Willow Rose and Sterling creep around the front of the black truck that faces away from the crowd. Quiet as I can, I get down from my father's truck and glide across the parking lot in the shadows until I am right there in front of them. Sterling leans against the front of the truck, head tilted back, eyes closed, a quiet moan rising from his throat. His jeans are undone, and my sister's hands are right there. If I could slash Sterling's throat I would. "Get away from her," I say and lunge at him. Willow Rose pulls away from Sterling and then pushes me as hard as she can when she sees me going in to pound Sterling's face. She yanks my shirt, but I get to his face first, and feel his cheek crack beneath my fist. Sterling tries to pull up his pants and swing at me at once, so I try to whack him again, but miss when he ducks. Willow Rose yells at me to leave them alone. She comes right up to me, and she shoves me and tells me to get lost.

"You look like a whore," I hiss.

She slaps me hard in the face. "Don't ever call me that again," she says and stares at me until I feel shame.

I turn to Sterling, who is rubbing his cheek, and I say, "Do you even know how old she is?" He knocks me over. When I pull myself up, Willow Rose is stroking Sterling's cheek.

It is so silent between us that over my heavy breathing I hear the croaking of the frogs.

"I guess we're even," Sterling says.

Willow Rose snorts. "A couple of jackasses you both are. Are you done now?"

"I guess so," I mutter.

"Why are you here, anyway?" she asks me.

"You left me and Mama. We need you."

"Aww," Sterling jokes.

"Shut up," Willow Rose says. "I'll come home soon," she tells me. "I just had to get out of that house. It was too sad and awful."

"I know," I say. I take a deep breath. "Is Lisette at the party?"

Willow Rose looks at Sterling and then reaches out to touch my arm. "Yes," she says.

"She's there?" I'm surprised — I hadn't seen her arrive. Willow Rose nods.

I shove my hands in my pockets and straighten up. My throat feels as if I've swallowed gravel. I edge away from my sister and Sterling. If she's there, I'll go find her. Willow Rose grabs me by the wrist and tugs me back.

"She's with someone, Jess," Willow Rose says, her voice real quiet.

"She's with Cole," Sterling says, like he actually feels bad for me.

"She's not," I say.

"She is." Willow Rose holds my arm.

"It doesn't mean anything," Sterling says. "She just likes to be with someone."

"She's not like that," I say.

"Maybe not with you, but this guy — he's just there to fill time," Sterling says.

"Fuck," I say. I kick at the gravelly road.

"She thought you were gone," Sterling says. "You *were* gone. She even told our mother about it. You left with no explanation."

I slam my fist into my palm. "It had nothing to do with her," I say.

"She kept waiting for you to call again, bro. She was so sad. Even I knew about it," Sterling says.

"Such a sensitive guy," Willow Rose says and snorts.

"I can be sensitive. I'm very sensitive," Sterling says and pats Willow Rose's head like she's a pet rabbit. She brushes his hand away.

"But seriously, why didn't you call her?" Sterling asks.

In truth, I have no idea how to answer that. Because I was too sad? Too fucked up to even go find a payphone? Because I didn't deserve someone like Lisette to care about me? Finally, I mutter that I figured I'd been gone for too long and she'd forgotten me.

"Naw, she didn't forget you. You forgot her," Sterling says, and it hits me in the chest that he's right.

When Willow Rose sees my sad face, she pipes up. "Hey, there are other fishies in the bayou, you know."

"Lisette's no fish," I say.

"Yeah, she's more like a dolphin," Sterling says. "You missed out." Then he adds, "Don't be a sad chicken, though. Things are always changing. If you like her, maybe you'll get another chance."

"How could she go for that jerk? Like I never existed." I hit the side of the truck with a fist.

Willow Rose takes hold of my arm. "Let it go. You can talk to her later," she says. "You're too…"

"What?" I ask.

"Too angry. You shouldn't fight anymore."

"Yeah, hitting me is enough for one night," Sterling says and laughs.

"You should go home, Jess." Willow Rose laces her arm through mine and walks me back to Daddy's truck. When she hugs me, all I can think about is what her face looked like when we stood beside the car in the desert that night, and I wonder how she manages to act so normal. The sound of exploding fireworks fills the air, but they are too far away for us to see them. "It'll get better," Willow Rose says before she leaves me alone to be a sad chicken, or whatever I've become.

When Mama catches sight of me the next day, I tell her I am done going after Willow Rose, that she'll come home by herself, or maybe Mama should go get her. "I guess I'll have to," she says. She gets ready for work almost like she's changing out of herself and climbing into the outfit — and life — of a stranger. She leaves and I wish I could erase the image of her dressed like that from my memory and never see her like that again.

That evening, I'm home alone and I snitch Mama's Pall Malls and smoke one after another while I sit out front where Daddy gave me his Colt the day he left. Looking at the orange embers as they burn away the paper of the cigarette, I think of fire and death and how easy it is for life to slip through your fingers. Fortune barely even got a chance before his tiny life was snuffed out. He was too little to know it was happening. In my memory, all he'll ever get to be is a baby. I never got to hear him speak or see him learn to walk. And all those men on the rig — they must have known the end was coming in that fire and that's an even worse hell. My father — whatever happened to him, even if he never tried to save anyone — he must have thought it was all over for him too. Antoine was right — *you think you've got life by the balls, but it's got you.* Daddy thought it was good to have that job, but all that oil never helped anyone I know, not really. I know from the radio that the men who owned the oil company and knew the rig might have problems got off with no punishment. I guess some people have life by the balls, but the rest of us — life has got you, whether you're a fuck-up trying to earn a living, or a baby born to a family like mine in the middle of nowhere. I inhale a smoke until the nub of it burns my fingers, and still I suck trying to get everything I can out of it. My stomach is empty, and inhaling hard like that, filling my lungs, makes my head feel light and buzzy and everything around me gets real soft for just enough time for me to forget.

While I sit there, Mrs. Salazar-Dulac shows up out of nowhere. I nearly choke and try to hide my cigarette, putting it out behind me. Mrs. Salazar-Dulac looks surprised as I greet her and then stand in the doorway, trying to block her view into our house, since no one bothers to clean anything around here anymore. She pulls a handwritten message out of her brown leather purse. Mr. Alvarez called her house. He was looking for me, and she wrote down everything he said. Her handwriting is elegant and loopy. My father. Mr. Alvarez has found him. Mrs. Salazar-Dulac has Mr. Alvarez's phone number. She asks if I want to come over to make the call, and she offers me a ride, but I don't want to go to her house. I don't want to see Lisette — I feel too sad and too ashamed, so I say no and hope she'll leave me alone. Mrs. Salazar-Dulac looks over my shoulder and into our house, and I brace myself against the door frame. "Is your Mama home, *mijo*?" she asks. I shake my head. "Where is she?" she asks. When I tell her that Mama's gone to work, Mrs. Salazar-Dulac nods. I know what's coming next, so I beat her to it and lie that she's working at a restaurant in Grand Isle, but she cuts me off. "Can I see Fortune?" Her question hangs for what feels like minutes. I cross my arms over my chest, shift to the other side of the doorway and say nothing. "Jesse, where's the baby?" she asks again. My throat suddenly feels dry, and my knees grow weak. Mrs. Salazar-Dulac pushes past me and I let her. She sticks her head in both bedrooms, looking for my brother. She puts her hands on my shoulders and asks again, "Where's Fortune?" Our house is dark, and outside dusk has come on. I want to run out into it and hide, but Mrs. Salazar-Dulac presses her hands into my shoulders and demands to know.

"He died," I finally say. Mrs. Salazar-Dulac draws her hands from me as if my words burned her.

She falls into a kitchen chair and cries out, saying "No, no, no." She pulls me into the chair next to her and tells me to tell her everything.

As if I am a zombie, I tell her the whole story, but it doesn't feel like me. It feels like I have left my body and someone else has captured the sound of my voice. When I finish, Mrs. Salazar-Dulac pulls me into her arms and holds on. She whispers that if there's anything she can do I should tell her. I damn near cry, but I won't let myself. When she pulls away, she looks just like Lisette. And then grabs me by my shirt and shakes me lightly. "That's for not coming to me for help," she says. Strangely, the anger and sadness in her voice make me feel better. Mrs. Salazar-Dulac asks me one more time if I want to come over and use their phone, but I refuse. I already know what I need to do.

Mr. Alvarez. My father. Fortune. The desert. My father. It will take me three days to get there. Two if I drive all night. I feel guilty as hell for taking food and money from my mama, but I can't stop myself. All I can think of is what I will say to him about Mama and Willow Rose. About how everything is his fault. I want to pound his face until flesh becomes pulp and bone becomes powder. I don't need a map. I find my father's Colt in the night table. Tucked beside it is a folded-up newspaper article I've never seen. It's about each of the men who died on the rig. My father has used a pencil to circle one name — Frank Allmendinger, and on the second page he's circled a picture of a woman and two girls who have the same last name. There is an address and a phone number in my father's handwriting. I stare at this man's smiling face and his pretty, blonde daughters. I crumple up the worn newspaper, but then I smooth it out and shove it into my jean pocket. I load the Colt, steal my mama's fresh pack of Pall Malls and I drive away before she comes home.

PART FOUR

FORTY-TWO

MONEY FOR NOTHING

I BEAR DOWN THE highway. I drive fast, glad that it's night so I don't have to look at the scenery as I pass it by. I smoke so many cigarettes that my throat grows raw. At first, it makes me feel real good, like pain dissolving as that buzzy feeling hums in my head, but then I start to feel sick. I keep on smoking because it's better to feel pain in my gut than to have all the thoughts run wild in my head.

By morning I'm past San Antonio and too tired and nauseous to keep on. I pull into some parking lot with a rest stop on one side and a giant church on the other, and a billboard in between advertising a place with dancing girls one mile down the road. I eat potato chips and buy a package of smokes. I go to sleep in the truck, the morning heat already heavy. I know the desert is ahead of me. I can already feel it on my skin. Barely rested, I press on down the highway and go towards it. Close to El Paso, I feel near collapse again from heat and exhaustion and thirst, so I lurch into a truck stop and tumble into the blackness of sleep. When I wake, it's night, and I go into the fast-food joint and stuff my face with French fries and a rubbery burger, drink a large Coke, and piss in a restroom where one stall is taken up by some guy snoring behind the door. Everyone else at this truck stop is way older than me and they all look grizzled and grey. I get back up into the truck to keep sleeping, but just as I am falling into it, a knock on the passenger door wakes me, followed by several knocks in a row. I fling the door open, and a woman — or a girl — jumps in. She's got bright pink lips and long eyelashes. Her blonde hair is pulled into a ponytail, her shorts tight, fake leather jacket over nothing but a lacy orange bra. She slams the door behind her.

"What the fuck. Who are you?" I say.

"I'm here to make you feel real good," she says and leans into me, trying to kiss me on the mouth. She smells like too sweet perfume and cigarettes and makes me think of one of Willow Rose's abandoned Barbie dolls. I back away from her, shrink into the driver's side. I tell her she should get out, but she's already got her hand between my legs, and even as I'm pulling away from her, I get hard, then angry that I feel that way. I keep telling her to get out, but she says it's too late for that, unless I want to meet her boss, who she says, is not a very nice man. The last man who didn't pay, she starts to say — and then she runs a finger across her throat and points out the front windshield — and I catch sight of a bearded tough guy with patches on his leather vest, and he's looking our way from just out front the restaurant. I pound an open palm against the steering wheel and the girl — she says her name is Maisie, spelled with an *ie* — tells me to take it slow.

She climbs on top of me and tries to press my face into her tits, then sticks her hands down my pants. I won't touch her, and her smell makes me want to wretch, but I'm still hard, maybe harder than I've ever been, and I both want her and want to throw her from the truck. "That's right," she says as she unzips my jeans, and then I feel it — she's got her hand in my back pocket and she's taking my Texas wallet with all the cash I've got in it. I shove her away. "Watch it," she says and clutches my wallet to her. I grab her arm, trying to get the wallet back. "My boss," she squeaks.

I don't mean to do it, but I panic and pull the Colt from the glovebox. "I'm not worried about your boss," I say, and I show her the gun. She drops the wallet, but she's not as scared as I expect her to be.

"Jesus. That loaded?" she asks.

I nod.

"Show me," she says.

I shake my head.

She holds her hands in the air as if in surrender, but she puts her mouth on my neck. "You wouldn't use that, would you?" she says.

The truth is, she looks barely older than me, all skinny like that. I lower the gun, grab hold of my wallet and tuck it back in my jean pocket. I keep my hand wrapped around the Colt.

"You should let me," she says, and she paws at me again, like she's used to doing it in trucks with guns just sitting around. The truth is, it feels good to be touched like that, like I've been dying for someone to pour myself into, but I don't want to want her. I don't want to have this kind of sex. I fool around with her for a couple of seconds, letting her kiss me some more, but it just makes me miserable. I push her off me again, but she keeps her arms wrapped around me.

"Can you just get out of here?" I ask, one hand fumbling to zip up my jeans.

"C'mon, let's just do it. It'll be fun," she says. "You're way more handsome than any other guy out here. Everyone else is old." She ruffles my hair with her fingers.

"You should get away from that guy so you don't have to do this," I say.

She groans. "Not you, too. Half of everyone I meet wants to save me. They want to fuck me, but they also want to save me," she says.

"Maybe you should try to save yourself," I mutter.

"Real smart. What do you think I'm trying to do right now?" she asks.

"You could leave," I say.

"Listen, how about we do it so that I can at least have the memory of your handsome face telling me to save myself, and then you pay me cash so that I can get a burger to go with that memory?"

"I'll drive you away from here if you want. I will."

"You're cute. Thanks, but I don't feel like being killed by my boss today. Hey, can I have one?" she asks when she spots my Pall Malls on the floor of the truck.

I light one up for her and one for me.

"You know, It's not like life handed me nice parents and fancy clothes, and I picked this instead. But you probably wouldn't understand that, driving around in this big truck all by yourself — someone give this to you?" she asks, gesturing to the dash.

"I do understand," I say and put out my smoke. And then I kiss her. I know it's wrong, and it's nothing like Lisette, but I kiss her anyway, and I don't stop when she climbs on top of me and takes hold of me between my legs. She strokes me and sucks on my ear, biting me so that I dig my fingernails into her skin and hang on. I am desperate and rough. She keeps her eyes open and so do I.

When I finish, I make a mess on her lap.

"You ain't the first," she mutters.

"I'm sorry," I say and lean my head into the steering wheel.

"Hey, don't get like that," she says.

I reach for my wallet, feeling like I want to puke. I hand her two twenties. She gestures for one more, just like I did with Antoine.

"Something for my boss, something for me. My little savings plan," she says and winks.

I hand her another bill. She stuffs this one into her bra and grins. Her teeth are still real nice. "He doesn't need to know everything," she says, and I think about me and Daddy with our hidden wads of cash and of Mama telling me that even people without money can dream. She plucks two cigarettes from my pack.

"I'm gonna need these later," she says.

Christ, I think, the way she twirls her hair is just like Willow Rose. Before she jumps out of the truck, she thanks me — real polite — as if I've been some kind of gentleman, but I know what I've become.

As soon as she's gone, I throw the Colt back in the glovebox feeling like the monster I am, and I speed out of there so fast. My skin crawls with the feeling of filth. I turn into a gas station off the highway and lock myself in the restroom, trying to wash as much of my body as I can with the sickeningly sweet-smelling pink hand soap and rough paper towels. I can't stop thinking of the look on that girl's face when I pulled out the gun. I want to cry when I catch sight of my face, my blue eyes staring at me in the mirror.

I know looking at the desert will kill me, so all through New Mexico and Arizona I speed past the scenery where every turn looks like the place where Fortune died. I crank up the radio and listen to anything and everything, only paying attention to whatever licence plate is directly in front of me. I won't stop until I arrive. I drive through the night and into the next day. By the time I'm safe in Mr. Alvarez's arms, I feel like battered prey.

Mr. Alvarez feeds me two ham sandwiches with cheese and thick bread. He pours me a tall glass of milk and then water and tells me everything he knows. He saw my father in town at the gas station, buying a hot dog. Mr. Alvarez tried to talk to him, but he says my daddy didn't have much to say. Mr. Alvarez didn't tell him about us, but he gave Daddy his phone number and told him to call if he needed anything and then he followed my daddy down the road until he figured out where he was staying. Outside of town there's an encampment where people live in trailers, shacks, tents, whatever they can scrape together. Survivalists, maybe addicts, Mr. Alvarez says. He tells me that my father is out there in a trailer called "Glam Life." I don't even bother getting rested or clean before I go.

FORTY-THREE

HERE COMES THE RAIN AGAIN

"WHO THE HELL ARE you?"

I'm knocking and then pounding on the door of a flimsy, broken-down trailer at the far edge of the encampment. There are about a dozen other trailers and shacks, most of them with busted windows or walls eaten through by rust and rot. The ground is covered with clothes, beer cans, a pile of cinder blocks and a sign in the middle of it all that says Pick Up Your Mess! and another sign that says Freedom! A man — maybe in his sixties, and who looks like he could be a regular grandpa in a cardigan — sits outside one of the other trailers reading a book and smoking. He waves at me and asks if I'm looking for someone. I tell him I'm okay. A dog yaps and the man puts down his book and brings out a chihuahua that he settles into his lap. They both stare at me.

My father won't open the door. He stands near the window. He holds a bottle of Jameson, and it's more than half-empty.

"Who the hell are you?" he hollers again.

I have no idea what to say to my father, who won't recognize me, so I call for him to open up. The man with the book whispers in his dog's ear and shakes his head. My father tells me to get lost. I plead with him to let me in until finally, I say through the screen door, "Let me in or I'll shoot right through this door." I show him I have the Colt.

My father moves up close to the door and says to me, "You would never do that."

"Fuck you," I say and I hold up the gun. I put my finger on the trigger.

"Language!" the man with the chihuahua says, and then he puts his bug-eyed dog back inside, comes back out and takes a piss right in front of his trailer.

"Fuck me? You're the one who came all this way just to act like you're going to kill me," my father says.

"I mean it," I say.

My father disappears into his trailer.

"I'm coming in," I say, and I jiggle the flimsy handle until it gives, and I burst into my father's dark space. There's nothing on the walls and almost nothing in his trailer except for a chair, a mattress, and a countertop covered in empty beer cans, and a dirty plate in the sink. On his mattress is an open book called *Fahrenheit 451*. My father stands at the end of it all and strikes a match to light a smoke.

"I guess you didn't need a gun to get in after all," my father says.

"I could still shoot," I say, and I point it at him.

"That ain't you," my father says.

"Try me," I say, but I am trembling.

"You wouldn't," my father says, and he takes the gun from me in a single swift move and laughs. "I knew you couldn't do it," he says.

"Bastard," I say. My father smiles like he likes hearing me talk like that.

We stare at each other, and I realize I don't know what to say. I thought I would know, but now I see that I don't even know the man my father has become. Finally, he breaks the silence.

"You like it?" he asks, waving his hand around.

"It's great," I say.

"Liar," he says.

"Okay, it's shit," I say.

"At least it's not a swamp. How did you find me anyway?" my father asks.

"Mr. Alvarez."

"I should have known."

"He's a nice guy. Helped us out when you abandoned us."

My father nods, silent. His trailer is so hot, and the sun burns in through the window.

"You should come home," I say. "Mama and Willow Rose need you."

He shakes his head. "That's another lie. I never helped either of them," he says and sits down on the only chair he has.

"That ain't true. Come home," I say.

"I ain't lying," he says. "I failed all of you. First, I brought Antoine around, and then we came here. And Fortune…"

"It ain't your fault what Antoine did," I say, sweating for real now.

"I damn well should have killed him for what he did to your mama," he says.

It is the closest my father has come to telling me what he knows. I let several moments go by, and then I breathe in knowing everything is about to change.

"Daddy, I saw him hurt Mama. I never told you." I nearly choke on my own words.

My father closes his eyes, and I remember how he wouldn't hear me that time in the truck. He stays silent so long I think he is pretending he didn't hear. Finally, he speaks. "I figured as much." He keeps his eyes closed.

"You knew?"

My father nods and looks at me. "I guessed."

"I wish I killed him when he came over. It's my fault," I whisper.

"I left you in charge," my father says.

"I'm sorry." I put my head in my hands to keep myself from crying because I don't want my father to hit me, though I know I deserve it.

"Sorry ain't nothing. We paid a real price for what he did."

"I know it. I tried to stop him, but when I got the Colt, I was too late."

"You should have pulled the trigger when you had the chance."

"It wasn't even loaded," I whisper.

"What kind of a man are you?"

"I tried."

"With every breath between now and the day I die, I curse that man. I'll never forgive him for what he did to Angeline and to us. If

I ever see him again, I hope it's through the barrel of a gun. You can take that back home with you when you go. You hear me?"

I wish my father would hit me or scream at me, but he won't even look at me when he cracks open a can of Bud, takes a swig and then hurls the can across the room. It slams against the wall, sloshing beer all over.

"Daddy," I say. "Mama and Willow Rose —" I start.

"Why didn't you tell me then?" he asks.

"I tried. That time in the truck, and… I didn't want to hurt you more. Why didn't you tell me what you knew?" I ask.

"Because I didn't want to know, and I couldn't do a goddamn thing about it. I wasn't the one taking money from him anymore."

"That money helped us," I say. "I'm not sorry for that. I took from him so I could help us. At least it was something."

"You lied to your Mama," my father says.

"You're calling me a liar? You've been lying all this time." I dig into my pocket where I still have that newspaper article. I unfold it and toss it at him. "I found this. And I read all about the explosion. I know you were alone when you jumped, that you lied about helping your friend. Frank. You wanted to be a big hero, but you're not."

"Where did you get this?" He grabs the newspaper up from the floor and throws it back at me.

"It was in your bedroom," I say.

"And you think you know something about this? You think I made it all up?" He's near to screaming now.

"The newspapers said all the men died together on the rig floor. You didn't help anyone. I know it. You lied to make yourself feel better. To make an excuse for moving us to the middle of nowhere when, really, it was just that you were a fuck-up," I say.

"You don't know shit," he says.

"I know what I read."

"You think those newspapers know more than I do? I was there. No journalist can say that."

"Then you should tell me what happened. Whose address is this?

Why do you care so much about these people?" I ask.

He pounds a fist into the counter. "Frank Allmendinger was a man who deserved to live. He died that day because of me."

"I don't know what you're talking about," I say.

"All those other men died because the oil company was too cheap to care if the rig worked right, if they could seal that well if they had to. They died trying to spare other men from that, but Frank died because I got him drunk. The good ones die because of me, but when a man comes around that really deserves to die, I don't do shit," he says.

"You were drinking on the rig?"

"Don't pretend you're surprised. You know who I am. I was drunk in a place I shouldn't have been drunk, and I got Frank wasted too." My father holds his head in his hands and bends over double like he's going to be sick, but all that comes out of him are sobs. "I thought it was real funny. We were fucked up and slow — we thought it was a drill, and then he busted an ankle in the first explosion. I tried to help him. I dragged him to the lifeboats, but we were too late."

"They should have waited."

"They couldn't wait. That fire was hell. We were too slow, so we jumped and he couldn't swim. That's on me."

"It ain't your fault he couldn't swim," I say.

"He wouldn't have had to swim if he'd been anywhere else but with me. He'd have been better off dying with the others. At least there'd be honour in that. He died for nothing. He died because I'm a degenerate."

"You tried to help him," I murmur. I am suddenly so much sadder than I was before I arrived in this terrible trailer, in this terrible place.

"I killed him. And Antoine knew that. That made him dangerous."

"I'm real sorry," I say.

"You have no idea how sorry I am," he says.

"I thought it was all a lie," I say.

My father keeps his eyes closed when he finally says, "If all I'd done was lie, it would be better. I drove all the way to Mississippi to tell his widow what happened. Sometimes it's better to keep the truth to yourself."

"You went to her?"

"I got nothing more to say about it. I shouldn't have done it. Frank's dead and his widow's heart is more broken than it was before she knew he drowned. Fuck the truth." He puts his head in his hands.

After a long silence, I say, "At least he wasn't alone."

My father shakes his head, and says, "He was. We all are."

In my father's trailer, an ancient metallic fan creaks but does nothing to keep the heat from taking up all the space. My father lies down on his mattress and throws an arm over his eyes as if to block me out.

"Come home," I say.

"I ain't never going back to that goddamn swamp. There ain't nothing more I can do for any of you."

My father is so skinny that his ribs look like a staircase protruding from his chest. I can see each breath he takes, the lines on his face, the blue veins that snake up his skinny arms. I want to sob, but instead I whisper, "I hate you. I've hated you ever since you came home from the rig."

"That's the thing. Sometimes when you can't help the people you think you love, you start to hate them, don't you?" he says and turns his back to me.

"Daddy," I say. He is silent. "Emmet," I say, and he looks out from under his arm. "Go to hell."

"I'm already there," he says and shuts his eyes against me.

When I leave, I pick up the Colt, but then I put it down next to the sink. I don't need it anymore.

FORTY-FOUR

ROCK ME LIKE A HURRICANE

WHEN I GET IN the truck, I'm breathless and shaking. I want to peel off my skin and throw my raw body from a cliff in the desert. The drive home is a black hole that I bore into, blocking out everything, including memory. I know that I spend days in a truck stop parking lot, eating Twinkies and burgers and smoking cigarettes down to the tiniest nubs so I can get every bit of relief, but I don't know how many days — or maybe weeks — go by. I have nowhere left to go. The heat in the desert is like a living thing, wrapping its arms around me, making me forget where I am or where I came from. After days of living out of the truck, I can smell myself, and the woman who sells me Twinkies asks me if I'm okay. I nod and tell her I'm great, but she looks at me real strange. I look at the rack of maps in the store: I could go anywhere. When we were at the Grand Canyon, I thought I'd never see anything so beautiful again. I thought it was the best day of my life and all I wanted to do was hold onto it. Now I'd do anything to forget it along with Mama and her short skirt, and Willow Rose and Sterling, and the tiny white urn in Mama's bedroom.

Awake one night, I leave the truck and walk up to the edge of the highway and feel the hum of so many trucks and cars blow by me, their headlights a blur, going somewhere. I rustle around in my wallet for some change and the newspaper article I still have. I will call her, I think, I'll call Mrs. Allmendinger and try to undo what my father has done. Tell her he's a drunk and a liar. At least I can do that.

I dump all my quarters — six of them — into the payphone outside the truck stop. I sweat and I dial. One ring, two rings, three.

And then, "Hello." The voice is a woman's. Sure, strong.

"Mrs. Allmendinger?" I ask.

"Yes," she answers as if she is asking me a question.

I breathe into the phone for a long moment.

"Hello?" she asks.

I keep breathing, my pulse jumping around like a jackrabbit.

"Is anybody there?" she asks.

She has a real nice voice, not even angry, and right then I think — *there is no reason to make this woman's life even worse.*

"I'm real sorry," I finally say, and I put down the receiver. I want to scream, but instead I walk back to the edge of the highway and spread my arms wide to feel the speed of the trucks rushing by like wind, while all the things my father said race through my head in circles. Even though I grow hot with rage when I think of him, I also think he is right. I fucked up. I should have killed Antoine when I had the chance. He's also right about this — sometimes it's better not to know the truth, but I do, and there's no unknowing it.

The stars are out — so many of them it reminds me of waiting in the desert for my father and then for Mama and Willow Rose. I have been alone like this before. But Mama and Willow Rose — they came back. They came back and now they need me. The only thing I ever wanted was to get the hell out of where we were, but now I know, I have to go back. Daddy's right. I've got to fix things on my own. I get back in the truck and clear out the shit I've left in there. I must have eaten dozens of Twinkies and smoked a thousand cigarettes. I used to wonder how Mama could sit there for hours doing nothing but smoking and staring, but now I understand. Thinking of my family, I drive the rest of the way home in a fit of speeding and stopping for a few hours to sleep and then driving some more. The air grows more humid, and as I get nearer to home, I grow less afraid.

As I drive down the last stretch of highway, the red sun slouches low in the sky and its reflection follows me in the water of the bayou. I breathe in the marshy smell, let it fill my lungs with its softness.

A flock of snowy egrets lifts like a wave off the road ahead of me and flies out over the water. I hum Mama's lullaby to myself.

The smell of Mama's cigarette smoke is the first thing that tells me I am home. She and Willow Rose sit in the living room and watch *Family Feud* when I burst in. They are snuggled up together. Mama's face is so soft and gentle. I am ashamed for leaving them and I know Mama will know everything by how skinny I've become and by the way I smell.

"Jesse!" I think my mama might hit me or scream at me and tell me to leave. But when I come into the dark room, she takes in all of me and her eyes flash from surprise to something warm and sad. She grabs me and holds me to her, hand on the back of my head, stroking my hair, soft like the way things were before everything happened. I haven't felt my mama's touch or smelled her mama smell in so long that when I do, I melt into sobs and tell her everything about the road, and the desert, and how I tried to bring Daddy back, and how I got everything wrong. When I cry into her neck, she keeps her arms around me and says, "Shh — cher, you're home now. You're with us."

Willow Rose comes up to me then and grinning she says, "You look like hell." When she comes in for a hug she adds, "And you stink."

"You do stink," Mama says and holds me some more.

In the shower, I linger under the water, scrubbing the heat and the smell and the sweat from my skin, but I know that beneath all that is something I cannot wash away.

My mother has a new job at the grocery store in Golden Meadow. She wears a white uniform and ties back her hair all tidy in a way I've never seen. Willow Rose stays home and does math homework from a textbook, her notebook open on the sofa. Correspondence classes, she tells me. It was all Mrs. Salazar-Dulac's idea. She came over with soup and a tuna casserole right after I left, and she helped Mama get her new job. She even brought Willow Rose some of Lisette's old clothes — a Saints sweatshirt, a pair of jeans with a red label — Willow Rose shows me these with so much excitement, you'd think she won a million dollars. Then she shows me the equation she's working on. I can tell she's real proud of herself, and she tells me I should try out correspondence school too. When I sit down beside her and ask her about Sterling, her cheeks turn red, and she tells me that one day Mama and Mrs. Salazar-Dulac barged in on them and talked Willow Rose into going home. Mrs. Salazar-Dulac also told Sterling he'd better move on, or she'd come after him, and Willow Rose said he turned all coward when his step-mama spoke to him like that, and she knew it was time to leave him. I don't ask Willow Rose about Lisette, but she knows what I'm thinking, and she tells me, "I saw Lisette a couple of times. She asked about you."

I mumble that it's too late, that I fucked that up for real.

"She and Cole are over. She dumped him," Willow Rose says. "You could try again," she says as she braids her own hair, and I think she means it.

From the marrow of my bones, I remember my longing for Lisette, and the sweet taste of her, and also the shame of how I treated her, knowing how much more she deserved.

"I just want to look after you and Mama for now. Get a fresh start." I say. And to myself, I pray for a chance to do better.

Willow Rose throws her skinny arm around my shoulder, pushing aside her math book. "I guess it's just us then," she says, and she sounds real happy.

"Just us," I say. Leaning into her embrace, I notice that her earring from Sterling is gone and only a pinprick of a reminder remains, the smallest scar on her flesh.

"We're going to be okay," Willow Rose says and tightens her arm around my neck. When she takes my hands, hers are soft like Mama's.

Dusk creeps into the living room, and in the falling, blueish light I close my eyes so that Willow Rose won't see them. I lean into my sister and hold on.

For weeks the heat and humidity sit over us, unmoving, and we all try to do as little as we can. We long for rain, for the crack in the sky that will bring us relief. When I go outside, even the pelicans are as still as the water and the motionless oaks. Mama works, Willow Rose does math, sometimes asking me for help. In the mornings, I make breakfast, and in the evenings, I cook things like spaghetti and hotdogs, and we sit around the table and eat dinner together. I wash the dishes while Willow Rose dries. Some nights, I read to Willow Rose and Mama from *The Old Man and the Sea*, and they let me read all the way to the end, when I catch Mama shed a tear. Willow Rose heaves a big sigh and I swear she puts her hand on her heart.

During the day, I look after Mama and Willow Rose as best I can, but when I lie awake at night, I am tormented with thoughts of Fortune and Antoine, and I hear my father's words echo like when you shout over the Grand Canyon and everything comes back to you. I go over all the scenes in my head: I should have kept Antoine out of the house when Daddy was away. I should have loaded the Colt. I should have kept Fortune safe. I should have been a different kind of son. I wake up every morning feeling like I'm lying in a puddle of guilt that has seeped out of me all night, and then I spend every day pretending to Mama and Willow Rose that I am okay. We are all trying to be okay and I won't be the one to crack. I promise myself that from now on, I will be the one who makes things right.

With our bodies roasting in the heat, we almost pray our thanks on the day the sky darkens and snaps with lightning and spits down droplets, but then the TV tells us we have only days to prepare: a storm — the first big one of the season — is forming over the Gulf. It's going to hit Grand Isle first and then come for us. Mama lights a cigarette and takes a long drag and says, "I always knew this day would come. We have to get out of here."

I pretend we're only playing. "Should we run to Uruguay? Or Yemen?"

Mama smiles into her smoke. "Nairobi — you better take that map with you."

"Mama — where will we go?" I ask.

"We'll find our way," she says. And then she adds, "Home is when we're together, remember?"

I nod and reach for one of her cigarettes, but she slaps my hand away good and hard. She tells me it's time to start packing.

In the evening of the second day of the evacuation warnings, PJ and Andy come knocking on the door. Andy smiles and calls me Halfass, and PJ claps me into a strange one-armed hug like he's shy or something, and he tells me he wants to make sure we know about the storm and the evacuation order. He asks if we're planning to get out and tells me our walls look too flimsy to withstand a hurricane like this one. I tell him we're leaving soon, which we are. I don't tell him that I don't know where we'll go once we're up past our stretch of highway. I guess it could be anywhere.

"If everything's gone after this one, I don't know if I'll make it back," he says. He looks real sad as he tells me all the things he left behind along with the only home he's ever had that was his alone. He tells me he's going up the bayou with Andy, who has family in Lafayette, but who knows where he'll end up. Even though he's been waiting for this hurricane forever, he has no real plan. Maybe there are oysters for coonasses like him somewhere else, somewhere without oil. He says, maybe I'll come find him wherever he is, and I agree that I'll look for him again someday. "Hey — if you come back here and I don't, you look after those cats. And take my boat if she's still there." He gives me a key from a ring and grabs me into a long hug, like he doesn't want to let go. When my mama comes to the door, she grasps him into her arms and he leans into her too.

"I'm glad to see you, cher," Mama says.

"Oh Angeline, I should have come around more," PJ says.

Mama shakes her head and says, "We're going to be okay. This could be a new beginning for all of us. Won't be much left of this place after this storm."

"Hey — you find me when this is over. You hear?"

"I will," Mama says. "Swamp people always find each other."

"It's the stench," PJ says.

After all the hugging, Andy and PJ drive away from here, the back of their truck covered with a tarp to protect, as PJ says, all the stupid things he has.

There is barely enough gas in Mama's car to get anywhere, but after PJ leaves, I leave too. My heart sprints as I remember everything Daddy said about fixing things. I know this is my last chance to get things right. I know what I did and didn't do and what I have to do now. I can still see my father all alone out there in the desert, and how hurt his eyes were when I told him what I saw, and he told me what I should have done, and I can see the terrible look on Antoine's face that night with Mama. The air swells with heat and thunder. The rain has begun to gust, and the road down the bayou is slick. All the way to Leeville, there is no other vehicle going this direction. Even the egrets and herons that normally hover at dusk at the edge of the bayou looking for a meal are all gone away.

At the cats' hideout, I pull over and find them, the ginger tom and about a half-dozen others. They pace, their backs arched. They know what's coming. I know they won't survive. I finger the kitchen knife — the biggest, sharpest one we have — that I brought with me. When I see him, I grab the ginger tom to me and I stroke him. I scratch his ears, and he purrs deep and fast into my chest. I whisper to him that I'm sorry for what I'm about to do. Real sudden I yank a pillowcase I've brought over the ginger tom's head. He fights me with his claws like little razors, but I tie up the opening and he's caught. Blood rushes in my ears as I hold the bundled cat to my chest. I could drown him or run him over with the car. I could spare him the hurricane, but he's filled with life, clawing through the pillowcase, slashing my arms and yowling even as I whisper reassuring words to him. Rain runs down my hot cheeks and slithers down my arms as I leave the ginger tom still frantic in the car and I go after the others. I chase the calico one, but she tears off into the abandoned house and wedges herself between a rafter and the wall, too high up for me to reach. Inside the house it is dim, and the rain pelts the sides of the building. In some spots, there's just enough roof to hide from the storm. I howl at the calico cat to let me save her as the sky grows darker each minute. Against the sound of the wind, I scream, but the calico cat presses her body, rigid, into her hiding spot and I can't get close. I should have brought food. I shouldn't have come here without a plan. I tell myself they're smart — and I promise them I'll come back for them when this is all over and we come home. I promise them out loud and then I run to the car, shivering. The ginger tom has stopped fighting the pillowcase, and when I put my hand on him and whisper "Shh," he growls, and I am relieved that he's okay.

The long bridge to Grand Isle is a massive shadow, looming and black. I don't know why I never took my bike across it. I could have. I could have gone back and seen my friends, but with everything that happened — I didn't want them to know what my family had become. And now, I can tell from the howling of the wind that our little blue house there, and maybe everything else I ever knew, will soon be gone.

Antoine's truck is in front of his house. I slip into his shop — it's unlocked as usual. Fast and half-crazed, I puncture every tire on every car in his shop. I stab them like I want them to bleed and with every loud hiss, I feel relief. Then I crouch in front of his truck and do the same. The rain lashes my face and plasters my hair to my head. I can hardly see. I think of Mama's face that night and again when Fortune died, and I think, this is the least I can do.

I have never seen a category five hurricane before. I have heard about Camille and what she left behind. On my way back up the highway, I begin to understand.

Back home, Mama finds me in the kitchen. I am soaking wet and shaking as I slip the knife back into the drawer, but she catches sight of it and she knows, the way you can smell evil, that something isn't right.

"What have you gone and done?" she asks.

I don't lie because I want her to know that what I saw that night mattered and I should have taken care of it then. The windows rattle. We have to leave. Inside, the house is electric with humidity and the feeling of waiting for the full force we know is coming.

"Antoine," I say.

My mama rests her hands on my shoulders. "What did you do?" she asks again.

I tell her that I had to make things right for Daddy, for her and for Fortune. That Daddy said I should fix things. That someone had to do it once and for all. Everything bad that ever happened was because of Antoine.

My mama pulls me to her chest and holds me. "Oh Jesse, that is not how we do. Not you. Not us," she says, and she cups her hands around my chin and looks straight into my eyes so that I feel sick when I see myself in them.

We have packed everything we can — including the ginger tom that we've put in a boxtrap — into the truck and pulled a tarp over it. I hold Willow Rose in my arms and she cries into my armpit as we prepare to leave behind our house. I tell her our home is with each other. We get in the truck, but instead of heading north, we turn south and drive back to Leeville where Mama tells me I better find Antoine and tell him what I did. When we pull up in front of his place, he is right there, looking at the damage I left behind while the storm pelts him with its anger. His face is a mask of terror and rage.

"What the holy fuck is going on here? You still trying to kill me?" Antoine bellows when I jump down from the truck. He is dishevelled, hair standing up, shirt wet. Beside him is a suitcase, bursting at the seams, tipped over with its wheels up.

He looks at Mama and Willow Rose high up in the truck, safe. "After everything I done for y'all," he murmurs.

"You ain't done shit for us. You hurt my mama and my whole family," I say.

"You going to help me get out of here or what?" Antoine's voice trembles and I think he looks like a fish on land, gasping, afraid.

"Say it. Say it. Say you hurt my mama. Say you're sorry. Tell me it's all your fault. Say it or we'll leave you here." My voice rises with the wind that shakes the trees.

"Your father was crazy from that explosion. I tried to help you.

All that money I gave you."

"You don't talk about my father like that. It's all your fault. You hurt my mama and then you made it so we had to leave. Fortune would be alive if not for you. My father would still be here."

"You little shit," Antoine says.

I rush at Antoine like I'm a bull. I try to bowl him over and in the slickness of the rain and with the sound of thunder gathering, we both topple over to the road where I cling to him, shrieking for him to admit everything, scratching his flesh, longing to feel his thick body yield to my rage. Antoine slides beneath me and I punch, my fist stinging and wet against his face. His three-fingered hand flails and he gasps at me to stop.

"Jesse!"

The truck door opens and slams shut. Mama stands over us. Her face is stone and fire, and her arms crossed over her body are her only armour.

"Mama," I gasp.

Antoine, lying on the road beside me, pulls his knees to his chest. I am crouched over him. I want to hit him again.

"Get up," she says.

I pull myself up from Antoine. I am sopping wet and feverish with rage. I hang my head and let my hair fall into my face so that I don't have to look at my mama's.

My mother's voice comes from somewhere deep inside her, so deep I think she is the voice of the storm, of the trees, the sky.

She looks at Antoine. "We do not owe you anything after what you did to me, but you will not turn my children into murderers. Get in the truck."

Lightning crashes and lights up the sky, illuminating the bridge to Grand Isle.

"I can't let you do that." Antoine shakes his head and rain pours down his face.

"Get in the truck or you will drown right here," my mama says. Willow Rose has rolled down the window to listen.

"It's what I deserve after what I did to you, what happened to your baby," Antoine says. He buries his face in his hands.

A branch from a tree nearby cracks and blows to the ground.

"That may be true, but no matter who you are and what you have done, my son is not a murderer. Get in the truck now."

A hurricane isn't a storm, it is a fury. It is a scream ripped from the sky. It will come for you stronger than the scorching desert sun, catch you in its inferno like an explosion. It will end you with wind or rain or flood.

Antoine pulls himself up and heaves his suitcase into the back of the truck. He hands Mama all the money he has stuffed in his pockets, and she takes it. He lowers his eyes, but she does not.

"Dying is easy," she says. "It's living that's hard."

The sky closes in as the black clouds gather. Rain batters the truck like fists. I am the one who tells Antoine *one wrong move, and we'll throw you out the door while the truck is still moving*. I am the one who sits squished between Antoine and Willow Rose, who clutches the small white urn, while Mama takes the wheel. And I am the only one who turns and looks at everything we leave behind as we drive up the highway one last time.

ACKNOWLEDGEMENTS

Thank you to my dear friend Katherine Atkinson who was there when this story sparked to life, and whose raucous enthusiasm urged me to keep chasing it down. Giant thank yous to the Fictionistas — Jen Gryzenhout, Julie Hartley, Ellen Keith, Laura Nicol, and Sarah Richards — whose brilliant insights lit the path that I followed on the way to this book.

I'm grateful to have been part of the UBC School of Creative Writing and especially thankful for the wise guidance and generous support of Linda Svendsen, John Vigna, and Susan Musgrave. Much gratitude to others who helped me along the way, introducing me to agents, putting in a kind word: Andrew Westoll, David Leach, David Chariandy, Daniel Scott Tysdal, and especially Chelene Knight whose vision helped to shape this work.

Much gratitude to my kickass agent, Carolyn Forde for navigating the business side of this baby. Big, big thank you to the Anvil team: Brian Kaufman, Karen Green, and Jessica Key for so much loving dedication to this book and for being editors and publishers who make real art.

Thank you to *Embark* magazine for publishing an excerpt of this work in July 2019, and to The Masters Review for awarding a section of *After We Drowned* third place in their 2022 novel excerpt contest.

Thank you to T.J. and Randy in Leeville who took me out on their oyster boat, and Kajun Kent who told me stories that echo in these pages.

Loving gratitude to my family near and far, especially my devoted parents, Avi, Lori, and Rubies, and the international network of excellent cousins everywhere.

More loving thank yous to every one of the Atwells, especially to Aunt Marty for the outdoor office where much of this was written, and an extra special bit of tender gratitude for my dearly departed and badly missed brother-in-law, Charlie who had the sweetest way of asking — *so, how's your novel, Jilly?* Damn, I hope there's a piano, a recording studio, and a forever Beatles concert wherever you are.

Crazy love and gratitude to my hilarious and whip-smart Montréal posse of friends, especially Marites Carino who vibrates with inspiration and reads all my grant applications, to my Vancouver pals for friendship and irreverent late-night texts and encouragement, and even more special thanks down the west coast to Catherine Lee for providing unflagging support and the most beautiful music.

Finally, I owe my most heartfelt gratitude and my sweetest love to Willie: comic genius, editor extraordinaire. Without you, there would be no story.

ABOUT THE AUTHOR

Jill Yonit Goldberg is a Prairie-born former Montrealer living in Vancouver. Recent work includes essays, short stories and very occasional poems that have been included in publications such as *Room* magazine, the *London Reader*, and *subTerrain* among others. She is a co-author of *The Fire Still Burns: Life In and After Residential School* (Purich Books; UBC Press, 2023). She teaches literature and creative writing at Langara College.